Virginia Duigan has worked in journalism, radio and television. She wrote the screenplay for the film *The Leading Man*, and the novels *Days Like These* and *The Biographer*, both published by Vintage. She was born in Cambridge, UK, and lives in Sydney and London.

The Precipice

VIRGINIA DUIGAN

VINTAGE BOOKS

Australia

A Vintage book
Published by Random House Australia Pty Ltd
Level 3, 100 Pacific Highway, North Sydney NSW 2060
www.randomhouse.com.au

First published by Vintage in 2011

Addresses for companies within the Random House Group can be found
at www.randomhouse.com.au/offices

National Library of Australia
Cataloguing-in-Publication Entry

Duigan, Virginia.
The precipice.

ISBN 978 1 74166 716 5 (pbk.)

A823.4

Cover image by Bodil Frendberg, courtesy Millennium Images Library, UK
Cover design by Gayna Murphy/Greendot Design
Text design by Midland Typesetters, Australia
Typeset in Bembo by Midland Typesetters, Australia
Printed and bound by Griffin Press, South Australia

The paper this book is printed on is certified against
theForest Stewardship Council® Standards.
Griffin Press holds FSC chain of custody certification
SGS-COC-005088. FSC promotes environmentally
responsible, socially beneficial and economically viable
management of the world's forests.

10 9 8 7 6 5 4 3 2 1

*For my lifelong friends in the JCH 'mafia': Anna Bowman,
Jennifer Bryce, Caroline Clemente, Elaine Counsell, Jean Deacon,
Penny Gay, Angela Munro, Jo Bell, Carole Pinnock
and, in memory, Jennifer Gibbs*

Now that it's nearly time for the invaders to move in, I'm not sure I want them to come here.

Not sure? Poppycock. Absolute, in point of fact, bullshit. I do not want them here, period.

Not that I can do anything about it now. Nothing whatsoever. I've sold the house and I've sold the land. It's not mine anymore – it belongs to them. What were their names again? Campbell and Carrington. It sounds like a poem by John Betjeman or Ogden Nash.

'The Campbells and the Carringtons are moving in next door.
They haven't any furniture, they're camping on the floor . . .'

Except that it's not amusing. Not one mingy, infinitesimal bit.

His name is Frank Campbell and hers is Ellice Carrington. In their twenties, I think they would be. Early to mid. Married? Maybe, maybe not, there's no knowing. Doesn't matter, in any case. Both names on the contract. They were thrilled to get the house, at least there's that. I could see they loved it from their reactions when I showed them round the first time. And why wouldn't they? What's not to love, as they say.

It's a very special house, no question. It was going to be mine to live in, once upon a time. Once upon a dream. No surprise that it's a wrench to part with it. But I can't live in two houses, can I?

Anyway, there was no choice in the end. I was always going to sell one – just not that one. It became that one quite suddenly, right out of the blue. It was a matter of money, that's all. My sad little cottage, rundown old humpy-dump that it is, with its small overgrown garden, wouldn't have fetched much more than a handful of beans.

There was no choice. So much in life boils down to two things: luck and lucre, and not having enough of either when the chips are down. Or having had enough money once, and then blown it. Having watched it blow away in a stock market crash, of all things, in common with swarms of other gullible fools like me. Financial birdbrains all. How banal that sounds. How truly, imaginary god-awfully banal.

You make your own luck, I've always believed that. And that includes your own bad luck.

I must not think about things that are in the past and cannot be changed. I have never done that, by and large, and I am not going to start now. It is dangerously close to self-pity, something I abhor in others. In oneself it is even worse, I think.

Yes, and yes again. I have fallen into all the above categories. I have been careless, gullible and – useless to deny it – trusting. And not only in matters financial. And not only trusting of investment advisers. This is not being self-pitying, it is being realistic.

Nothing to be done about it now, any of it. Now is the time to roll out the homilies. No use crying over spilt milk, grin and bear it, take it on the chin. Dust yourself off and whistle a happy tune. Alternatively, I could give myself a hundred lines. Write out one hundred times: *do not dwell on what cannot be changed*.

Although this is not the kind of punishment I ever meted out, or not that I recall. It always struck me as being singularly pointless, having endured it myself as a pupil. But right now I am prepared to concede there may be some point in mindless repetition. It may even produce the desired effect, on occasion.

It could be time for it. Maybe I should mete it out upon myself?

~~

No doubt I could have got more for the house if I'd been prepared to wait. One of Mr Murphy's laws, these days better known as Sod's: buy at the top of the market, sell at the bottom. What goes down must go up, of course. But with the market in the state it's in (and the world too, for that matter) there's no knowing how long you'd be waiting for the upturn. And how long have I got? How long does any of us have? Meanwhile, there are bills to pay and another mouth to feed.

It was quite simple. I was not in any position to wait.

I liked the way the couple responded to the house. In spite of everything, I reacted to them a fraction favourably. Their unabashed enthusiasm, even the endless questions, which came mainly from her. Had I really, *really* designed it? The long living room with the soaring roof – how fabulous is that, Ms Farmer? All that humungous floor-to-ceiling glass – stunning. The flagstones on the kitchen floor – they look so wonderfully old and venerable – they can't be *new* tiles? Surely not, Ms Farmer! And all that timber and light – like, wow! You'd feel you were living outside among the gum trees.

Like, yes, indeed you would, Ms Ellice Carrington.

I'd thought, being young, they might have been put off by the emptiness and the isolation. No clubbing around here, no little corner shop for when you forget the milk, I told them. No dens of iniquity. No neighbours at all, apart from Teddy and me. Just impenetrable bushland stretching to the horizon.

They professed to see this as the plus that it is. They're a pernicious influence, those iniquitous dens, Ms Farmer, she declared, fluttering lush eyelashes, and my husband is dragging me away by the hair. We just love that the house is surrounded by a terrifying wilderness. He chimed in at this point, claimed they wanted to come to the Blue Mountains for a 'tree change'.

I'd call it more of a tree-and-sea change, I said. The valleys are like oceans ringed by sheer cliffs. When you look down on them you are looking at a sea of rippling green leaves. They nodded with the empty, uncomprehending smiles of city dwellers. How cool is that image, they chirruped to each other.

Put down in selective quotes like this, they (she in particular) sound gushing and ghastly, and insincere. But they weren't, if the truth be told. They were young, that's all – young and enthusiastic. Full of beans and anticipation for the future. All the things I am not full of. But I'm not curmudgeonly enough to resent them in others, I hope. Not quite yet, at any rate.

So their response to the house endeared them to me. They got it, as the saying goes.

Well, it endeared them to me slightly, to a certain grudging extent, let's not get carried away. Lead us not into pollyanna-land, O non-existent lord.

~~

You don't have to beat about the bush in a journal, and there's the beauty of it. You can be as bloody offensive as you like, as Oscar told the group last week. He said that the beauty of writing a diary is that it allows you to vent. Lets you roll in the mud, vomit spleen and express all those things you think and do not (for the most part) say. Frees you up to be brutally honest, he said.

Charge out of your comfort zone, thou trusty troops, he ordered. Glory in being naked and unashamed on the page, or on the screen. And interestingly, after a slow start, I am getting to rather like the screen. You can see your most unworthy thoughts up there, laid out before your eyes in pitiless black and white.

All very well for Oscar to say, but most of his troops have a few decades on him. I doubt if there's anyone in the writing group who finds it glorious to be naked and unashamed anymore, if indeed they ever did. They're a fairly buttoned-up lot. I include myself in that. And for brutally honest we may read misanthropic in my case. At least where the young Campbell-Carringtons are concerned.

But, and here is a silver lining, a sole sliver of one – they got the point of the house. The point being that I wanted the transition to be as seamless and unobtrusive as possible, so that from within you might always feel as if you were out in the bush. Under a sheltering roof and yet out there among the tall timber, lit by the constantly changing moods of natural light. From the first glimmer of dawn to the blinding shafts that flare through the leaves at noon. The pillows of evening shadows. Tendrils of mist snaking down the gully. The swooping black and white flashes of cockatoos, and the blaze of parrots.

The poetry of light. Even I, who can't write poetry for toffee, let alone for love or money, cannot entirely avoid it.

Because there was more than plain elbow grease put into that house. More than just wood and glass, and calculations and measurements. That house was made with love. And if I couldn't have it myself, I wanted whoever bought it to buy it for love, and not for any other reason.

~~

They loved it immediately, I could see that, and neither of them made any attempt to conceal it from me. None of the games people often play, with estate agents for example, when they don't want to appear too keen. They had the same openness with each other, I would guess they haven't been together very long. They reminded me of a pair of doe-eyed teenagers, wandering around the house hand in hand, or with his arm draped across her shoulders. I took notice of that. And they communicated. He wasn't one of those young men who just look and grunt, and leave it all to the wife. They talked to each other, quite intensely.

It occurred to me that she might be pregnant. They didn't say anything, and there was nothing showing, but he was solicitous. In the absence of furniture, a couple of times he suggested she sit out on the step or lean against the kitchen bench. She's very pretty in a gypsyish way, with tumbling black hair and dark eyes. She's more vivid than him, and more effusive, which is potentially worrying. I don't remember very clearly what he looked like. Sandy colouring, I think, and slight of build. He's more elusive.

'*She's effusive, he's elusive.*'

I can't be bothered to think of a follow-up line.

I made the house with love, and that is why, of course, it is so very hard to part with it. I think it must be rather like having a child that is ready to spread its wings and take off into the world. Your precious thing, but you just have to let it go.

~~

Write out one hundred times: *do not dwell on what cannot be changed.*

I tried writing this bald sentence five times on the blackboard. It did seem to have some sort of residual effect, oddly enough. I saw Teddy sitting on his rug and watching me, with what I interpret as his ironic expression. His ears were pricked. He and I exchanged ironic looks before I rubbed out the words.

Perhaps I should have left them there as a salutary reminder. Nobody's likely to see them, except us.

~~

These foolish things . . .

It was a perfect, cloudless day today, and I did a very foolish thing. Went for one last look. Knew I shouldn't, knew it was a bad idea, couldn't resist. Well, and isn't that a characteristic of bad ideas?

It is only a stone's throw away, and always will be. Mentally as well as physically.

Teddy padded alongside. He waited as I unlocked the front door, then pushed past me and became quite animated, bustling about and sniffing the walls. The air was dancing with sunbeams and bright amber light. In unison, we breathed it in.

I walked through the kitchen into the long living room, that splendid, soaring space. Then I saw other more mundane things, like cobwebs in the corners of the fireplace. The glass wall, the transparent demarcation of house and bush, was surprisingly dusty. I had a sudden urge to take a mop and cloth to it. A resistible urge.

The otherwise untainted emptiness of everything affected me deeply. I thought, this is the last time I will ever see my house untouched, just as I left it. The last time ever that it will be my creation alone. If I can bear to set foot inside again, in some unthinkable future, it will not be the same. It will have taken on the patina of other people's lives.

There was one additional thing I can hardly bring myself to mention: an expectancy. I sensed it, felt it hovering lightly in the air. The house was awaiting its new owners, impatient for its life's work and purpose to begin. It was almost as if it was – repudiating me, but that is too strong.

Yet I was aware that a distance had opened up between us. The intimacy of our relationship, the three-way interplay of myself, Teddy, house – it was no longer there. And more than that, it was as if it had never been. It had blown away, just like my money. Vanished without a trace, and from this day forward I could be nothing but a casual visitor.

I felt I was trespassing in my own house.

I sank down on the floor and drew my knees up to my chin like a child. There is a shame in writing this to myself, but also, perhaps, some kind of primitive release. Teddy had never seen me like this. He hurried to my side, and we grieved together in a silent requiem that may have lasted,

I am compelled to say, for some considerable length of time. My head supported by his soft, comforting fur.

It was a foolish impulse to go inside again. I should not have given in to it.

~~

The aliens have landed. A good title for a science fiction film? Perhaps I might auction it on eBay.

Yes, the invaders moved in today. It was strange to see a large removals van trundle up the drive; strangely unsettling. I was unprepared for quite how much the sight of it distressed me. I should have been prepared for it, imaginary god only knows, since the reality has been in my thoughts for months. But somehow I wasn't.

Teddy and I witnessed the invasion briefly from our vantage point on the verandah. Teddy was very excited at first, barked for five minutes and growled for a further five before he settled uneasily at my feet. He remained restive and jumpy for the remainder of the day. It will be strange for him too, having them living over there in our immediate vicinity. Those intruders who are occupying our former territory. I wonder what he will think of that, and of them.

Teddy is my comfort. My other precious thing, come to think of it. My first, and my enduring.

It started off misty and for a while I thought it might even rain, but it cleared and was cloudless all day. Not too hot, perfect moving weather. The van came soon after two and didn't leave until about five. I went inside and worked at my writing. Tried some poetry, hopeless as usual, then Oscar's assignment: a page of one's earliest memories. It shouldn't be difficult, but I am so painfully slow. If I were trying to write short stories, at this rate it would take until next Xmas to finish just one.

There were extenuating circumstances, however. I felt like one of Oscar's hand-picked platoon, a solitary sentinel trying to concentrate while knowing that an occupying enemy was taking up residence only a hundred metres away.

Would Oscar accept that as a reasonable excuse? I am unlikely to find out, because I do not intend to mention it. To talk about this wound, the takeover of my house by the Campbell-Carringtons, is unthinkable. And it is a self-inflicted wound – the unkindest cut of all.

I forget where in Sydney they said they were coming from. The Inner West? Not the North Shore or the Eastern Suburbs. He struck me as more faux bohemia and she more faux upper crust.

There were three of them, much to my surprise. They have a daughter – I was quite wrong, obviously, about them only having been together a short time. I saw her getting out of their car. Round-shouldered. Couldn't see how old she was, of course, but she wasn't a little girl so her mother must be a fair bit older than I thought. These days I find it hard to assess how old people are. They all tend to talk the same ungrammatical patois and wear identical clothes.

When they arrived they both looked over and saw me – the original two, that is – and waved. I saw this out of the corner of my eye and inclined my head. Rather grimly, but they couldn't see that. There was no question of eye contact, I did not once appear to look in their direction; I barely acknowledged them. Which wasn't difficult.

Much better to leave them alone for a bit, let them settle in. I suppose I'll have to gird my loins, which are monumentally reluctant, and pay a duty call down the line. Drop something in, a quiche or a bottle of champagne? That's the traditional welcome. Might it strike the right note, when it is a barefaced lie? Because I am not welcoming. I am not welcoming in the slightest degree.

For the moment I think I just can't face seeing my house with other people in it. The thought makes me feel quite ill.

This will surely pass.

The aliens have landed. It could be the opening scene of a horror movie. What happens next? If it were up to me, if there were none of the restraining bonds of civilisation, what would I do? Without the constraints of a strict and sheltered upbringing, to what depths might I descend?

Lead us not into idle speculation, O fanciful lord.

One thing I must be very careful about: to make the boundaries quite clear from the start.

~~

It was cool and windy today, and I went the full distance of our favourite walk, mainly so I didn't have to go past my house. Teddy came all the way with me. He was firing on nearly all cylinders for a change, almost his old self. Touch wood, the injection and the new pills are working wonders.

Yesterday I had to drive by my house on my way to the village. Their car was parked outside. It looked new. A black Subaru. Even seeing it parked there was a violation. I couldn't help seeing a few bits and pieces around too – chairs on the deck, flattened cardboard boxes, a girl's bicycle. Signs of life. Signs of invaders' lives.

We are not in a movie, however, and their occupation is not a violation in any way, shape or form. To write down such a word, even to think like that, is unacceptable behaviour. I wonder if a psychologist might think it verges on being dangerously unhinged behaviour. The house is not mine anymore, it is theirs. I may have brought it into being but it no longer belongs to me, or indeed has anything to do with me at all.

But the fact that I brought it into being and then lost it is like a hole in the heart. It remains in place. It cannot be filled.

~~

Their house.

I made myself print that phrase, that incendiary pair of words, very slowly on the blackboard, three times. It is theirs now, yet I still feel there is an umbilical cord between us. I need to sever that cord. Begin the long process of disassociation.

The long process. How long will it take? How long is a piece of string? How long do I have?

It is absurd to think like this. Everyone has disappointments in their lives, and in the scheme of things this is a minor one. I am talking about a material possession. A house is an inanimate object, not a living thing. A large part of the trouble, I realise, is that it was like a living thing to me. I brought it into being from nothing, and I suppose for me it symbolised a new life. The chance of a new beginning, long delayed. The chance, as they like to say, to reinvent myself.

Which at my age must be manifestly absurd.

When I saw the van move in I felt a physical ache. As if there had been a death and I'd only just found out. Well, that is in character, I'm afraid. I was slow on the uptake in my previous life, was I not? The emotional uptake, if there is such a thing.

Reinvention. To reinvent. Before, we never talked in such a way about ourselves, but it's common now and rather useful, I think. It was in my own eyes that I wanted to reinvent myself; it had nothing to do with the eyes of others. I don't care what others think of me, and never have.

If I were to be really pretentious I'd say it was to do with a rehabilitation of the sense of self. Because – I'll say it here but nowhere else – my sense of self was dismantled. It may be a long time ago now, a great many years have passed, but damage was done. Profound damage that lingers on.

It taught me that everyday life is a bit like wading into the sea. You may not see the hidden depths or the treacherous rips, but you know they are there. Experience has taught you that they are always there.

I wouldn't go on like this to a person, to an animate Homo non-sapiens, but on the blank, accepting screen you can go the whole hog, as Oscar puts it. A blank computer page accepts anything you type onto it, every incendiary thought – the sea, *their house* – that comes into your mind. Oscar is right, it is curiously liberating. I could get addicted to it if, indeed, I had an addictive personality, and I doubt if I've ever shown any tendencies there.

But I don't think I've ever been a particularly acquisitive person either, so it's a shock to have such a violent reaction to losing a possession. It's even more illogical since I received good money for it. Money that should, with any luck, unless things escalate into a major world depression, enable me to live in modest comfort for the rest of my days.

I say a possession, but it occurs to me that in a way it was the other way round. The idea of the house possessed me, and good can never come out of that, can it? I might of course win the lottery next week. Wouldn't that be a thing. Could I persuade them to sell it back for a profit? Should I jettison the habit of a lifetime and splash out on a ticket?

I hope I am not turning into a materialistic, embittered old trout. Or do I? Who cares? Who gives a fuck, as they so tediously say? I'm sure Teddy doesn't. He doesn't want me to reinvent myself, let alone rehabilitate my damaged sense of self. It's not damaged to him, he loves me whatever I'm like.

He anticipates my habits. We know each other's little ways. We two creatures, so different-looking, have an unconditional love for each other.

I should get a grip, whatever that is, and make myself go round later. There's no need to cross the invaders' threshold. I can go, dump the bottle at the door and come back without taking a single step inside.

I fear it is up to me to make the initial gesture. And if I do that I can also lay down the ground rules in a relatively tactful way. So what are they? Number one: we do not drop in. If we want to contact each other, we telephone first. The fact that we're near neighbours and isolated here makes it all the more important to respect each other's privacy.

However, I don't yet know their phone number. The gesture must be made, the conscience money delivered. There is no alternative but to let the drawbridge down and trudge across the moat on this occasion. I'll make a point of apologising, make it clear that I regard coming to their door as an intrusion and wouldn't normally do it, nor do I intend to make a habit of it. I can ask for their number, for future reference. That will be a smooth way of introducing the subject.

Basically, it boils down to one ground rule, and it has to be hard and fast. We're on pleasant terms, but for the most part we leave each other well alone.

~~

Ha. That plan came to naught. I was pre-empted. I got back from the village this morning with the paper and milk to find a note on the mat. It was sitting under a wooden wombat, one of those carved ones from the shop at the top of the Leura mall.

Dear Ms Farmer,

If you are around this evening, and if you feel inclined, please join us for a house-warming drink any time after six. If you can't make it, any other night this week would be fine for us – as long as you don't mind the mess…!! You could let us know by wombat mail.

From Ellice Carrington and Frank and Kim Campbell.

P.S. We would be extra-pleased if you could bring your lovely Red Cattle Dog, so we can meet him or her!

Kim Campbell's name was encircled by a line drawing of a wombat. Rather well done, but the note was written in an extremely badly taught, childish hand. It sloped at random, left and right, with lots of whorls and loops. It would be the girl's writing, of course, hence the 'extra-pleased' and the capitals and exclamation marks. At least she didn't show up in person at the door. They must have waited to send her over until they saw me drive past.

The 'if you feel inclined' bit didn't sound like the girl, though. I expect her mother dictated that.

I heard the sound of their car going off not long afterwards, so I scrawled an impulsive acceptance on the end and took it across. There was music coming from the house – a Gershwin song, oddly enough, from my childhood – and I was resigned to seeing one of them, but didn't, and was able to return note and wombat to the kitchen door unobserved.

The song was called 'Love Walked In'. And how ironic. I might have shed a bitter tear, were I the crying kind.

•

15

I need not have done it. I needn't have said I would come. It was a perfect opportunity to write a note to the effect that I was busy. It might have strained credibility, though, to say I was busy every night of the coming week. I suppose I wasn't prepared to be quite that offensive. They have made the gesture, I should force myself to make the best of it.

Our relations need to be distant, but cordial. Best to grit the teeth and get it over with.

~~

On the dot of six we went over. It was a balmy evening and they had put out chairs on the western deck. The door was flung open, and as we approached I could see the couple in the kitchen. He was standing on a stool while she handed him things to put on the high shelves. There were garbage bags full of crumpled newspaper. Music, some singer with a guttural voice. Bob Dylan? Is he still alive, or did he die of an overdose? I saw a jumble of boxes through the door into the living room, though I was trying not to look. The long, soaring room I used to think of as the house's crowning glory.

They greeted me with a show of warmth. She switched the gravelly voice off, and he hustled me outside and onto an incongruous dining chair with a red satin seat. The unpleasant Queen Anne kind you sit on and not in.

They had been Ellice's parents' dining room chairs, he explained. Antiques. Way too stuffy for him and Ellie, but they'd been landed with the entire set of ten − *ten*, Ms Farmer, can you believe it? − *and* a table the size of a footy ground when her parents downsized. They'd be getting rid of them as soon as her parents lost their memory, he said, gazing skywards, which would hopefully be next week.

After saying that he darted a furtive glance at me. And meanwhile, he continued hurriedly, they'd be on the lookout for some cane seating for the deck. Or wicker – like the funky old chairs they'd noticed on my front verandah. Could I suggest some junk shops?

I had a glass of nice cold Möet placed in my hand before I could say anything. Vintage, first of a case sent by Ellice's dad as a house-warmer, he said. They'd gone to some trouble. The daughter, Kim, followed the mother out silently with a tray of nuts, dips and biscuits. A coffee table, a fussy number with shapely bow legs – the parents again? – was placed at my elbow.

They were most insistent that I shouldn't set eyes on the rest of the house, not until everything was unpacked and straightened out. They said it would be too upsetting.

'Your wondrous creation, turned into a pigsty,' Ellice said. 'You'd never forget how it looked and never forgive us.'

That touched me, briefly. They do seem to understand, at some primitive level.

The girl sat quietly on the deck next to Teddy. She had a book but spent most of the time obsessively patting and stroking him. He lapped that up, of course. She was given a splash of champagne topped up with orange juice. Like her parents, she must be older than I first thought. Eleven or twelve, perhaps. She has her mother's colouring, in an intensified version. Very straight, dark hair, with an alice band. Almost blue-black hair cut short in a boyish crop, unlike Ellice's long waves. Olive skin, whereas her father is a classic paleface with thick, tightly furled gingery hair, worn longish. She does have his distinctive turned-up nose, however, but not his hazel eyes or freckles.

She presents as a shy, withdrawn child who hardly says a thing. Scrawny, caught in that awkward hiatus between childhood and adolescence. She calls them by their first names. They probably think that's cutting edge. It always sounds a trifle odd to me.

The occasion called for small talk. It reminded me of meeting young parents I had nothing in common with. I told them I was impressed that they had managed to locate the champagne glasses from the chaos.

Ellice said that was Frank's idea. 'He insisted on bringing them in the car with us so we could have you over on our first night to celebrate. Then he wouldn't let me do it. He put his patriarchal foot well and truly down, didn't he, Kimmie?'

'You were well and truly whacked, sweetheart,' Frank said, patting her arm. The next night they were catatonic from the unpacking and could only face takeaway pizza.

'We've been catatonic from the unpacking ever since,' Ellice said. 'Haven't we, Kimbo?'

The glasses were works of art: elegant, trumpet-shaped flutes engraved with kookaburras, cockatoos and waratahs. A wedding present, they informed me, and *majorly phenomenally* – not that we want to alarm you, Ms Farmer, don't even blink if you smash yours into a thousand pieces on the deck – they had not managed to break one in three years. I handled mine with mild paranoia after that. The set was made by a local artist I've never heard of, a woman whose studio is in a cave near Lithgow. They offered to take me there some time.

If they've had the glasses for three years, that means they married when their daughter was nine, or thereabouts.

There were no awkward silences. I was civil, calm and collected. I was quite proud of myself. We talked a bit about the area. And an inordinate amount about the ubiquitous 'stuff'. Where they should do stuff, and where they should go for stuff. And we talked about my house – *their house* – for some length of time too. I had my back to it but I was always aware of it there, presiding in my shadow.

They were curious to know where I'd sourced the materials. Pleased all the timber was recycled, commented on the leadlight windows and old panelled doors with porcelain handles. Good on me, though, for installing modern plumbing as well as an almost state-of-the-art kitchen. It spoke to them, they said, having the old and the new thrown together like that.

In what way it spoke to them they didn't say. *Almost* state-of-the-art? What more do they want?

I shouldn't be such a sourpuss. They were doing their best.

He stood up and proposed a toast. 'This is the house that Ms Farmer built.' He proclaimed this as if to a massive throng concealed in the surrounding bush. 'We feel very lucky and honoured to be here. Ms Farmer, and you too, Teddy: here's to your health and happiness.'

Even then I didn't bat an eyelid. Their sullen child was cajoled into the happy chorus. I was reminded of the old children's chant, this is the house that Jack built, this is the malt that lay in the house that Jack built, this is the rat that ate the malt, and so on.

'And here's to the three of you, and your new life here,' I added gamely. Gamely, and lamely.

They were lucky and honoured to be there, he said. How very true. At least they seemed to be aware of it. Blissfully unaware, of course, that their good fortune came at the expense of my bad luck. Or rather, my atrociously bad judgement.

They didn't mention the magic ingredient that got them there. It was their moolah, had they known it, that paid off the *almost* state-of-the-art kitchen. Money and timing, the two magic ingredients. Good timing doesn't receive due recognition, yet I suppose that is what luck is, most of the time.

When he heard himself toasted Teddy looked at me,

thumping his tail on the deck. There we were, the two of us, on a summer evening. Sitting in golden air scented with eucalyptus. Sitting under the tall, luminous trees outside the house that should have been ours. The two of us, who should have been in our own domain enjoying our own company in blessed solitude, instead of making stilted small talk with three barely tolerated strangers. It was as if we were the intruders, not them.

I had managed quite well up to that point, until that thought engulfed me like a cloud of poison gas. It threatened to undermine my composure far more than the stab of hostile envy that accompanied it.

Teddy and I took our leave rather abruptly, I realise. And it completely slipped my mind to ask for their phone number. But we had stayed an hour and fifteen minutes. That is perfectly legitimate, for pre-dinner drinks. I even went to the lengths of setting up a return arrangement. It sounded automatic and inane, like the social convention that it is.

They're invading the hovel for a drink next weekend. Saturday. I'd better write it down on the blackboard so I do not suppress it.

And why on absent god's earth did I bother to do that? Ingrained good manners? A morbid attraction to martyrdom? Surely I am of an age and inclination to be past doing something because it happens to be polite. Long past it. Perhaps Frank's frequent top-ups of his father-in-law's unusually good champagne had mellowed me in spite of everything. Made me weak in the head.

They jumped up with alacrity. No doubt they were as glad to get rid of us as we were to go.

~~

I don't feel like dealing with them on my own. Perhaps I should line up some reinforcements for Saturday. Which sounds as if I have legions to choose from, when there's barely a scratch team. Is there anyone from my meagre hockey team of mates they might like to meet? Or who would consent to meet them, more to the point?

They're not all like me. Some of them profess to enjoy parties. Davy Messer, for example. I believe the old Davy genuinely likes meeting new people, strange though it sounds. Especially if they're young and glamorous, and what he still insists on calling hip. He hopes some of it will rub off on him. Some hope.

Ellice should go down well. Does Frank Campbell qualify? He's not conventionally handsome but he's young, and he has a certain foxy appeal. They're bright and well-educated, or as much as you can hope for these days. They might find the old Davy a bit of a giggle. He's a cultured little luvvie, even if he is pocket-sized and a bit clapped out. I hope his breath's all right. It tends to go off when he hasn't been to the dentist for a while.

I know − Sandy. Sandy Fay, the Leaning Tower of Lisa's. Davy's polar opposite. I knew there was someone in the back of my mind. It's a perfect opportunity to have Sandy over after the Xmas drinks in the bookshop. He's an oddity, they may well think, but endearing in his oddness. His enthusiasms keep him youthful.

Joan's in China. Barb's ill. Bill and Monique would like them, they like everybody, but they're so old too. I wonder if their grandson could be roped in. He's their age, and he comes up here most weekends. And his girlfriend's pleasant enough. What are their names? Oliver, no − Olivier. And hers is what? Was it Polly? Ollie and Polly, that's right. Easy to remember.

If they all came that would be six, plus the newcomers. And me, of course. A grand total of nine. Quite a party, more than I've had in the dump for donkey's years. What about the morose daughter – Kim, wasn't it? She was much more interested in Teddy the other night, which showed good judgement. She'd be better off staying home and watching a DVD. I'll suggest that. They're sure to have a DVD player. Everyone has them now, except us. I don't like modern films as a rule, and I've seen all the old ones of any interest.

Teddy would be much happier out of the house. He responded well to her, I could even let her borrow him for company. It might do him good, be a little adventure for him. He's not himself when there are other people milling about. One or two others is the most he can handle, he prefers it when it's just us. We're alike in that, as in so many other ways.

Lisa's is a silly name for a second-hand bookshop owned by a man called Sandy Fay. It sounds frivolous, whereas Sandy is seriously devoted to what he does. It's typical of him that he didn't bother to change it when he took over. He must have had the shop for twenty years at least. Most people would rush to change it to something catchy or punning, like Pre-Loved Pages or Ye Olde Hoary Tomes. That's not Sandy's way.

Why in the name of fanciful heaven am I doing this? Correct etiquette was drummed into me, but I have long outgrown my dismal upbringing, surely. Am I obliged to do it?

No, absolutely not. One of the consolations of old age, and imaginary god knows there are few, is that you don't *have* to do anything. You can say whatever you wish and behave as badly as you like. No one gives a fig because no one even notices. Not only are you invisible in our youth-centred world, you're also inaudible and irrelevant.

When do they say women become invisible overnight? After the age of fifty? Isn't that the cut-off point for women? In that case, no one except Teddy has noticed me for twenty-seven years.

But this is not quite the case, to revert to my novel habit of brutal honesty inculcated by Oscar. I was noticed for a time, I think I can safely say that, even though I was over the cut-off point by then. Over it by what, getting on for ten years? When that little idyll was abruptly terminated I would have jumped at invisibility. The option was not on offer at that stage, however. I had to roll with the punches, in full public view.

But now that it is the only available option I find it suits me very well.

It wouldn't matter who had bought my house, I would feel the same towards them. I expect I would feel the same about Sandy, for example, if he had bought it.

Do I feel guilty about this? I don't think so. Should I feel guilty that I am as fallible as everybody else?

Nine people. I need not go to those lengths. Perhaps I'll simply have the three of them over and be done with it. On the other hand, it does provide an opportunity to announce, in no uncertain terms, that no one should be concerned about me because I am perfectly all right, in my imperfect way. I may have taken a second body blow in my life but I am rolling with the punches, just as I did before.

I'll sleep on it.

~~

I wonder how old they think I am? I suspect that once they see you have arrived in the country of the elderly, the tundra of the irrelevant, the young cease to think of age in gradations of years. You're just generically ancient to them. Not that I or most of my acquaintances are yet toothless and babbling, or excessively deranged. Or not that I know of. Verily, for such consolations let us all be truly thankful.

But would I necessarily know? For instance, I've noticed that the local chemist is full of incontinence pads. People must be buying them up in droves, and the odds are I know a few of their names. My bladder's not perfect, not by a long chalk, but it does a tolerable job. Teddy's might be more of a worry. There's been the odd dribble lately.

If I were lost in the land of dementia, the worst ogre of all, certain characters such as Barb and Davy would undoubtedly have let me know. But would I remember if they had?

I thought I was going fairly well today but I got worse as the day wore on. The invaders went backwards and forwards outside *their house* like a team of scurrying ants. I think he and the girl took a load of empty boxes to the tip. There was some friendly waving. I pretended not to notice.

If I hadn't made the calls already I would have decided against the blessed drinks business. Now it's too late, unless I invent a sudden-onset catastrophe. Spleen ruptured from excessive venting? Mad cow disease? Rinderpest, perchance? I don't want to saddle myself with something terminal.

Why, exactly, am I going ahead with this? I think it must be true, that I feel some remnant pangs of conscience. A few residual pangs, nothing like fully-fledged guilt. I would certainly recognise that, would I not?

It's not their fault that they, an ordinary, inoffensive young family, happened to buy my house. They couldn't have had any inkling of the baggage they were taking on. Does this twinge of conscience mean my character is not completely irredeemable after all?

What a waste, when the Great Redeemer is so conspicuous by her absence.

Sandy seemed pleased to be asked. I could hear that in his voice, as well as surprise. He probably thinks it's good for me to invite people over because I'm too reclusive. They all think that. A hermit without a permit, according to Davy. To that I say this: thanks be to imaginary god you don't need one to be one.

I could point out to them that real hermits do not attend writing classes. Oscar wants us to dredge out our first memories. What on earth could they be? At my age one is supposed to have no short-term memory left, but I don't seem to have much of a long-term one either. Which could just mean I don't like looking back.

And why would you? I've never seen the point of deliberate self-abuse.

~~

Only five of us there today. Bearded Greg was a no-show. He is the sole man in the class and only in his forties. I've already said I wouldn't be at all surprised if he drops out, and he may have done so already. If so it was Gilda who drove him away. Gilda, the faded lily in need of gilding. She said she thought he was feeling intimidated by a queen and five old bats. She talks nonstop and only ever says the obvious and/or the offensive. A common characteristic of people who talk too much.

My first memories were as dull as ditchwater. But so were those of the others, with one fanciful exception. They were all along the same, inconsequential lines. Being lifted into a cot, or walking downstairs holding on to a banister. Fleeting, formless memories of no conceivable interest to anyone. You couldn't even say they were privileged glimpses into the past. You couldn't do anything with them, as a writer, but perhaps that was the point of the exercise.

Except for the Gilda-lily, who claimed to remember a temporary nanny, a Bulgarian with warts who force-fed her

25

until she was sick on her hamster. It was clear to everyone she must have been at least six, even assuming it happened, which I doubt. The details were a giveaway. How could she have any idea of a fill-in nurse's nationality, or know what a nationality was?

I believe I am the only one who has obeyed Oscar's order and embarked on a journal. I stayed behind to tell him. He asked if I had been veracious, or mendacious? Brutally and *vora*ciously honest, I said. Aren't I always? To which he replied: 'You're blunt, Thea. I don't think that's quite the same thing.'

He added a further enigmatic postscript: 'I'd like you to keep it up for me. I think you may find it liberating. Even,' and he tipped me a wink – I'm not at all sure they're right about Oscar being gay – 'madly therapeutic.'

Interestingly, that seems to be true. Although *madly* could be overstating it.

Our new assignment might have been tailor-made with me in mind. We are to give a detailed description of a place that has special meaning or significance in our lives. Perhaps a particular city, house or room, a garden maybe, or somewhere exotic in a foreign country.

Or it might be a certain landscape formation.

Unlike the last session, when I had nothing to say, this time I have an embarrassment of riches. I have a choice of three. There have been three places of life-changing significance to me. They are a house, a rocky outcrop and a narrow ledge.

'Think of somewhere that you are not ambivalent about,' Oscar prescribed with an expansive gesture. 'Somewhere with such potency in your life that you can't even think of it without your heart skipping a beat. The place where once you gathered wildflowers in spring, perhaps. Or where you were *wildly* deflowered.'

I rather like the outré way Oscar talks. It's alarming at times, but in a way exhilarating to a member of my wildly more stitched-up generation. Is it spontaneous? It certainly gives that impression.

Thinking it over, I wonder whether he gave us the first memories assignment in order to identify those who are prepared to be honest from those who cheat. If so, it achieved its objective.

I suppose I could ask him to the drinks thing, but I have a feeling it would be too stuffy for him. I think he's the kind of person who prefers less conventional pursuits, whatever they may be. He knows Sandy because he frequents his shop. Sandy is very tolerant, but even he might find Oscar at close quarters a fraction in your face, so to speak.

~~

I feel liverish. Nobody calls it that today, but it must be the aftermath of the drinks. I had too many drinks, that's the trouble. Odd, to get to this advanced age and still be doing stupid things. Some of the same stupid things you did in your youth. Well, perhaps that's a blessing in disguise. It gives you a point of contact with the young, should you ever desire one.

But I felt exceptionally foolish when I introduced the invaders, euphemistically, to Sandy. I told him they and their daughter had come to live opposite me, in my house. Sandy was late, and I suppose I'd already sunk a couple of Davy's lethal martinis. But two egregious blunders in one sentence.

Ellice and Frank spoke at once. Oh no, Kim wasn't their daughter, she was Frank's *niece*. She couldn't be theirs, she was half-Vietnamese, hadn't I noticed that? Kim was Frank's brother's child, Frank was her uncle. And besides, she was twelve years old.

'Ms Farmer must have thought we were thrillingly precocious,' Frank said to Sandy. Davy was listening in. He enjoyed that.

'I would have been pregnant at thirteen,' Ellice laughed. Gurgled, actually. They high-fived each other with delight.

Sandy was in a world of his own as usual, but of course the old Davy couldn't resist. 'You have to make allowances for Thea,' he said, pursing his lips in that arch 'thespian' way that is so irritating. 'She's not losing it yet – at least, we must give her the benefit of the doubt – but she's always had a touch of the innocent abroad. Doesn't always draw the obvious conclusions, do you, love?'

He cocked an eyebrow, also in the way he does. He thinks it looks whimsical and endearing, when it induces in one an urgent compulsion to dry retch. The little speech meant nothing to them, of course, and I could see Sandy wasn't even listening, but I could have taken an axe to Davy's head.

'Shit.' Ellice was looking aghast. 'You must have thought I was thirty at the very least, Ms Farmer. Mid-thirties even. Aaagh, the horror!'

I had to smile.

'Uh-oh.' She lowered her voice. 'Franko. That makes *you* over forty.'

The sepulchral way she pronounced it – thirty was the gateway of doom, the beginning of the end. Forty? Might as well be six feet under.

They fell about a bit more, then remembered they were hemmed in by three old codgers who were over the forties hump by several decades. We were concentrating on knocking back our drinks, the time-honoured way of drowning out what you can do bugger all about, like death and taxes and bloody old age. Not to mention bad luck and wretched judgement and the whole damn thing.

Then they launched into voluble apologies. How could they have been so rude? Each had assumed the other had told me. Honestly, give poor Ms Farmer a break, how could she be expected to know?

All the evidence aside, Ms Farmer, Davy murmured. They didn't pick up this sly little dig, of course, but once again I could have kicked him.

My second gaffe, the one about 'my house', seemed to pass unnoticed.

Ellice and Frank recognised the name Davy Messer. They'd even seen his last performance, as it happens, his dribbling Polonius, which gave the old boy a kick he didn't deserve. He's a vain little sausage, like all actors.

He professed bafflement as to why they'd come to live here. 'Out in the back of beyond, miles from anywhere, with only *Thea* as a neighbour? What can you have been thinking?' He performed his gargoyle grimace.

But that's the whole point, they chorused. Where else would you find such an incredible place to live?

'They came here specifically to get away from suburban professional bores like you,' I said. Just because Davy prefers to live slap-bang in the middle of a country town, he always insists on calling this the back of beyond. He dislikes driving on the long, unmade road, which is why he hardly ever comes here. He cadged a lift this time with Bill and Monique.

The old perve was visibly taken with Ellice. She was wearing sandals with heels and an ankle-length skirt in some filmy red stuff, with a sleeveless orange top. Quite daringly low cut. We were taught never to put clashing colours together, but the effect was rather stunning with her full figure and dark, wavy hair.

It was the first time they'd set foot in the dump, of course. It must have reeked of neglect to them – I haven't done any upkeep here for donkey's years. I always thought I would be leaving that dubious pleasure to somebody else. It did seem incongruous having a pair – no, a quartet, with Ollie and Polly – of lively young people in the hovel. Ellice of course made a point of wittering on about how cute it was. Such a terrific period, the Victorian, wasn't it? I corrected her in mid-gush: I think you mean Federation.

Then I said, pity about the *un*state-of-the-art-kitchen, isn't it? I could see the reference was lost on her. Then Frank came up later and said what a charming Federation cottage it was. She must have tipped him off. Well, I suppose the old bones are all right in their way. If you overlook the prehistoric kitchen and bathroom and the lack of light and the miniscule, mouldering verandah.

What they neglected to mention was what a contrast it is to my house. To *their house.*

Still, nine people crammed into cramped quarters tends to make a party. Especially if they're drinking gin martinis mixed by Bill, or worse, by Davy. So much so that nobody would make the first move to leave, and finally I served a pot of scrambled eggs and a pile of hot buttered toast. The youngsters did most of it. I think they bonded.

Luckily there were plenty of eggs to supplement my two. The Nugents had arrived with a bag, still messy with chook feathers, and Ellice sent Frank over to raid their fridge. He reported that Teddy and Kim were perched on cushions eating baked beans and watching a DVD of *Gone With the Wind.* Teddy's seen *Gone With the Wind* on TV, I said, but not with baked beans on his lap. He's having his horizons broadened.

Later, after he'd brought Teddy back, Frank insisted on staying to help me clear up. I was in two minds about this. I'd planned to do it in the morning at my leisure, but he wouldn't take no for an answer. It would take no time at all with the two of us, he said.

We had a little chat. It turned out they thought I was an architect. Had been one, I mean. When I said my career had been in teaching he expressed surprise. English, I told him, but I ended up as a school principal. A careless thing to say. Reckless. The martinis speaking. I could have bitten my tongue off.

'Did you souvenir Year Three's blackboard?' he asked. We were in the kitchen. I explained it's an aide memoire, for my lists. Just as well I'd remembered to rub off my lines.

Then he touched me on the arm. Could he let me into a naughty secret? 'I hope you don't mind, Ms Farmer, but we've all been a bit intimidated. A bit in awe of you. Our Wombat especially. Now we know why.'

It's always disconcerting when people come out with things like that. You don't think of yourself as an awe-inspiring figure. Not in the least. Although I did wield some power for a time, in a small pond. If I had chosen to use it.

Now I am more a figure of no consequence one way or the other. A woman of negligible importance, as Wilde might have put it.

He asked what schools I'd worked in. I gathered my scattered wits sufficiently to say, vaguely, that I'd mainly taught in the public sector. True, as far as it goes. Thirty-five years for the ghastly government versus three for the abominable Anglicans.

Then he inquired if I'd been a terrifying headmistress. I knew from the way he dropped that passé word he imagined I had. It was exactly the same way as his wife pronounced the dreaded forty. A *headmistress* was a Dickensian, Dotheboys Hall species of female.

I had no intention of going there. No idea, I said. I had my back turned to him. Then added, 'How does any of us know what impression we make? It's just as well we don't, in my book.'

31

That was being both honest, my dear Oscar, and blunt. Although in the interests of accuracy you might prefer to say it was honest *up to a point*.

Frank's response was, 'We never have the shock of seeing ourselves as others see us, right? One of life's little mysteries instead of one more in its never-ending sequence of disappointments, as Ellie's dad often says. I always think he's referring to me.'

'Oh, I doubt that,' I said, disingenuously. I quite like the sound of Ellie's dad. Maybe it was her mum who chose the chairs.

Frank wasn't quite done with this. Actually, he reckoned I wasn't fearsome at all. He reckoned as school principals go, Ms Farmer, I was probably a bit of a pussycat. He smiled blithely at me. What he probably reckoned was that he'd ventured out of his depth, and was scurrying back. Little did he know.

Pussycat, owl or pea-green boat, I said, it was time we dispensed with formality. No more Ms Farmer. They had better call me Thea. Immediately after saying that I regretted it.

He responded with another smile. 'Cool.' It was a tentative, rather charming smile. He couldn't imagine the Wombat was up for that yet though, not quite. He thought he might need a bit of practice, too. He took a deep breath. 'Thea. There, I did it. Did I do okay? Did I pass?' We shared a little laugh.

Frank didn't seem in the least tired. That's youth for you. Wombat must be his pet name for the niece, of whom he seems fond. Said he wanted to sit me down and tell me all about her. The circumstances, why she was with them. Not tonight you won't, I said firmly, another time. Another time may never come, I thought to myself, but this may be being unduly optimistic.

It's probably some kind of trendy, extended family business. Divorce, or perhaps there's been some awful accident. Best not to know? Anyway, it was late, and Teddy and I wanted the place to ourselves.

Before he left he said I must come over for coffee soon. With no time to dredge up an all-purpose excuse I avoided a response. I daresay I can come up with something. But he was probably just saying that for politeness' sake. He seems a well-mannered young man, more personable than I rated him initially.

I must admit I was quite pleased when I got up this morning to find everything shipshape. The place looked less of a shambles than it has for some time. I kept getting little whiffs of Sandy's pipe tobacco, not unpleasant. You get the same savoury whiffs in the shop, even though he confines his pipe to the back room.

The other good thing was having no blasted bottles to deal with. Frank had taken them. He said he'd drop them in the recycling this morning as he was catching an early train to Sydney.

He turns out to be something in music. A composer? You couldn't make a living from that, surely. Perhaps he writes advertising jingles, or are they obsolete? Ollie Nugent was talking to him about whatever it was, and they seemed to get on. Ollie's in IT. He's been raking it in, according to Monique, but she thinks the economic downturn might scuttle all that.

Apparently Frank can work from home much of the time. He enthused about how great it is being able to 'chill out' up here. 'Give me the simple life,' he sang in a light baritone. What does she do? I've forgotten already. He didn't say how long the niece was staying with them, and I didn't ask because I had no interest in knowing.

Still, I approved of their use of my surname until invited to do otherwise, even if it was prompted by my unimaginable level of seniority. You hardly ever hear this nowadays. And their conscientious use of Ms was to be applauded. No trespassing on the thin ice of Miss, or the hallowed ground of Mrs. No assumptions either way, which is as it should be. Gruesome pronunciation apart, Ms is one of the few contributions of modern etiquette that is a resounding improvement. Modern manners being a contradiction in terms, as a rule.

Anyhow, I've discharged my social obligations. Now I can safely ignore them for a while. And vice versa, let us undevoutly hope.

~~

So they see me as an intimidating figure. Out of touch too, I imagine. Well, they're probably right there. I wonder what emotional history they have constructed for me, if any. However inventive, it is unlikely to be accurate.

Admittedly, I did find myself warming to Frank somewhat. No doubt the martinis were responsible for that. But he is a very open, rather likeable young man, and not unattractive either, upon closer inspection. Thinking it over, I can see it was exposure to this openness that made me unnecessarily uneasy. It led me to believe he was interested in my career history when he was merely being polite.

~~

Felt better today. In a penitential mood, went for the two-point-five hour undercliff walk to make up for the sloth of the last two days. Left at six-thirty and completed it in under two hours. Teddy didn't mind me going too much. He's always sluggish at that hour.

My powers of recovery remain strong. Physically, that is. Walked briskly past their house without giving it one glance, let alone a second. Could have walked longer if I hadn't known Teddy would be awake and waiting for me.

Fifty yards from my gate I thought I was home and hosed, then heard my name hesitantly pronounced. The girl Kim, needless to say, shoulders hunched and proffering an envelope. I took it from her with a cursory nod and kept going. I'd finished my water bottle and Teddy needed his breakfast.

After we'd both eaten I remembered the damn thing. Had the usual hunt for the reading glasses. They were in the bed. Is that the fifteenth time or the fiftieth?

Inside the envelope was a handmade card, a folded sheet of thin cardboard with a drawing of a cattle dog and girl sitting side by side on cushions on the floor watching television. The figures were unmistakably Teddy and Kim. Teddy had his tongue lolling out. It was surprisingly well done, painted in watercolours. Signed K. Campbell, in the bottom right-hand corner, with a small *PTO, and please see PS.*

Overleaf were two messages:

Dear Ms Farmer,

Thank you for lending Teddy. I hope he enjoyed his evening as much as I did, from Kim xx.

It was written in that undisciplined hand that slopes off in all directions. Her name was enclosed again by a line drawing of a wombat.

Underneath:

Many thanks, Thea, for a great night, warm wishes, Ellice and Frank, in more sophisticated script. They'd all signed their names in different-coloured inks. At the bottom was the small PS, which I nearly missed, in spite of the reminder:

Frank helped with the finer points of Teddy's visage.

The finer points? Visage? Curious terms for her to use. I looked at Teddy's face. It was a remarkable likeness. Very observant. I placed the card on the mantelpiece in the living room. I suppose I should have opened it in her presence, but how was I to know?

At least there are some people left who still write thank-you letters.

Davy called. He's old school about things like that, always punctilious. Had a right old time at my knees-up, he said, very jolly. They were quite *hip*, my new neighbours, weren't they? Oho, yes, they'd keep me on my toes.

Oho. Lucky old me.

~~

I went out early again in the hope of seeing no one, but still ran into three separate groups. Mainly French and Japanese, map-reading couples with serious backpacks, overtaking me. They looked as if they were heading for the canyon, a full day's hike, or maybe a more adventurous expedition and camping out for two or three days. Strong, striding young people, all saying hello.

Walkers always greet one another as they pass. They're that kind of person. Being out and about in a spectacular setting tends to make you well disposed to your fellow humans, even if you're not especially that way to start with. Is this a motherhood statement or is it true? I suspect it may be more true of others than of me. Any amiable tendencies that trickle my way are liable to disperse, I find, rather swiftly.

All the paths and hiking trails winding along the cliff tops and down into the valleys can take in only a tiny fraction of the national park. The area covers hundreds of thousands of hectares. Those in frequent use are well-kept and the rump of humanity sticks to them, thankfully. But if you venture further afield many tracks, often well over a century old, overgrown and assailed annually by deluges of stormwater and fallen trees, are impossible for any council to maintain.

Fortunately, Teddy has the unerring instincts of a homing pigeon. Without him, in years gone by, as we explored half-obliterated trails together, I would have come to grief many times.

Nowadays the walks are rated according to grades of difficulty. What happened in the past, when plump and perspiring tourists found themselves confronted with a succession of perpendicular iron ladders? I haven't done one of those demanding walks for some time, but I can still do the uphill trudges. Just as well, because there's usually a fair amount of climbing. If I take my time I can tackle plenty of steps, but not the hundreds I used to do, and sadly no more ladders.

Teddy loved our daylong rambles, but you hardly see dogs at all now. People are much more obedient and stick to the few trails where dogs are permitted. They keep them on leash, usually, as they are supposed to do, even in areas where you rarely or never see a ranger.

I used to be naughty. But Teddy was far too well trained to think of hurtling off into the bush. The worst thing he ever did was catch that lizard. It was a fairly small one, about five inches, but I felt bad about it for weeks. Longer, I suppose, because I still think about it.

People are more aware these days about conservation and the fragility of our wildlife. They're more informed. If Teddy were suddenly, miraculously rejuvenated I would think twice about taking him on the public trails where we might be challenged. Or if I did I'd keep him on a lead. Have I become more law-abiding in my old age? If you're invisible it should be the other way round, shouldn't it? You can get away with more.

It's a different matter on our own private walks, the ones only Teddy and I know about. The ones that harbour our secrets. We've never encountered another living soul there, human or canine. May that goodness and mercy continue all the days of our lives, O imaginary lord. All the remaining days.

~~

I always did have a mutinous streak. Which is odd, considering my profession. There are few more responsible jobs than teaching, let alone being head of a school. As I know to my cost. Did that irresponsibility intensify, I wonder, as a reaction to my work? I don't know that I was ever particularly fond of children as a genus. Had I been more fond I might have been more vigilant on their behalf, might I not?

Some were all right. If anything, I identified most with the troublemakers, because they were generally the individualists, the ones with the most gumption and disdain for authority.

I think of landscape as having similar characteristics to children: introverted or outgoing. It can be passive like England, dreamy and civilised; equally, it can be unstable or high-spirited. I inhabit an ancient, swashbuckling land whose weather and topography are dramatic – and unpredictable.

Is that why I respond to it so powerfully? And not only me, of course. It is a World Heritage Site. Even after living here for twelve years and spending weekends for decades before that, I am never oblivious to what is on my doorstep. This vast, secretive wilderness.

~~

Apart from restoring Teddy's youthful vigour, and obliterating the invaders breathing down my neck, my third dearest wish is to write poetry. But my best efforts continue to be pathetic. Bathetic, to be brutal about it. Elementary rhymes, not unlike the scatological doggerel everyone wrote at university, seem to be my limit. I could never show them to the writing class. There is no future in them. Perhaps if I liked children more I could write a book for them in simple rhyming couplets.

As Oscar says, a journal is a way of keeping one's writing muscles toned, a generative, quotidian task. When he intoned those words I caught his eye. He and I have fallen into the mischievous habit, now and then, of using words only the two of us understand.

I do get something resembling enjoyment from this diary. It is a continuing dialogue with myself, a daily – quotidian – autobiography. I can think on the computer page, express things I wouldn't normally say to anyone. Even to Teddy. It's true that it is an outlet, Oscar is right about that. I seem to be becoming downright expansive. Or is it longwinded? Teddy, who was always a rambunctious boy, might find the details tedious, even if he understood them.

~~

I am going to have to pull back. I'm worried things may be taking too familiar a turn. Best if we keep right out of each other's way for a while. What I emphatically do not want is for them to construct a sad existence for me. I don't want them to imagine I'm lonely.

I had to take Teddy to the vet. Nothing serious, only his prescription and check-up. Occasionally these expeditions are harder than they used to be, because of his dickey back leg. Sometimes it plays up, and then he has trouble jumping on to the seat.

The Campbell-Carrington trio saw me struggling a bit and came over. The couple went back promptly, saying the electrician was coming to put in a few more power points. I thought there were plenty of power points, I'd made a point of putting in more than you need. But they said you can never have too many of the damn things.

The tiresome girl was still hovering over Teddy. Close up, you can see she has some Asian input, around the mouth especially and the eyes. I don't know why I didn't notice it before. She was chewing gum, a particularly unsavoury habit. Didn't seem inclined to leave, but nor did she want to say anything to me. Instead she murmured away to Teddy in a sing-song voice, ruffling her fingers through the thick fur around his shoulders in the way he likes. Chattering away to him as if there were all the time in the world and they were the only two in it. She flashed me a quick sidelong glance in which there was a hint of provocation.

I responded to that by saying loudly, 'We're going now,' and opening the driver's door. She came round and muttered a question about Teddy's leg. We had a perfunctory exchange about medical matters before I cut it short. I don't disparage her concern, but she seems not to understand that this hip business is quite normal for his age. He is in perfect health otherwise. She talks too fast and has a tendency to mumble. I was impatient to go, and completely forgot to mention her thank-you card.

She was still hanging about after I'd climbed in, scuffling her bare, dirty feet in the dust. She said, 'I like how Teddy gets to sit beside you on the passenger seat. It makes him feel important, like he's a human.'

Then I spent what should have been a pleasant drive feeling guilty about being brusque and having forgotten about her drawing.

The school year starts soon. She'll be going home. That will be one invader less.

It was a mistake, having the drinks party. It was a rush of blood to the head, I can't imagine what came over me. It gave the wrong impression, because I don't want this neighbourly business. I don't want to feel guilty or beholden – I want none of it. Next thing we know they'll be racing over for a cosy little chat whenever I have a shopping bag to unload.

I think I'll start parking the chariot in a different place, behind the house where it can't be seen from over there. I could start using the back door, I'm sure I can rig up something for Teddy. A plank, so he can walk up onto the seat when he needs to. Or I could get Giorgio to make another set of steps, like the ones he installed for Teddy at the end of my bed. That would work well, if they were permanently in the same place. I'd just have to be a bit more precise with the parking. Unloading him is no problem because his front legs are fine.

Reading this over, I am aware that my behaviour might be judged unreasonable, but I cannot be held accountable for that. Who is there to judge? Reasonable or unreasonable, it is of no consequence. I am responsible only to myself and to Teddy. If they label me selfish or unneighbourly – or just plain *blunt* – it's fine by me. It's how I like it.

~~

That's nothing to what happened today.

I took Teddy on his sixty-minute circuit. It's essential he gets his exercise every day. But as he plods along in front of me and I slow my pace to accommodate him I think of his youthful, bounding self. The exuberant way he fetched balls and sticks. He'll still chase gamely after a ball, but I suspect he is only doing it to please me. We humour one another, rather, I imagine, like a contented old married couple.

We were pottering along the downhill stretch, skirting the fallen tree and approaching the white scribbly gum that grows out of the outcrop. Approaching what I think of as my magical place, the rock formation Namatjira might have painted.

We were about a hundred yards away when Teddy spotted something. He stopped and stood stock-still in front of me, ears pricked. At first I thought it might be a rare sighting of a lyrebird or a swamp wallaby. He barked once, then darted ahead with a spurt of energy, tail flying. There was a blurred flurry of white and red, and Teddy's excited noises.

This was unprecedented, and so shocking that it took me a moment to register what was happening. Then it dawned on me. It was that infernal girl again, the niece Kim, in a white cotton hat and red T-shirt, perched up inside a crook of the sandstone where it rolls under itself into a cresting wave formation. If not for Teddy I'd have missed her completely. She was only just visible behind the leaning tree trunk. I think she must have been sitting in the hollow of the wave, reading.

I felt winded, as if I'd been punched in the solar plexus. I had three distinct thoughts in quick succession. First: this is our private sanctuary. Second: in all these years I have never known another person to come here. And third: I will not have it.

Teddy was bounding up to lick her face, untroubled by any of these thoughts. One of the rare times when we were not in accord.

I didn't linger or hesitate. I whistled him back and turned on my heel. He trotted after me obediently after a short interval. Nor did I once look behind, although in my mind's eye I saw the girl standing up in confusion, staring after us. Teddy was disconcerted too. He wanted to go back and see her and continue the walk, I could tell.

I found myself breathing heavily as I strode home. An uphill gradient, but that wasn't the reason. I should have said something. Confronted her? With what? I have no legitimate grounds for confrontation. It is public land. She is as entitled to wander through it as Teddy and I.

But there is no need for any of them to encroach on my territory. There is virgin bush in abundance behind their house. It stretches way beyond the twenty hectares that are now on their title.

All the same, I should not have turned my back on her without a word. Bad behaviour on my part, no question about it. Uncalled for and rude. Moreover, I'm afraid, rather childish. I'm in my eighth decade and she is an actual child. An awkward, solitary child, too. Why don't they let her bring a friend to stay? They have plenty of room. Was she perhaps looking for us? Waiting for Teddy and me? If so, she will have to learn that some places are out of bounds.

Why should I have such an immoderate reaction to what is a natural feature, an exposed sandstone outcrop? Is it because I know it has a secret, interior life? The idea of another person, an intruder, discovering what is concealed there – it is anathema to me. It enrages me at a pure, visceral level. I can't pretend it does not. The rage is boiling inside me and I cannot suppress it.

The notion of inner lives has always appealed. The auto-nomy, the impregnability. Which, of course, is only apparent. Only an illusion. However much human beings may believe their secrets are impregnable, out in the natural world they are always vulnerable – to the plundering of their fellow humans. That is what I am fearful of, and always have been.

I wish to be the only one who knows the secret. Because it is the single, certain way to keep it safe.

~~

Why do I feel like this? I feel a compulsion to justify it, in order to explain the extremity of my position. To explain it to myself, perhaps, as much as to anyone else.

On an aesthetic level alone the rock is a still life of rare perfection. Its undulating architecture has been forged over centuries into a noble composition. This is its 'public' face. I have tried – fruitlessly, of course – to write poems about the public face of this rock. How it has lain under the sky down the ages. Down the lifetimes. 'Since time immemorial' is a hackneyed phrase, but I find it apt.

There are curvaceous channels where rain has swept along in torrents and burrowed into the compliant mass. The girl was nestling in one such sinuous hollow, and I have done so myself on endless balmy days. Sat for hours contentedly with Teddy and a good book, cradled by the ancient warmth.

These shapes bring to mind Japanese paintings of towering waves curled over, poised on the brink of breaking. Elsewhere the sandstone is honed into sharp edges, honeycombed with indentations that suggest giant prehistoric clams. Or some elemental creature's monstrous fingerprints.

Some contemporary residents live in the crevices. Teddy and I are well-acquainted with the blue tongue who stalks out to squat or stand alone in one favourite spot. It is a creature of habit, much like ourselves. Teddy has never once chased after this particular lizard, it is far too intimidating in its stillness – a primordial waxwork defying a melting sun. We are old friends, I like to think, who observe each other with companionable acceptance. Like Sandy and me, come to think of it.

But the rock is not just the ancestral home of lizards, snakes and marsupials. Back in the distant past, in the realms of what we presume to call prehistory, it attracted the attention of another species. A very different proposition, this one: adventurous and propelled by curiosity. Relentless too, and destructive. But also – and uniquely – artistic.

Concealed among the labyrinth of rock forms, very well hidden, is a low aperture leading to a small cave. Teddy found it first, and excavated some animal bones. Then one day I brought a torch and wriggled after him. I found myself in a tiny room, a miniature chamber curved like a vault and as dry as long-entombed dust. It was just large enough for me to stand, but not quite straighten up, and to take four steps.

In the thin arc of the torch I saw some marks directly facing me on the wall. At first I thought they were natural chalky smears. Then, as my eyes slowly adjusted, I saw they were drawings. Cave paintings, two of them, one above the other. Centuries old, in all probability. Thousands of years old, conceivably.

In the years following that first sighting I have gazed at those marks countless times. One is the outline of a wallaby. The other is harder to read because it is more like a diagram. It looks like a group of squiggles and wavy lines inside a television set. Which it can't be, for obvious reasons, but I have never managed to decipher it.

Not long after that first discovery, I think it was on the third visit, I noticed another set of marks placed down low on the cave wall. I couldn't believe I had missed them, I could hardly credit it. What I saw now was the print of a left hand with the thumb and fingers spread. When I crouched up against it using a stronger torch, until my eyes were almost too close to focus, I could just make out what seemed to be tiny irregularities in the pigment. I was seeing what may have been the pores of the artist's skin.

I laid my own outstretched hand against it, my hand that was dry and cold but very much alive. I found it was shaking a little. My hands are largish because I'm tall and big-boned.

The print was smaller than mine. It could have been made by a man, but I like to think – I feel it in my bones – that it was a woman, left-handed like myself, someone nobody will ever identify, who chose to leave a signature on her clandestine work. Who left behind the message of her creativity.

Lately I haven't gone in, not because of any fear that I might expire in there. With the torchlight fading away in the dark and the gleam of light from the opening, it would not be such a terrible end. No, simply because the contortions required are a bit beyond me now.

There are other cave paintings in the mountains, but as far as I know these three have never been documented. I took some flash photos once with a throwaway camera. They came out surprisingly well. I told the girl in the chemist when I collected them that I'd been on holidays in the Northern Territory. Her total lack of interest or curiosity was a relief. I keep them in a drawer in my desk.

It may be presumptuous to say so, but I think of these paintings as being in my custody. I think of them as my own, and myself as the sole curator of this tiny art gallery. It is a museum in miniature. For a long time I have been aware that, in all likelihood, I am the only living human being who knows it is there.

The outcrop is only visible when you are nearly upon it. In order to find it at all the girl must have followed our route through the dense bush. Because when you leave the dump that is my cottage, you have to follow certain landmarks before you arrive at anything approximating a path. Landmarks? That's a highfalutin word for what are particular trees, trunks and bushes, configurations I have come to recognise. There are no other guiding signs. The path itself could hardly be more obscure.

It's scarcely a path at all. Just the ghost of a trail, often camouflaged, winding through a thicket of stringybarks, grass trees, grevilleas and banksias. A fragrant tangle of foliage that Teddy and I have pushed through and trodden down together over the years, invariably in single file because Teddy likes to lead the way. He is my protector, checking that it is safe to proceed.

How did she find her way there? She must have made a deliberate search for it. She risked getting hopelessly lost. Is it conceivable she waited and watched us setting out one morning? Careful to stay so far behind that Teddy was unaware? His hearing and sense of smell are not what they were.

Was this her first visit, or had she been there before? Did she fossick among the twisted curves and crevices? Is that as far along the track as she went?

I find these thoughts deeply unsettling.

~~

I felt bruised. I felt a need for some human contact, a rare event, to be sure. It's always a mixed blessing, contact with our infuriating blessed species. This was no exception.

I dropped in to Lisa's. Sandy had just had a delivery, all the books from Arnold Monleigh's estate. No one in the shop so I went through to the back. He and his sidekick, whose name always escapes me – pleasant enough woman – were on their knees, sorting and cataloguing. Sandy was all folded up like a concertina.

She's pleasant but unremarkable; I suppose that's why I can never summon up her name. I can't imagine she and Sandy have a thing going, in spite of what Monique and Bill say. Davy's convinced too, but then he always thinks everyone's on with everyone else. Except Teddy and me, presumably, which is the just the kind of bad taste remark Davy would enjoy.

I was rather sorry I hadn't asked her to the drinks. Seeing them together away from the shop, one might have had more of an indication either way. But I would have had to ask her husband, the pharmacist, who is even duller.

Sandy clambered to his feet when he saw me. He was positively animated, all smiles beaming down on me from his great height. There's nothing like a good deceased estate to bring the corpse to life, I teased. He was nice about the drinks too. You didn't ring me, I forbore to say, unlike Davy. Nor, moreover, did you send a thank-you drawing of yourself enclosed by an elongated wombat.

He gave the invaders the seal of approval. Said my new neighbours had already been into the shop.

'The father and daughter lobbed in,' he said. 'He was after CDs and music books.'

Frank wasn't her father, he was her uncle, I reminded him. She was half-Vietnamese. I could see this was news to Sandy. And after all that palaver the other night. He obviously hadn't taken it in at all, the funny old thing. He's so unworldly he had trouble working the relationship out.

I mean unworldly in that he lives in a parallel universe made up of music and thousands of second-hand books. It's not that he's naive. As Davy says, he may not have done it but he knows how it would be done. Very droll. I wonder if Davy says that about me?

As we went back into the shop Sandy remarked, 'The young girl Kim is an intriguing kettle of fish. What do you make of her?' He knows her name already. I was surprised by that. He forgets the names of half his regulars.

For a second I was transported into another landscape. I saw the girl in her red T-shirt perched up in the cradle of the rock.

'That girl? I don't make anything of her, in particular,' I said. 'Why?'

'Because I think she's an unusual girl, Thea. We had quite an interesting little talk.'

That turned out to mean a talk about books, of course. What else interests Sandy? I waited while he mused over it, puffing on his pipe. For someone who has smoked all his life he has an amazingly unlined face. A kind face, I've always thought, under that floppy thatch of white hair.

'The thing is, you see, she has the mind of a reader but an erratic experience of reading.' There were some things you'd expect, Harry Potter, of course, and the odd vampire book, even Agatha Christie. But it was scrappy, all over the place. Surprising things like dog training manuals, and *Reader's Digest* condensed. He looked properly outraged. Condensed books are among Sandy's pet hates, to the extent that he refuses to stock them.

'You expect one thing to lead to another, but with her it's been curiously random, as if she's had no guidance. Self-*help* books . . .' He trailed off with a groan. If there is one genre that Sandy cannot fathom at all it is self-help books. He has to stock them because people bring them in all the time, but he gets very upset when someone wants to buy one. He tries to deter them. Consequently, it is the fastest-growing section in the shop.

That wasn't curiously random at all, I told him, it was depressingly normal for nowadays. Reading is badly taught, school reading lists are abysmal and dumbed down, and you're lucky if they read at all. Sandy only mixes with rarefied circles, people who read because it's encoded in their DNA. I could see he was unconvinced.

'What about this, then?' He was getting quite worked up. 'All those old boyhood adventure stories. R. M. Ballantyne and John Buchan. Rider Haggard. Jeffery *Farnol*, for Pete's sake. She'd actually read *Black Bartlemy's Treasure*, circa 1920. This is a girl, mind you. Pirates and torture. Yo–heave–ho, me hearties! Boiling water in his ears!'

He was so excited he pumped my arm. 'Now you can't tell me you don't think that's odd. How could it have happened? Most kids wouldn't touch those books with a barge pole. Nobody reads them nowadays.'

Well, I did, I pointed out. And I was a girl too, once upon a time back in the dim, distant past, you know. To please him, I conceded it did sound unusual. Sounds as if you had quite a ball, the two of you, I added, reminiscing about those ripping yarns.

Sandy never normally smokes his pipe in the shop. Must have been the rare combination of juicy deceased estate and that all-but-extinct species: eager young female customer. Most of his customers are our vintage, give or take twenty years.

He'd found the perfect book for her. *The Greengage Summer* by Rumer Godden. About right for twelve, didn't I think? Suffused with nostalgia. Romantic but seemly. Rural France, grapes, growing up. As far removed from pirates as you could hope for. Not too old for her, was it?

Really, I've never seen Sandy so carried away. There was no stopping him. She might turn out to be a bit of a find. Get them young and you'd got them for life, hadn't you? She was painfully shy, but she seemed like a sweet kid, didn't she? It must be rather satisfying, after all, having them living just across the way. Rather refreshing.

Satisfying, after all? Refreshing? My jaw must have dropped several inches.

He saw that but it didn't faze him one whit. Satisfying in the sense that although I had lost my dream house, there were appropriate people living there and appreciating it. And refreshing in that, having lived out there on my own for so many years, there was an injection of youth and change.

Appropriate: what an odd word to use, was all I could think to say. And I was never alone. I've had Teddy for nearly fourteen years, he knows that.

After a pause he added, 'I'm sorry, Thea. Don't imagine I underestimate the pain of your loss.'

Just before I came in, he said, neatly changing the subject, Monica had unearthed Arnold Monleigh's copy of *Lost Horizon*. American first edition, no less. Mint condition. That would be good for next time, wouldn't it?

Monica, that's her name. Monica ha! Harmonica, how could I have forgotten?

They'd never dare say it in my presence, but the possibility occurs to me that people secretly think it's a good thing I had to sell the new house instead of the dump. The dump is really only suitable for one human and dog, whereas the new house is spacious and flexible. I might have found myself with only one neighbour, and most likely a doddery one at that, instead of a bevy of youthful charmers, as Sandy would doubtless have it.

What he said is probably what everyone is thinking. It's good for me, I've been living a reclusive life out in the sticks for too long. It's unhealthy to be so set in my ways, and at my age even a bit risky. Better to have people around.

He understands the pain, I do believe that, but why is it so hard for Sandy, for everyone, to accept the rest – that I was not lonely and I did not and do not want change? Is it perhaps because it diminishes them? Their role in my life, I mean. Real or imagined.

First edition *Lost Horizon*, my foot. Frank couldn't afford it, or if he could he wouldn't. Good for next time? I have an idea Sandy feels his Pygmalion period coming on.

~~

Even in the café I cannot get away from those people. My fault for going into one, but I needed a strong flat white. The moment I set eyes on Joan Mills I regretted it. The peripatetic woman is back from her latest extravagance. China, this time.

I'd left Teddy outside. The laws in this country are absurd. If we were in France he could be sitting at the table, perched up beside me on a chair with a napkin round his neck and no one would bat an eye. They're talking about changing the rules but nothing seems to happen.

No sooner had I reluctantly sat down at her table (no avoiding it) when I heard my name a second time. The young woman dispensing menus was none other than Ms Ellice Carrington. She seemed amused at my astonishment. After she'd taken the order I went out and smuggled Teddy inside under the table, where I fed him bits of ham and cheese from my toasted sandwich. I'm told my new neighbours find me intimidating, I explained to Joan, so she's unlikely to have the temerity to object.

'Intimidating!' Joan exclaimed in her hoity-toity voice. '*Toi?* No, surely not.' The idea that sarcasm is the lowest form of wit has never lodged in Joan's minimal cranium. And she is loud – Ellice, emerging from the kitchen, gave me a quirky look.

It wasn't my intention but Joan ended up gleaning more information about the intruders in my life than I heard about China. In any case, she was obsessed by the pollution in China, to the exclusion of anything else of interest. The state of the world is horrific.

Ellice has a degree of some sort – I can't imagine what she thinks she's doing working as a waitress. Joan, who is easily impressed, was quite taken with her. She announced her intention to invite them to one of her famous dinners. I'll make an excuse, as usual. She's welcome to them.

Joan brought up the subject of her financial advisers, as I knew she would. She always boasted about them, and after what happened to me she is unstoppable. Nonetheless, I should have taken my head out of the sand and listened to her when she offered to put me on to them, should I not?

I had no wish to pursue this train of thought. Luckily Ellice had spotted Teddy's tail and chastised me for bringing him inside. Wasn't I the naughty girl, then? If she wasn't careful the boss would whip her ass.

Not a punishment I wished to witness, I said. Just the excuse I needed for getting out of there.

~~

We were pottering along the road. It rained heavily last night, the ground was steaming, but too wet and muddy to take the usual circuit. A car chugged up behind us. It could only be theirs. Frank, leaning out. Hi there. Did I want anything from the village? Bread, milk, newspaper? Caviar or truffles, *peut-être*?

No, thank you. We have everything we want, I said pointedly.

53

The car did a few sputtering kangaroo hops before driving off. It was only then that I realised it was Kim who was in the driving seat. Frank must be giving her driving lessons.

She's only twelve, but it's a safe enough place to do it, on an unmade road with no passing traffic. All we country kids learned to drive even earlier than that in the school holidays, dodging rabbit holes in the paddocks. Self-reliance is a fine thing, especially for girls. It tends to be in shorter supply than it used to be. Children are over-protected. Parents have succumbed to the modern disease of mollycoddling, the blight of bloated Western countries.

I suppose I could have asked Frank to pick up the paper. But that would risk setting an unhealthy precedent.

Everything we want. Wasn't that a lie? White, polite and disingenuous. Because we do not have the single thing we want the most. That is the eternal complaint of my species, is it not? Teddy's species, on the other hand, is content with whatever it is given.

What we really want is the one thing we cannot have. We want them not to be here.

~~

Car, café, bike — I cannot escape these people. The girl ran slap-bang into us, coming round a blind corner concealed by heavy scrub. Or rather, nearly into poor Teddy, who was ahead of me as usual. She was riding far too fast and skidded on some loose stones. Showing off. She wobbled, came off the bike and gashed her leg.

'I'm so sorry, Teddy,' she said. Not a word to me.

I said she should have rung her bell, then saw there was no bell on the bike.

'Didn't think I'd ever need one, not on this road.' She was chewing that awful gum again. 'There's never anyone here,' she said, rather mulishly.

I told her that was a foolish thing to say. Even on a deserted bush track you never know when anyone's going to be here. We were here, for a start. I could have added, I didn't know you were going to be up in the rock, did I? But, hey presto, there you were.

Of course the uncle and aunt had to be out. Probably at the café. And if they had a first-aid kit she didn't know where it was. Then she should tell them they'd better get one quick smart, I said, because of just this kind of mishap. And besides, there are snakes.

I was obliged to take her back to my place to wash and dress the wound. It wasn't a deep cut but there was a lot of blood. I dabbed Dettol on it and applied a bandage, as she seemed hopelessly ignorant of elementary first aid. I was taught what to do in the very thorough St John's Ambulance class I attended when I was about her age.

'I missed that, didn't I?' she said, as if this was obvious to any bonehead. 'Had to change schools. *Again.*' A significant emphasis. Was she expelled, perhaps on a serial basis? I didn't ask.

We hadn't said a word after this. The silence became oppressive, even to me. Teddy was happy, he was lying on his back having his stomach tickled. Her head was bent towards him, but I knew from long experience there was something fizzing away inside. You can always tell when a girl is brooding over something.

Eventually she muttered, 'You didn't like me being there, did you?'

I gave no sign of having heard.

Louder, with an undercurrent of truculence: 'You thought I was trespassing on your personal space.'

'Trespassing? On our personal space?' I assumed an obtuse expression. It occurred to me I was descending to her level, behaving childishly again.

'Those rocks out there.' The words tumbled out. 'That's where you and Teddy go just about every day, right? You think it's, like, your place? You don't want to see anyone else in your place, do you, Ms Farmer?'

It was more statement than accusation. But I felt suddenly absurd. Awkward and gauche in a way I don't think I have felt for quite some years.

I said, 'Kim, you must understand that you are staying opposite someone who has lived here since well before you were born and is very set in her ways.'

A nod, rather too vigorous. Riffling Teddy's fur. 'Yeah, right.' She looked down and frowned, screwing up her eyes. 'I hear what you're saying. I won't go there again if it drives you nuts.'

I was about to deny that it did this, then thought the better of it. No point in succumbing to the indignity of rising to the bait. 'You're perfectly entitled to go there if you wish,' I said. 'It's not my land. I have no right to ask you not to.'

'But you think of it like it *is* yours, yeah?' Rather than accusing, the words sounded tentative and exploratory.

'I don't own it. Nobody does. But, yes – I suppose I have thought of it like that.'

'Because I guess you always had all this whole entire place to yourself, before. You and Teddy.' He thumped his tail.

Because we did have it all to ourselves before, that's just it. You've hit the nail squarely on the head. I said none of this, however.

'Do you wish we weren't here?'

Only a child would have asked that direct, confronting question. But I was momentarily taken aback. She looked at me searchingly with wide, dark eyes. Unfathomable eyes,

I thought, like a pair of ink blots on an exercise book. Or, more charitably, like a pair of black opals. Flawless and rather beautiful.

I thought it more tactful not to reply. Although I'm told tact has never been my strongest suit.

She said, 'I would, if I'd had this all to myself for such a long time. I'd wish we'd never come here.'

There was my chance, Oscar. Wouldn't you have wanted me to say, with brutal honesty, of course I wish you had never come. I wish it more than anything in the world except for Teddy's wellbeing.

Instead of which the girl found herself transported to the principal's study. I said in a carefully measured tone, 'You had better tell me how you came to discover it, Kim.'

'It? What do you mean, *it*, Ms Farmer?' The ink-blot eyes had now taken on a look of wilful obtuseness. A childish expression irritatingly reminiscent, I had to concede, of the one I had assumed earlier. We regarded one another with this surreptitious mutual awareness.

'That rock is not at all easy to find is what I mean. As you know perfectly well.'

'Well, I did. I just found it. It was easy. Easy-peasy.'

Goaded by the singsong intonation, I said sharply, 'It is not easy-peasy in the least. It took Teddy and me a very long time indeed before we discovered it. It took you a matter of days, did it not?'

She shrugged.

'Did you follow us, Kim?'

She darted a covert glance at me, then looked away. She had the same shutdown look I have seen on the countenances of any number of miscreants.

I waited. She said, 'Anyone can see where you go on your walks, can't they? Like, you know, where you take off into the bush? I just went the same way, didn't I?' Unapologetic.

And faintly pious, with a new undercurrent of impudence.

'I just came to them. Exactly like you did, Ms Farmer. *No way* was I spying on you.' She had assumed an emboldened air of wounded innocence. 'No way known. Or on your own, *private, secret* rocks.'

I suspected that the heavy emphasis on the adjectives was intended to annoy. If so, it succeeded. The word spying was the giveaway. I thought of all those old adventure books Sandy mentioned. The methods of their sleuths might be old-fashioned but they were still effective: broken twigs, snapped-off branches, the smudged imprints of shoes in the dust. Prying eyes and prying hands were never out of date; it was as well for me to remember that.

In my mind was a fingerprint on the wall of a tiny museum.

I said tersely, 'Not rocks plural. It is an intact sandstone rock formed in one piece, but weathered and moulded into many shapes. It's not mine and it's not exactly private or secret anymore, is it?'

The eyes widened, brimming with righteous indignation. 'It *so* is, Ms Farmer. I haven't told anyone. Not Frank, or Ellice, or anyone, that's the honest truth. I don't have anyone else to tell anyhow, do I?' The hint of a grin. I sensed she knew it was risky. 'Teddy knows already and the others are totally clueless.'

But you have a clue, I thought. How long will the secret be safe from you? We were in the kitchen. She peered out in the direction of the rock. The windowpane, I noticed, was crusted inside and out with baked-on dust. She seemed to be distracted by it, and simultaneously to be trying to second-guess what I was thinking.

'I can go somewhere else to read and stuff. It's not like there's a huge shortage of spare room round here. We don't need to trip over each other, right?' She gave me another fleeting grin and a direct, impish stare.

'Right. We have no need to get in each other's way,' I said, 'but you were fortunate not to get lost, you know. Do you live in the country or the town, Kim?'

She didn't reply but gave me an odd look. I decided to deliver a little lecture that was obviously overdue.

'You may not be sufficiently aware that you have to respect the land when you're staying up here.' The area behind her aunt and uncle's house was virgin bush. If she tried to go walking in there she would almost certainly get lost, so she shouldn't think of it. 'Even if you intend to stay close to the house. Off the beaten track you have to be very careful until you get some sense of the lay of the land. Most people never get it.'

'I've got my mobile. A *mobile phone*.' Pronounced with cheeky emphasis, as if talking to a Luddite. She fished it out of her pocket and flourished it for proof.

That was all very well, I said, but mobile reception was notoriously erratic here. It dropped in and out, and mostly out. You couldn't count on it and she should never rely on a phone.

'I guess you always had Teddy when you went exploring,' she said. 'You knew he'd get you home okay.'

This was true, I granted. Without Teddy I'd never have gone into the bush. She should leave a well-defined trail for herself if she ever ventured out of sight of the house, even for one minute. A brief lapse of concentration was all it took to get disorientated. Only last summer a bushwalker had vanished.

'People disappear here, you know, and are never found.'

She seemed unworried. A sagacious nod. Oh yeah, she knew about all that stuff so as not to get lost, no worries. Stuff like tying bits of brightly coloured string on branches.

Then, before I could comment on that, she said, 'It's important in life, right? To have somewhere sort of private of your own where you can, like, get away from people, and commune with nature?'

Commune with nature. Odd phrase, coming from her, but fitting. She must have read it somewhere. She's not as well spoken as her aunt and uncle, nowhere near, but she comes out with the occasional surprising word.

'You're quite right. Getting away from people is most important in life,' I said.

The brittle atmosphere between us seemed to have eased somewhat, also rather surprisingly. I asked how she was getting on with *The Greengage Summer*. Her mouth fell open. I explained that Mr Fay at Lisa's Second-Hand Bookshop was a good friend of mine.

'Phew, I thought you must be, like, incredibly *psychic*, Ms Farmer. Yeah, he wanted me to read it that very night. I haven't started it yet, but. Don't tell him, will you?'

'All right. I won't.'

'He must be a cool guy to have as a close friend. It's awesome how tall he is. I think he's the tallest guy I've ever set eyes on.'

I thought the awesomely tall Sandy would be quite tickled to hear himself described as cool. I might even tell him. Then I wondered if close friends was an accurate description of our relationship.

'It'll be back to school next week, won't it?' I said. 'I suppose you'll have to be going home.' I still haven't established where she lives.

'Home? Huh. Okay, right!' She shot up like a jack-in-the-box. I hadn't meant that home or that precise moment, but she was already halfway out of the open door.

'Thanks for doing the bandage, Ms Farmer. See ya. See ya, Teddy.' And she was gone.

Just as well the school year starts next week. I wondered idly how many schools she has attended.

~~

I can't imagine what possessed me to think I had the luxury of three choices for my homework. The house is far too painful a subject. Far too raw and recent. I couldn't begin to write about it and I doubt if I ever will. You need a measure of emotional detachment for writing.

Or do you? I am not exactly detached emotionally from the other two subjects, but it's a different kind of attachment. I didn't bring them into being, and therefore they exist on an altered level of consciousness.

Or do they? Perhaps the only difference is, I haven't loved and lost the other two. Or not yet, I mustn't tempt fate. In two out of those three cases fate has so far treated me kindly. Perhaps it feels it has a deficit to make up.

Rock dreaming. Does Oscar go for timelessness and serenity? Does he go for ancestral hidden treasure? I'm sure he would, but he probably goes for the adrenalin rush more, I suspect. The rush of danger. For that, coupled with awe-inspiring spectacle, there is no contest.

It has to be the ledge, the precipice. The forecast is good for tomorrow. I will take my notebook.

~~

Beyond the rock where Teddy and I had the shock of seeing Kim, about thirty minutes' brisk trek further on, our route intersects with the public walkway. This is the popular, well-maintained track that clings to the top of the ridge. Our ghostly path appears to end at this junction, but that is an illusion. It doesn't end there at all. This is only the halfway mark. We resume a little further on, hidden from the inquisitive gaze of others.

Just past the junction the public track is diverted by a deep fissure between the cliffs, a vast gorge of eroded sandstone. And very early one morning many years ago, one bright morning when he was a young and frisky puppy and we were both more energetic and agile, Teddy and I made a seminal discovery.

Instead of staying on the official path as it veered inland, we struck away to the side like a pair of reckless skiers venturing off-piste. Keeping as close to the fault line as we could, we forged a scratchy passage down through a maze of brush until we hit a creek – a thin, fast-running stream of ice-cold water.

We followed it, stumbling and scrambling and sliding downhill. Eventually we pushed through into an arc of sunlight and found ourselves at the foot of a steep overhang. The water was heading in the direction of a narrow aperture, a cleft in the rock. Coming closer, it resembled the two arms of a bridge, nearly but not quite meeting in the middle. An almost intact arch framing a theatrical vista of valley, blue ridges and sandstone cliffs.

The ground levelled abruptly there and the bubbling water fanned out and flowed around our feet. Teddy stopped and lapped it up with enthusiasm. I cupped my hands and drank.

I remember Teddy taking a few bounding leaps towards the gap ahead and coming to a skidding halt. I froze momentarily. Then, as I reached his side, I saw just where we had emerged. We were standing on a flat remnant of layered rock, a ledge flush against the escarpment. We were at the top of a waterfall.

I stood recklessly close to the edge on that first day and looked down, the water spilling over my boots. From this slippery footing it was a vertical plunge to the floor of the canyon, a sheer drop without obstruction. Not an obstacle below, not a single tree or rock shelf to break a fall.

There are many lookouts on the official walking trails along the cliffs and canyons. Mostly they are fenced and quite safe. They may be tame and touristy, but they're no less striking for that. This one has not been tamed. This pristine place we stumbled upon is the second great secret of our lives. It thrills me even now, after so many years, to describe it. I have never encountered anyone else here – not man, woman or dog. Nor a child on a bicycle either, thankfully.

It has remained safe from such casual intruders because it's hidden from view until you are upon it, obscured as it is by towering cliffs. Only from the slender aperture in the rock wall is it exposed to the wide blue yonder. To the blue-grey ridges unfurling away to the far horizon, and the blue-green floor of a valley, whose shimmering leaves move in unison like the surface of the sea.

Out here it is as untouched as it has been for millennia. There are no rubbish bins, no fences, no warning notices, no sign of human pestilence. It is a gateway to a wilderness, undefiled and primeval. And over everything lies this quality of intense stillness. It's not a brooding silence, there is nothing disturbing or eerie about it, but I feel a sense of eternity (as opposed to religiosity) in the absence of noise that I have never experienced elsewhere. Certainly not in any man-made cathedral.

It is not an implacable silence because it's not absolute. There is the light, trilling fall of the water punctuated by other orchestral sounds, the music of bush life. The fluting of bellbirds, and the raucous tambourine screeches of the white and black cockatoos. The soft feathering that is the rustle of wind among the leaves. These sounds exist within the overarching silence and are part of its definition.

Did my left-handed cave painter come here? I have a conviction in my bones that she did. When she was alive there must have been human voices echoing across the vastness of this canyon. Explorers foraging in the remotest corners, people who were adventurous and spirited, in tune with the landscape they roamed. And animals that used to populate the mountains in their thousands – kangaroos and koalas, rock wallabies, bandicoots, wombats, dingoes. Nearly all these original inhabitants are vanished from here now.

I too am an intruder, on this reckoning. And Teddy as well. I should never let myself forget that.

I remember standing there on that first morning, a restraining hand on my puppy's collar. He was an excitable boy, but I think both of us were silenced, struck dumb by our surroundings, just as we have been on every subsequent visit since that first momentous discovery. We were both affected by it. Equally moved, I firmly believe, in our own ways.

I think of it as a trinity, ironically enough; secular yet sacred. The enveloping silence. The grandeur, which is profound. And thirdly the danger, whose profundity is of a different order. The danger, potent in its allure, of one misstep, one single false move.

This is why I sometimes leave Teddy at home these days without too many qualms. He is a little clumsy now, a little careless. One small slip is all it would take.

~~

This is what I think of as my one truly spiritual moment, when I stand out, alone and exposed, on the very tip of the escarpment. It sheers away under my feet and plunges five hundred metres into the fathomless, shifting sea of the valley floor.

No one can see me here. Framed by the arch's incomplete embrace, my figure is dwarfed by ochre-striped cliffs that soar out of the sea of rippling leaves. Vertical cliffs that rear up from the depths of the ocean like gigantic ships of war.

There's nothing headmistressy or intimidating about me here, thank you very much, Mr Frank Campbell. However irresponsible I may have been in my life, however careless and out of touch, here in the timeless silence it matters not a whit. And neither do I. The small speck of materiality that is Ms Thea Farmer is unimportant. One might even say, sublimely irrelevant.

Yet I have a rather diverting thought, as I gaze today across golden gorges and hazy, violet ridges to the distant horizon, as I balance on the lip of the precipice with the foaming water rushing over my boots. I have a feeling Oscar would appreciate it.

I imagine I might remind an onlooker, fleetingly, of a figurehead on an ancient galleon. The carved female warrior on the prow of a pirate ship.

This is my fix. This is how I imagine a heroin rush must feel. It floods over me and stops my breath. It catches me by the heart, and I have to take a step back for my own safety. I want to define it in verse, because it is the essence of poetry, but I can never pin it down. It always eludes me.

I have never spoken about this to anyone, since that first visit. But perhaps in prosaic prose I might attempt to capture it.

~~

I found the writing exercise, an endeavour to transfer my visual pictures to words on the blank computer page, strangely exhilarating for the first time. Uplifting, even. What made it so different from all my previous assignments was that it came without my having to unearth it. Normally writing is such an arduous excavation, it's like digging out the impacted roots of a dead tree. This time the words flowed. They arranged themselves in coherent sentences almost of their own volition, without my having to think about it. With scarcely any intervention from me, or so it seemed.

I was amazed to find that nearly three hours had passed since I sat at my desk. Teddy must have traipsed in and out without my noticing. Must have padded in and out, in growing puzzlement, several times, before sighing and subsiding on my feet.

~~

Oscar read out my description of the precipice. When he stopped there was a brief silence, then he clapped and they all followed suit. My spine prickled.

'That came from left field, Thea. Bravo, bravissima,' he said. 'No, I mean, really. You put your warrior heart out there for the first time.'

My warrior heart. I could tell he was pleased. He didn't cut it off halfway, perfunctorily, as he mostly tends to do when he reads out our homework. Of necessity, of course. Some of them can be very long-winded. Not me though, if anything I'm usually too succinct and to the point. Constipated, Oscar has caustically said, more than once.

But even though this was the longest piece of writing I have submitted, I knew it wasn't too long. The material will dictate the length, troops, he always says, if you lie back and enable it. Just let yourself fall into the caressing hands of the material and allow it to transport you, if you know what I mean.

I didn't, of course, and doubtless no one else did either, although we all nodded. Until today. For the first time I knew what he meant. I was transported by the material.

Of course, they all clamoured to know where the unique place I had described actually was. Could I take them there? We could have a writers' expedition, couldn't we? A little field trip? No, I'm afraid we couldn't because I don't know where it is, bugger it, I said airily. I could see Oscar wasn't too keen on a field trip, either. Two hours with this little group is probably his limit. It's hard to see Oscar in bushwalking boots and a floppy hat. He's probably never worn shorts in his life.

There was nothing in my account to identify the location. Anyway, how could you possibly describe how to locate it? You couldn't – you can only find it by going there. And unless you already know where to go you won't find it. Not without a guide, which means us, and Teddy and I are not in the business of initiating anyone. It's a catch-22 type of situation.

I fed them a little story. We had stumbled upon it once accidentally, when we were lost. Which was half true. And although I tried many times I could never find it again. Which was a whopping fib, but they swallowed it, as the saying goes, wholesale.

I expanded on the theme. I was there only once but it engraved itself indelibly on my mind. I could close my eyes and see every detail, I told them, even from this distance. It was on a three-day hike in autumn, many years ago. We came upon it accidentally when we lost a badly marked trail and got ourselves comprehensively bushed. We were more energetic and intrepid then. And a fair bit younger and more reckless.

They gobbled up this farrago with no trouble at all. Lost in the bush, they all repeated in hushed tones. How long for? There weren't any locator beacons to carry with you then, were there? It must have been terrifying!

Gilda–lily leaned forward. 'And who is *we*? I think we should be told, Thea.'

Oh, *we* was just a friend, I said. No one you'd know. Satisfyingly, some eyebrows were elevated.

We were lost for about eight hours, I said. But I wasn't unduly worried because we had a good compass and were well equipped. It was not too hot and there was plenty of water. As we stood on the precipice at the top of the falls we could see the lay of the land, and plot our direction. We could see it quite clearly.

Surely even intrepid little *we* must have been visited by a sliver of unease, Oscar put in. I think he was prompting me to milk this for all it was worth, and I didn't need much encouragement. All the spontaneous invention came as something of a surprise, however. I was quite entertained by the virtuosity of my own performance, the unhesitating way it emerged, like a bright streamer unfurling. I never realised I had such a talent for improvisation.

Or do I mean lying? That's something else Oscar makes a big thing about. Good writers are usually bloody good liars, he says.

Someone on high wrote it for me, I told Oscar afterwards jokingly when the others had gone. It was her up there.

He looked complacent. 'That's what writers mean when they say they were channelled,' he said. 'What they mean is, it wrote itself. That, in a nutshell, is the beauty and the mystery of creativity.'

'Why a nutshell?' I said. 'Shouldn't it be in a precious stone, like a black opal? Or perhaps in a scarab beetle?'

Oh, for pity's sake don't quibble, he scolded. We fell silent together for a moment in that dun-coloured utilitarian room, with the circle of empty plastic chairs and a couple of coffee mugs people had forgotten to take out and wash.

Then he smiled at me and crooned in a dreamy, off-key voice, 'I think she's got it. By George, she's got it.' What 'it' might be he didn't attempt to say. He wasn't being bombastic, for once. He looked and sounded like a different person. He sounded like a teacher who was startled by the homework of an unexpected and hitherto rather gormless pupil.

I recognised the response to 'it' because I had felt it myself, on occasion. Not very often, in fact quite rarely in my career, but when it did happen it made up for some of the drudgery and tedium. It made teaching, for a fleeting moment, worthwhile.

The experience was described to me once, by a considerably younger member of staff. He seemed quite bowled over and expressed this in a roundabout way, like Oscar. Very much in that kind of way. I remember the incident well, because it was the first time I had really noticed this particular teacher. He was one of the few males on the staff, of course, so he stood out, but he wasn't the good-looking one.

There was one young man with classic film-star looks, although I can't at this distance recall his name. He was the standard tall, dark and handsome type. The girls were always getting crushes on him – seniors, juniors, you name it. Not to mention the female staff. I was always having to deal with the fallout. A nice boy – well, he was in his late thirties. Apparently unaware of his appeal and rather bewildered by it. Always having his picture surreptitiously taken.

He was the school pin-up, his face mingling with magazine photos of the heartthrobs of the day on the inside doors of the sports lockers and the boarders' cupboards. Since it was a girls' school nearly the entire population was susceptible. Hardly anyone was exempt. I'm not sure I was exempt myself to begin with, though later I found him as bland and unexciting as a male model.

The other one's face was not pinned up inside any girl's cupboard door, as far as I know. I say he wasn't the good-looking one, but that was my initial assessment. Later, when I came to know him a great deal better, I started to see him differently. That sometimes happens. As you get to like them, certain people's looks grow on you.

He'd made a special appointment to see me. He brought me the student's handwritten composition to read for myself. Oddly enough, in spite of him making such a big thing about it, I can't recall anything about it now, not even the subject, although I certainly recall the student whose essay it was. She was one of a hand-picked group of year eights and nines, in my special literature class. The names and faces of the majority of my students have been swallowed up in a black hole. Not this one. She was my star pupil.

I remember the young man's barely suppressed excitement, the particular quality of artistic reverence with which he handed the essay to me. As if it were a precious object, like a flawless diamond. This made an impression on me. An indelible impression.

And I do, needless to say, remember his face. And his name. It was Matthew, Matthew Rhode. Not Rhodes as in Cecil, I teased him a while later. Or even Rhodes as in Xandra. Merely a singular Rhode. A very singular Rhode. The Rhode less travelled.

I think this may be the first time I have typed out that particular name for a great many years. Is this a milestone? If so, what kind of a milestone might it be?

My warrior heart. Where was it when I needed it?

~~

Today I reached another milestone. I award myself a pass – certainly not a distinction, not even a credit. But a creditable pass, which is an achievement in itself, under the circumstances.

Frank turned up. Called through the open door just before eleven. The sun was streaming in, he had the coffee on, could I be tempted? Wombat was at school, Ellie was at the café, and he was all alone. In short, it was safe to come on over. Safe, was it? He is a mischievous young man.

I hadn't expected this. The other night he mentioned it, but I hadn't taken it seriously. Now he had caught me on the hop. Put on the spot like that I couldn't pull out of the air a convincing excuse.

He must have seen I was flustered. After a pause in which he regarded me expectantly with his head on one side, I said, 'I don't think I can. What a shame. I'm on the point of going out. I was planning to grab a coffee on the run, in your wife's café.'

The colloquialisms – grab a coffee, on the run – sounded phony even to my own ears. Living out here in isolation leaves one singularly short of plausible pretexts. This has never been an issue until now.

He groaned. 'Don't go to the café, the coffee's shithouse. Ellie's got no idea how to make it.' He gave me a pleading look and put his hands together prayerfully. 'I'd do anything not to start work, Thea. Well, you know – *almost* anything.' Not the most disarming of invitations, one might think, but delivered with a knockout smile. There was nothing for it. I caved in, feeling craven and full of misgivings.

'Very well, I suppose. You win.' It sounded ungracious. 'But only if you're sure we won't be rumbled.' I added this as a sweetener. It must have been the effect of the writing class last night. I'd felt bathed in a rosy afterglow all morning. Dispersing now, however, by the nanosecond.

We walked across together. 'The coffee's not exactly on – I

lied in order to inveigle you over. It's switched on,' he said, tucking my arm through his. He's very familiar, but somehow you don't object. There are men I would object to taking my arm (is that grammatical?) and there are men I wouldn't.

Teddy was trotting alongside. He paused at the threshold of the house with an uncertain air, tail at half-mast, looking at me as if to say, drinks on the deck was one thing, but this was quite another. This was more significant. The invaders were properly in residence now.

As I walked through the door on Frank's arm I had a swift, unsettling vision. It was as if I were a new bride being waltzed across the threshold by my young husband. I was not tempted to say anything to that effect, not remotely tempted, but as I glanced at Frank's face, which is unusually mobile, I could have sworn he was thinking the same thing.

I repressed the vision as we went into the almost state-of-the-art kitchen, but a cinematic sense of unreality persisted. *Their kitchen*. It looked different, occupied and messy. There were frivolous fridge magnets, Michelangelo's David in boxer shorts and bra. A professional-looking electric espresso machine took up a prime position on the bench.

Frank was maintaining a constant patter. A diversionary tactic? I found myself trying to keep up with it – instead of having to deal with the inescapable reality of where I found myself. Ellie had given him this fabulous new gizmo for Christmas, Thea. It could grind and foam and do everything you'd ever thought of doing to a coffee bean. Or almost everything, maybe I had some refinements? He threw me a teasing glance.

He demonstrated, with a transparent sense of enjoyment, what it could do in the form of a flat white for me and double espresso for him. 'You're like a tub-thumping evangelist from the Deep South,' I told him. 'Only spruiking a shiny boy's toy instead of superstitious mumbo jumbo.'

He grinned. 'Yes, *ma'am*.'

He put the mugs on a tray and ushered me through to the living room. If the kitchen looked different, this lofty space I had designed to be so spare and unadorned was nearly unrecognisable. It resembled a commonplace suburban living room.

Rammed up at the kitchen end was the parents' famous dining table. Repro, I'd guess, like the ten overblown Queen Anne chairs with their padded crimson seats. Beyond were two conventional sofas, piled with cushions, and at the far end, grouped around a vast flat screen TV, one of those angular L-shaped seating arrangements in black leather. Magazines, DVDs and CDs everywhere. And several of those impractical floor cushions obscuring the lovely timbers. At least there were books in my built-in shelves beside the fireplace.

There was nothing I would have chosen for that spacious, airy room. I had planned on the bare minimum, two or three comfortable armchairs with loose covers in natural linen, lots of books and some interesting lamps, and a sturdy farmhouse table. I was going to leave the space to speak for itself by eliminating extraneous objects. My desire was to pare my life down to essentials. Instead of which it seems to be becoming increasingly encumbered.

Frank, of course, was oblivious to such feelings. He stood there, surveying the room with a pride of ownership that pierced me. What did I think? All their stuff had fitted in amazingly well, hadn't it? Even the crap dining suite wasn't too crap.

'So, Thea, how do we look? I haven't tidied up for you, I'm afraid. Well, actually I have a bit, but you can't necessarily tell.'

That was certainly true. 'How do we look? We look lived in,' I said. Which displayed a capacity for tact I didn't know I had.

I sat down heavily on one of the unyielding navy sofas. It was on castors and immediately took off across the floor. The windows, shimmering with olive-coloured leaves, flashed by as if from a train. Frank put down the tray and hurried over solicitously, as the sofa and I collided with one of the black couches. I've never liked leather seating or those ugly modular things.

He put the mug of coffee into my hand and patted my shoulder. He apologised for the athleticism of the sofa. Teddy lumbered up and collapsed on my feet with a heavy sigh. I remembered the last time he and I had ventured here. I had slumped to the floor of the empty room.

I struggled to put this shameful picture out of my mind. Teddy remembered it too, I'm sure. I'd been consumed with self-pity then. What did I feel now? Blank, like an empty black-board waiting for something to be written on it. Something to ease the pain, which will probably never be written.

'Did you say your niece is at school today?' I asked Frank. At least my voice sounded normal. There were no audible tremors.

He looked amused. Hadn't I realised she was of school age?

'But isn't she going home? To her parents, or,' I hazarded a guess, 'her guardians?'

'Do you mean we haven't bored you with the Wombat saga?' He rolled his eyes in amazement. It was a long one, he said apologetically. Was I sure I hadn't any pressing engagements?

To cut the story short, Kim is the accidental child of Frank's much older brother – seventeen years older, I think he said – and a Vietnamese woman. The brother, as described by Frank, was a ne'er-do-well drug addict, a drifter who only lived with the mother for a matter of months. He disappeared well before his daughter was born.

'We lost track of him years ago. He fell off the planet. He's probably dead by now.' Frank looked unconcerned. He didn't sound regretful, rather the opposite. I could understand that.

The rest was the type of history that was depressingly familiar to me from many years working in under-funded, inner-city schools. Kim's mother had been a refugee, a Vietnamese boat person. She was uneducated, spoke little English and struggled to cope. For a while she kept the child, but jobs with low pay and long hours, and midnight flits from overcrowded flats, and from no-hoper boyfriends, all took their toll.

Eventually she was charged with neglect and the child, then a few years old – around five or six, Frank was vague – was taken into care. They were interstate at that stage, in Tasmania. Two years later, back in Sydney, the mother took up with an Iranian who wanted no truck with previous offspring. Pregnant again, she went to Queensland with him, where the trail petered out. Kim ended up in several more foster placements before Frank and Ellice took her in.

'But before that happened, Thea,' he said, 'we had come up here, met you, and bought this amazing house.'

I was finding the view from the windows quite startling after the dimness of the hovel. Almost hypnotic. Frank turned and looked at me. Possibly he had just registered something untoward about my demeanour, even if he didn't know what it was. He seems to be a perceptive young man, or more than most, which is not saying much.

'We thought, you know, she could come and live with us. There's plenty of room. We could do it. We *should* do it. Ellie was really keen, probably more keen than me. So, yeah, we went ahead and bit the bullet.'

He leant back contemplatively with both hands clasped behind his head. 'Know something, Thea? D'you know what really made us do it?'

He wanted a response, so I shook my head and said no, I had no idea what really made them do it. Men often tend to talk at you, I have found, but he clearly prefers a two-way conversation. By then I was hardly listening, however. I had no idea what was coming, not one speck of intuition.

Frank said, 'If we hadn't found this house of yours, Kim wouldn't be here now.' His eyes rested on me. 'This house was the catalyst.'

I did not show any reaction. Or none that I was aware of. There was a pause. I put my mug down. He sighed, and looked faintly disappointed. 'I hope you think we did the right thing.'

There was no doubt it was the right thing to do, I said. It sounded abrupt. After a short silence in which I tried to gather my thoughts, I added, on impulse, 'She seems a trifle solitary, though. Which is not in the least surprising, given her history.'

The Wombat was not used to being looked after, Frank said. And not very interested in other kids her age. Had never related terribly well with them, or at least that was his feeling. The social worker they dealt with said being the new kid at school had become her default position. She never expected to stay anywhere very long.

'I can see she loves animals. Perhaps you might think about getting her a dog. It would give her something of her own to look after.' I hadn't thought about this or planned to say it. It just came into my mind of its own accord.

Frank put a hand on my arm. 'Perhaps that's an inspired idea, Thea.'

He reached down and tickled Teddy on the head. His fingers were spatulate and flexible, I noticed, covered with wiry, ginger hair. I don't normally go for ginger hair, but on him it's not unappealing. 'You're double-jointed,' I said, surprised.

He laughed and put the tips of his fingers together. The end joints of fingers and thumbs bent backwards by more than ninety degrees. I was entranced. 'My party trick,' he said. 'Never fails.'

When Teddy and I got up to leave not long after that, he took my arm again and walked me back jauntily. At the door he planted a little kiss on my cheek. 'That was cool. Any chance of a return date?'

'Perhaps we might risk it,' I said.

'Hey. Same time next week?'

The way Frank related it, the decision was made by him and Ellice alone. I wonder if the girl's feelings on the matter were ever sought. It seems more likely that she was simply informed that her life was about to change again. Just told that this was to be her new home.

My house was the catalyst.

This sentence lingered in my mind for the rest of the day and into the evening. It was like getting an annoying tune on the brain. Or perhaps it was a haunting refrain, I'm not sure which. One or the other.

~~

I forgot to park in the new position, fatally, and she spotted me. She'd changed into after-school gear: rubber thongs and a singlet with skimpy shorts. It made her look even thinner but less childlike.

I assumed the main attraction was Teddy. He had scrambled down the steps from his lookout post on the verandah, as he always does when he hears the car. She hung back while we greeted each other, then knelt down and squeezed him in a bear hug.

I was nearly inside when I heard her say, 'Um, excuse me? Ms Farmer. I've got some interesting information. To tell you. Do you want to hear it?'

Somewhat jerky, and offhandedly posed, but I assumed the question was rhetorical. I wondered if I'd been right, initially, about her aunt's pregnancy. With my newfound sensitivity I had decided against raising the subject with Frank. She was still on her knees, and had adopted the eager look Teddy used to have when he waited for his stick to be thrown. Endearing on him, irritating on her, although it turned out to be rather apt.

I suppressed a sigh. 'I think you're going to tell me whether I like it or not. All right, out with it.'

Then I had a twinge of conscience when she confided, with more animation than I'd imagined she possessed, that they were getting a puppy. Well, they *might* be going to. Wasn't this amazing? They were really, probably getting one! Frank had said that I was responsible. It was my idea, right, and if it did happen she would always be incredibly grateful for ever.

She is still on the diffident side, but now that she is a little more at ease with me she tends to lapse into speaking as she writes, in exclamation marks. I find myself mentally inserting them. On balance, I think I probably preferred the mumbling.

A response was required. I returned to the verandah and dumped my bag with an ungracious thump. Really, probably getting one?

She looked earnest and shifted, with an enviable suppleness, to a cross-legged position on the ground next to Teddy. Yeah, well, it might not actually happen, but that's what they'd said. This morning at breakfast, you see, they'd said she could choose a puppy as a pre-birthday present. Her birthday wasn't for six months actually, in fact it wasn't until August. She was a Leo. August the *tenth*. A light stress on this piece of news.

'I've no memory for dates,' I said. 'Never have had. Can't remember my own birthday.'

She looked sceptical. 'But how do you know how old —'

I cut this off. 'So you'll be having a second birthday halfway through the year. The real one. The Queen does the same thing. Her official birthday is a public holiday.'

'The *Queen*? She has an official birthday? Like, a virtual one, as well as a real one?' The notion grew on her, visibly. 'Hey, what a brilliant idea. She gets two lots of presents, right?'

I've always thought this was rather a dreadful idea, and I'm fairly sure the Queen agrees with me. It had to be exactly six months before your real one, or after it, I said, so that made hers this week, didn't it? What kind of dog were they planning to get, I asked briskly, to move things along. Not a corgi like the Queen's lot, I hoped. I'd never entirely seen the point of corgis.

She shook her head. 'Me neither. Not entirely.' She said she had once lived with a golden Labrador for nearly a year, and since then she had always wanted a dog of her own. The Labrador was named Pippi, after Pippi Longstocking in the Astrid Lindgren books. Pippi had been five years old. She was brilliant, an awesomely perfect dog in every respect.

I found this information rather mystifying. I said, without thinking, 'You only had her for nearly a year?' Had the dog died? Been run over? Then I recalled, with a jolt, what Frank had said about the various foster homes. She blinked and looked away, mouth compressed, forehead crumpled. I waited for a decent interval before asking again, more cautiously, what breed she had in mind.

Not another golden Labrador, she said. It was better to make a fresh start, right? It might be hard on a young puppy, to have this memory of an ideal predecessor sort of hanging over its head. The new one might suffer in comparison, might always sense that it was less than perfect.

I agreed that this might well be a burden for a puppy. So if not a Labrador, then what?

She brightened up. Teddy was a one-off. She could see he was like Pippi. Fab, totally. But perhaps to have another red cattle dog so close by might not be a good idea either, in another kind of way?

She came to an abrupt halt and seemed to be debating something in her mind. I found myself suddenly disconcerted for no apparent reason. Almost apprehensive.

Her face contorted in a grimace. She said in a rush, 'Um, I was just sort of concerned, you know, that Teddy might be offended. I wondered if he – Teddy, I mean – if he might wonder if he was being – like, usurped, somehow. Or even *worse* than that. Replaced. Kind of, you know, *in advance.*'

A look of alarm came and went swiftly, replaced by acute embarrassment. Her face flooded with colour. She buried her head in the fur ruff around Teddy's collar.

I couldn't tell whether it was the idea itself, or the reference to the inevitable. I think she may have been shocked at her own temerity, the fact that she had alluded in my presence to the prospect of Teddy's inevitable demise. The unthinkable prospect. And perhaps, by association, alluded to my own equally inevitable, if less inconceivable, demise.

It certainly had the effect of knocking me for six. Before I could think of a suitable response she had jumped to her feet and was banging herself on the head with a balled fist.

'Shit. *Shit*! That was a fucking, like a totally *dumb* thing to say. I'm really sorry, Ms Farmer, to be blathering on and everything and taking up your time.'

And she was gone, slim olive-brown legs haring across to the other house.

~~

I felt deeply unsettled for the remainder of the afternoon, and annoyed for having been made to feel like this. Teddy sensed it and stayed around my feet. Every time I looked at him I felt a surge of unease. I saw her rush out of the house and ride off down the road on her bike, without looking in this direction. An hour or so later I heard the sound of their car and saw Ellice get out. Frank must have been in the house. Working, one assumes. What about keeping an eye on his niece and making sure she does her homework?

It was acute of Sandy to say she was an interesting child. Also of interest, some of the words she uses. Usurped. Blathering on. They're old-fashioned words, bookish, I suppose, as Sandy said. Typical of a bright child who is largely self-educated. No doubt her first language would have been Vietnamese. Books were a way of catching up.

Her manner is rather awkward too. Tries to sound grown up, then lapses back into immature jargon. She seems more naive and less pseudo-sophisticated than most girls her age. That's a relief. But it also means there is something unguarded about her, a vulnerability. Which is only to be expected with that messy, unstable background.

What she said may have been tactless and clumsy, but it was well-intentioned. And sensitive in its way, I suppose. I cannot deny that. I suspect she was really talking about me and not about Teddy at all. Teddy might like to have another young cattle dog over there, but I'm not at all sure that I would like it.

And why not? Sometimes my own reactions give me pause. They can be hard to explain away, even to myself. Verging on bloody-minded to a confused child, I suspect. I don't recall ever having bothered myself with such questions during my teaching career. Should I have bothered?

In retrospect, I think some people may have tried to tell me I was too aloof and unapproachable. Not my chummy young colleague, Mr Rhode. We were very simpatico, he said. I wasn't too aloof and unapproachable with him. Not that he would have confided anything he didn't wish me to know, I can see that now. Our growing friendship became a bulwark against the rest of the staff. I can also see that it was in his interests that I should be chums with him and no one else.

If I had been more 'approachable' would it have made any difference to the outcome?

~~

I have always tended to feel that others, not this particular child necessarily but most people, are more of a piece than me. In the American self-help, psychobabble sense, they are more 'together'. In my rarer rational moments I am perfectly aware that this belief has to be a snare and a delusion. One can see inside one's own mind, perhaps regrettably, and people on the outside cannot, which is decidedly fortunate.

And I should never forget that certain individuals are very adept at appearing together when they are nothing of the sort. Mr Matthew Rhode was particularly adept, and I was accused of being a bad judge of character because of that. But that was one lapse. Admittedly it was a terrible lapse, but should one be damned for a single, catastrophic mistake?

    'Now hear ye the drama,
    of poor old Ms Farmer.
    They gave her the heave ho,
    a ticket of leave ho!
    And filled the void,
    with schadenfreude.'

Matthew Rhode was a special case. It was my misfortune that he happened to be at my school. Doubly unfortunate that I was responsible for appointing him, but I could not be blamed for that, surely? There was nothing untoward in his interview or his cv. Nothing to ring any alarm bells. No omens or portents of any kind.

On the contrary, as I began to see his influence on the students and the results he was achieving, I was proud to have him on my staff. The insights he brought to teaching literature and the originality of his approach struck me as exemplary. To the extent that I think I came to see in him the dedicated teacher I might like to have been.

What an admission that is. I have never made it before and I would make it nowhere else.

This is an uncomfortable train of thought, I don't know what brought it on. I am not given to bouts of introspection as a rule, and for good reason. But if I were losing the plot I would not have been capable of writing my last essay in that lucid way, would I? Although, according to Oscar, creative people are always mad. They are all basket cases to a greater or lesser degree.

Ha. Embrace your inner loony, is what he says. Is that what I'm doing? One successful exercise and I'm putting myself in the creative basket?

She does seem more comfortable with me since the trespassing conversation. I am unsure if this is anything to be pleased about. Or whether I have any attitude to it, for that matter.

No doubt she is worried now that I have taken offence.

~~

There was a soft knock on the door. I knew who it was going to be. Teddy gave only one half-hearted growl. Even the knock sounded hesitant.

I'd put the Sunday paper, dire as it is, on the table on the verandah and was in the kitchen about to deal with the shopping. I considered not answering, then reconsidered, taking into account some of my recent behaviour and the fact that she knew I was there. And her chequered history. Better not compound the deplorable.

Ellice and Frank had gone down to Sydney for the day, to have lunch. (Yes, I'd observed them going off in the car.) She appeared to be about to say something, then bent down and stroked Teddy. She seemed a bit jumpy. I wonder if she is less self-sufficient than I thought. In which case they are very remiss in leaving her alone like this.

She looked up, taking a deep breath. Would I, possibly, like to come and have a cup of tea? I could see it took an effort to ask the question. I could also see there was a lot hanging on the answer. I would be her guest in their house or she would be mine, here in the dump. The second option was preferable. I wasn't ready for the alternative venue again, not quite this soon.

'Tea sounds good,' I said, 'but I'll make it because I have strong views on tea and it needs to be made in a teapot.'

'We've got a teapot.' She shifted from one leg to the other, blinking. Teddy was licking each foot in turn.

'Come inside. And keep still, for goodness' sake. You'll drive Teddy mad, not to mention me.'

'Sorry. Sure you don't mind?'

'I would have said if I minded.'

She nodded sagely. 'Yeah, I suppose you would.' This was more conversational than offensive.

I went in and started unloading the bag while she hovered at my elbow. I rejected her tentative offer of help. There's hardly room to swing a cat in this kitchen, if you had a cat to swing.

She picked up on this, but misinterpreted it. 'Other people

always put things away in the wrong places. And they always make the tea wrong.'

I thought these were acute remarks, for twelve years of age. 'Or they don't know where the tea is to begin with,' I said. Not that there are a wealth of possibilities in this decidedly unstate-of-the-art kitchen. I saw her look intently around and spot the tea caddy, balanced on a pile of journals and paperbacks on top of the fridge. She handed it to me with a muted air of achievement.

'You can go and inspect my bathroom library if you like,' I said, 'It will give me more room to move.' I'd seen her eyeing the books. They're visible from the kitchen though the open door.

She went in with alacrity. The shelves between bath, loo and basin are packed and spilling over. A bathroom is not good for books, they're falling apart with the damp, but where else can I put them? I can't bring myself to throw them out. Sandy wouldn't want them and neither would the Salvos, they're too mildewy. I would have had floor-to-ceiling bookshelves in my new study. I was planning to clean the books up a bit, put them in some kind of order. That will never happen now.

When she heard the kettle whistling she trotted back. 'It's really cool how you don't only have books in the lounge room. You have them in the kitchen and bathroom. And, like, everywhere else.'

Like everywhere else meant piles of books on the floors. I remembered she hadn't set foot inside the hovel before.

'Well, books do furnish a room. That's the title of rather a good novel you can read when you're older, by Anthony Powell.'

'Shouldn't it be books do furnish *every* room?'

'Yes, it probably should. Especially when there are only four poky rooms to furnish. Snug and charming with

85

limitless potential, as the estate agent would have burbled. Dark, decrepit and dwarfish, more accurately. A Black Hole of Calcutta for pygmies.'

When I built the new house I suppose I was reacting to years of feeling cramped and stifled. That's why I endowed it with such grand dimensions. If I hadn't been so profligate I might have been able to hang on to it. Delusions of grandeur – they were my undoing, like others before me.

Her mouth had fallen open. I realised I'd got carried away and was talking loudly. Usually I keep my rants to myself and Teddy, who's used to them and thinks nothing of it.

'Don't you like this house, Ms Farmer?'

'As a matter of fact I loathe it,' I said.

'Yeah?' The emphatic black eyebrows shot up in cartoonish astonishment. 'But I like it.' She saw my expression and made a faint sound, like a smothered snort. 'Well, it's not *that* bad. It's kind of *homely*. I think it's nice.'

It struck me that she'd very likely lived in a lot worse than this. 'Your house is much nicer,' I said. And thought: your house is also the catalyst for you being here, if you only knew it.

I remembered I had three quarters of leftover ginger cake from the fire brigade stall. It was a few days old and looked on the dry side. Anyway, she probably didn't like ginger; it was an acquired taste.

Oh no, she'd acquired that taste already, a while back, actually. And she was sure it would be totally fine if we cut off the desiccated bits. We could feed them to Teddy, yeah? Or hadn't he acquired the taste yet? No he hadn't and we certainly could not, I said. Sweet things are bad for his teeth. Teddy still has excellent teeth because I give him lots of bones and proper meat, none of that tinned muck, and he's never tasted anything sweet in his life.

'So he doesn't know any better, right? Any worse, I mean.'

Quite so, I said. And she should make sure her new dog didn't either, when she got her new dog.

'Yeah, if I ever do,' she said, looking wistful. 'They've never had pets so they don't know much. About how to look after animals and that. I s'pose I could check on all that stuff with you, right?'

'I suppose you could. As long as you don't make yourself into a menace,' I said.

'Good point. I'll do my best not to make myself into a menace. My level best.' This was said solemnly, with just a hint of acceptable cheek. I was always good at categorising cheek. There were entire repertoires of it. Some crude, some insolent, others I quite enjoyed.

I employed her to carry the tray out to the rickety garden table for a change. The table and four chairs live outside and have done for years. She looked the chairs over critically. 'Hmm, reckon these've seen better days, right? Will I try and wipe all the bird poo and gunk off? Or, you know, *some* of it?'

'Very well, you can take a dishcloth to them if you insist. Dampen it first.'

True, a great deal of gunk had accumulated. Bird poo, dead insects, leaves, twigs, snail trails. I hardly use the table these days, it's easier to sit on the verandah if it's just Teddy and me. But it's nice in the garden, even if it is overgrown.

She did some surprisingly energetic scrubbing, and then dried the chairs with kitchen paper before we sat down. Paper was better than a tea towel, she said, because it didn't have to be washed. For a girl of her age she seems unusually domesticated. It probably comes from having had to fend for herself.

So, how was the new school? She took a large bite of cake. Screwed up her eyes and shrugged. It was okay. She obviously didn't want to talk about it.

'When's your birthday, Ms Farmer?'

'I can't remember. As I told you.'

'You can but you don't want to?'

'Not in the slightest. Birthdays are best forgotten at my age. An annual intimation of mortality that needn't concern you.'

'But they're an excuse for a celebration.' She must have heard that phrase from some other old fogey. A pollyanna type, of which there are legion.

'I don't go in for those.'

'But didn't you use to, once? Go in for them?'

'Don't speak with your mouth full.' I considered the question. 'No, I don't think I ever did.'

She chewed and then swallowed with a degree of emphasis. 'Why not? *If,*' lips pursed, 'you don't mind me asking.'

'I don't mind. Because there wasn't a great deal to celebrate.'

'No? Not ever?'

She leaned forward intensely, chin in her hands. She looked so concerned that for a moment I toyed with the notion of promoting myself as a giddy party girl just to please her. After all, I had recently shown a flair for creative embroidery.

'Twas a fine demonstration
Of wily improvisation
When with a touch of artifice
She raved about the precipice.'

The lines floated into my mind. Better stay honest with this particular child, I concluded. She probably deserves it.

'Not ever is probably overstating it. Nearly not ever is probably more like it, I should say.'

This elicited a wry smile. 'Yeah, right. But dogs are different, they like a good party. When's Teddy's birthday?' He was lying in the shade under the table and she was resting her bare feet comfortably on his rump. Like I do from time to time.

I said that Teddy detested parties even more than me. And I never knew exactly when his birthday was because he was an abandoned puppy from the pound. He was two months old when I got him, which was in October, so that meant his birthday must be some time in August.

Same month as mine, she said. From a pound? Did I mean a lost dog's home?

Some of them are lost and some are abandoned, I said. I saw her take this in and stow it away for later.

August. Then he was most likely a Leo. A lion dog. That'd be right, Teddy was so a Leo it wasn't true — much more than her. I was not going to dignify this with a response, but she was waiting for one and I relented. Astrology, I said, was gibberish. It was bogus, unmitigated drivel, on a level with Scientology and every other mystical belief, and all intelligent people should make it their business to shun it. As well as all the other nonsensical superstitions.

She looked momentarily startled, then made the stifled noise again, midway between a snort and a giggle. Then she surprised me by agreeing. Yeah, astrology was a *total* waste of space, but it was really odd, right, how often people seemed to conform to their star sign? My turn to shrug. This was merely the gullible seeing what they want to see.

'You have such —' She broke off, chewing her fingers and burrowing her feet in Teddy's fur.

'Go ahead,' I said, 'I won't bite.'

'I like it that you have such strong opinions, Ms Farmer. You know, about things and stuff.'

'Opinions are usually about things and stuff. Doesn't everyone?'

A pause while she thought this over. 'If they do, they don't express them, like, how you do, exactly. You're very —'

she raised her eyes to mine. I saw a gleam of humour. 'Very certain. And very, um – *emphatic.*'

'That's probably because I know I'm right. When you get to my age this happens. And I'm not used to being argued with.'

'No. I guess Teddy doesn't usually contradict you.'

'Usually not, no. Mostly he agrees with me. He knows which side his bread is buttered.'

'That must make him a dream to live with. Kind of like,' she searched around, 'you know, kind of like an ideal husband, only with four legs instead of two.'

'Yes,' I said, 'kind of like that.' This had never occurred to me before, oddly enough, but it has a whimsical kernel of truth.

Then she wanted to know Teddy's story. Was he lost, or was he abandoned?

I explained how I'd made two previous expeditions to the pound, which was quite a drive from where I lived at the time. How there were dozens of adult dogs there, which was very distressing because they were all jumping up and down in their cages, wagging their tails, barking hysterically, doing anything to attract your attention. Willing you to take them home with you.

I told her I'd have taken almost any one of them home. But I was adamant I wanted a puppy.

A nod. I'd set my heart on bringing it up from babyhood, she could perfectly understand that. And then? she prompted. The third visit. It was a case of third time lucky, right?

'Third time lucky, yes. There were several puppies to choose from.'

I found I remembered them quite well. A dachshund, a spoodle – spaniel-poodle cross – two Jack Russells and a Doberman. Very sweet and engaging, every one. But somehow, I felt they weren't quite for me. None was the just-right dish of porridge.

A serious nod. Ah, no. *And then?* This is not a child who suffers from attention deficit disorder. Her concentration was total. The lustrous black eyes were fixed on me.

And then, I said, in an enclosure all to himself, I came upon another puppy. He was lying down in one corner, seemingly relaxed, but I could see he was keeping a weather eye on everyone as they went past. He was a scrap of a thing, with pricked ears that were far too big for his head. A pretty boy with thick, red-brown fur and black markings, amber eyes and a handsome white blaze on his chest. On the board attached to the pen was a chalked sign: 'red cattle x'.

What was the x for?

Cross, I told her. They didn't know what he was crossed with, but I'm pretty certain there is some brindle Staffordshire bull terrier in there. Either that or some thylacine, the extinct Tasmanian tiger. Her eyes widened even further.

'The attendant was an Indian girl. She opened the pen, picked him up and handed him to me. He was so thin and light he hardly weighed a thing. I cradled him. He was unusually calm and settled in my arms. He observed me with a steady, unafraid gaze, looked directly into my eyes, and then all of a sudden sprang into action and licked my face.'

I had asked the attendant how big he was likely to grow. He would be medium-sized for sure, she said. You could tell that from his paws. He had nice macho paws, but they were not huge.

Kim listened to this recital with a small, inward smile. I found the recounting as absorbing as she did. I found I remembered it all quite vividly. She leaned forward with her elbows on the table. We were taught never to put our elbows on the table, but this was not the time.

'You were smitten, right? He was the just-right dish of porridge. Was it like, you know, love at first sight?' Her eyes were rapt and shining at the idea.

91

'Just like that, indeed. It was love at first sight. There was something about him, you see.'

She nodded and wiggled her feet. 'Oh yeah, of course there was, I can see that exactly. Anyone could.'

'Yes. I knew at once he was the one for me and I didn't hesitate for a minute. I'll take him, I said to the attendant. She said some other people had liked the look of this little chap too, and they were maybe going to come back later. You can tell them they've missed the boat then, I said in my most authoritarian, not-to-be-contradicted voice – I was used to being obeyed then – because I want him right *now*, and I mean now this very minute. I'm taking this little chap home.'

'Yay!' She clapped her hands. 'Brilliant. That would've sorted them. Your school principal voice, right?'

'I'd retired by then.'

'But you still had it.' She looked at me, assessing. 'You've still kind of got it now, actually. Like, I don't mean on a regular basis, but when you need to dredge it up for something.'

Perhaps I still had it on a regular basis then because I had only just retired. And not retired, exactly. Resigned, to be honest. Been induced to resign, to be brutally honest. Been toppled from the perch.

They gave her the heave ho, the ticket of leave ho . . .

How lucky that you cannot read my mind, I thought.

She was still focused on the story. Questions came thick and fast. Did I ask them about the puppy? Did I find out anything else? Like, where he came from and what'd happened to him and how he'd been found?

I told her what they said. There wasn't much more to tell, but this was the bad bit.

'He had been picked up late one night by the side of an isolated road outside Wollongong. It was a deserted country road on the South Coast. A lorry driver spotted something in the headlights, a tiny bundle lying in the road. He pulled

92

up just as he was about to run over it and got out. It was a shivering little puppy, half-frozen in the cold.'

A shocked '*Oh.*' She gazed at Teddy.

'There were unseasonable gale-force winds that night. It was pouring with icy, sleety rain, and he was soaked through to the skin. His fur was matted with mud, the man thought he'd been in the ditch and managed to drag himself out. He must have been abandoned there. Thrown out of a moving car. Teddy's always had a tendency to arthritis, and I'm sure it was caused by that experience, alone for hours in the wet and cold. If that man hadn't come along just in time and rescued him, he would have died of exposure.'

There was silence. I glanced at her. Her face was set. Then I saw the tears welling. Two spilled over and ran down her cheeks. She got out of her chair and knelt down beside Teddy, and hugged him round the neck, convulsively. She looked stricken.

She said, in a whisper I could hardly hear, 'And then he was rescued again. You rescued him for the second time.'

I said, 'I don't think I've ever told anyone the full story before.'

I would like to have added something else. Because although this was all true, it wasn't the whole truth. It wasn't what really happened. What really happened was that Teddy rescued me.

I forgot to mention her card again. It was still on the mantel-piece. I hope she saw it there.

The gingerbread cake was quite all right with the cut edge removed, as she suggested. Between us, we finished it all up.

~~

I went to Lisa's and said to Sandy, 'What have you got for a twelve-year-old girl?'

'That one, Thea?'

'Yes, that one.' The waif and stray. She identified with Teddy, that was obvious.

Sandy bustled about the shelves. Young adult fiction – he was thinking of setting up a separate section. Trouble was, he didn't get that many young adults in the shop.

'Still, if I build it they might come,' he murmured obscurely.

'Isn't that a misnomer?' I said. 'They're pre-teens and teenagers first, surely?'

No, no, they were all lumped into young adult these days. It was contracting by the day, childhood. It was being abolished, like old age, while middle age was getting longer and longer and taking over everything.

'You and me, Sandy, we're teetering on the verge of our prime.'

We chortled together in an unforced way. The woman Monica wasn't in the shop, thankfully. Sandy is always more fun when she's not around, I've noticed.

He came up with several possibilities. I left with *Beau Geste* and *The Yearling*. I dithered between that and *The Scarlet Pimpernel* for a while, but three books might be overdoing it. I remembered reading these when I was around her age and finding them exciting, as well as romantic and inspiring.

These days young adult fiction was all about drugs, date rape, incest and suicide, Sandy said. He confessed to relief that I was opting out of all that hairy realism in favour of flights of the imagination. Fiction that was unafraid to take the moral high ground.

A moral tone of any height was in short supply nowadays, I observed. Children badly needed it, in my opinion. And were today's in-your-face stories any more realistic, really, when it came down to it?

We considered this. It might be selective realism, I concluded, but the way they shoved it down the throats of the poor, unfortunate young adults verged on the prescriptive. Sandy, who is unworldliness personified, said he was a fence-sitter on this one. He said he'd keep the *Pimpernel* aside for another time, no worries.

Both books still had their dust jackets, very tattered and torn, but I always think children like to have the coloured picture on the front. The titles are a bit – well, they are *very* old hat, as Sandy did comment, but Kim doesn't strike me as a conspicuously modern girl, not at all what Davy calls a hip chick. Although she does possess a certain awkward maturity. Not physically, especially, and not in any unpleasantly precocious sense, but she has what I think of as a nascent mature sensibility. And she is much more respectful than many.

We had an interesting discussion about what Sandy called her 'readerliness'. This is one of his favourite words, although I am not entirely convinced it is a word. He said it was particularly surprising because she learnt to read unusually late. When she was about seven, he thought. Or it might even have been eight. She was staying with friends at the time and the mother of the family gave her lessons.

'She said, and this is verbatim, Thea,' Sandy reported, as if it were information of great import, '"the mum took pity on my ignorance."' He seemed struck by this sentence and repeated it over again to me, rather unnecessarily. Learning to read had been a revelation for the little girl.

As you would expect, I said.

The friends had a library in the house and she had become a bookworm, more or less immediately. The idea filled Sandy with rapture. Although her stay had been cut short, evidently.

I enlightened him as to the reason for this. It wouldn't have been friends she was staying with; it would have been a foster family. He looked mystified. I outlined Kim's disadvantaged background. Sandy clearly knew nothing about this at all.

'It's wholly understandable that reading would have enabled her to escape into another world,' I explained, 'as well as being the means to an education. When did she tell you this?'

The other day. On closer questioning it sounded very much as if she might have left school early on that particular afternoon, although Sandy seemed unworried when I called it to his attention.

I'll wrap the books and deliver them next time I see her. They can be an official birthday present.

She badly needs friends. A dog would be a good companion for her. A necessary companion.

~~

Teddy and I were on the verandah. We spotted her coming home on the bicycle. I think she must leave it chained up at the bus stop in the morning. I beckoned her over. When she saw us she rang the bell on her bike. Shrilly, several times, for emphasis.

'See, Ms Farmer, I got one,' she said. 'I obeyed your command.'

'I'm pleased to hear it, and even more pleased to hear you using it. Been at school all afternoon?' She looked slightly nonplussed.

I put the parcel in her hand. I'd found some wrapping paper full of animals and jungle greenery. Very Douanier Rousseau. At first she seemed not to quite comprehend she was being given a present. I had to remind her it was her official birthday. She seemed astonished that I had taken this seriously. Astonished and, I could see, touched. It occurred to me that she may not have received many presents in her life.

She hadn't heard of either book. Well, she wouldn't have. They're from another era. The era before the era before last.

'Don't worry if you don't like them,' I said. 'If you'd rather read about date rape and drugs you can always sell them back to Mr Fay. He's got plenty of realistic modern books, too. These are more on the escapist side. Funny old oddities, I'm afraid.'

'Yeah well, that's what I want. And I'm kind of a funny young oddity myself, right?' she said. She was in her school uniform, an open-necked blue gingham cotton dress. Too short, the way they all wear them.

I'd found a birthday card with a photo of lots of puppies, all different breeds. How awesomely appropriate, she said.

Inside I'd scribbled a silly little jingle:

'Take Kim and Queen Liz. You wouldn't necessarily think
With two persons so diff'rent there could be a link.
But when birthdays are mooted they won't settle for one,
It's two each or nothing, and double the fun.'

'Wow, you're an incredible poet, too, Ms Farmer!' she exclaimed.

I only write doggerel, I said, the lowest form of verse. But it seemed to amuse her. I wondered what she'd meant by 'too'.

'I've got more news,' she said. She'd told them the story of Teddy's rescue. Them being Frank and Ellice. They had made a joint decision that the new puppy should come from a pound, just like Teddy had. Frank said that they should give one imprisoned canine spirit a joyful liberation.

'But only, you know, if you don't mind. I mean, like us rescuing a puppy as well? The same way you did?'

97

Why in the name of unmerciful heaven should I mind, I said. The finest dogs come from the pound. The very best. Pounds are the only places one should ever think of going to find a dog, in my opinion.

'Absolutely in mine too,' she said.

She had looked on the internet and the nearest pound was about forty minutes away. They were planning to go there on the next available weekend. Sunday, she confided in a whisper, had a good chance of being the red-letter dog day.

'Um.' She looked down at the ground, scuffling her school shoes, which were badly in need of a clean. Did I think – would I perhaps, maybe – like to come with them? It was an abrupt return to her former constraint that took me by surprise.

The question caught me off balance, too. Well, let's see, I said neutrally. Perhaps, maybe, I might.

Frank came over, gave her a kiss and chided her for not wearing her helmet. He fished it out of her schoolbag and plonked it on her head.

'Wombats without helmets get picked up by the fuzz and thrown in the clink. Don't they, Thea? And we'll have to pay a queen's ransom to get her back. Probably have to mortgage the house.'

'Or else they get knocked off the bike and rendered quadriplegic,' I said. I hadn't noticed the absent helmet. There were no such things in my day. I'm in two minds about them. I never bothered to wear one up here, in the days when I rode a bike and Teddy ran along beside me. Don't recall ever owning one. But perhaps they're a good idea.

She turned to Frank diffidently. 'Ms Farmer might come to the pound with us. Maybe she might, she said.'

'Cool. Gimme five,' he said to her. They slapped palms in this curious habit young people have. He did seem genuinely pleased.

I declined their invitation to come in. We all had things to do, I said. Frank threw a protesting arm round my shoulder. He's a very demonstrative young man. About the same height as me, five ten, which was tall for a woman in my day but is unremarkable now. Not short, but not tall for a man these days. He hadn't heard of the two books either, needless to say.

'Don't forget our assignation, will you?' he said to me in an intimate voice. 'Monday, eleven am sharp, coffee machine, staff common room. Right?'

Kim looked at me. 'Hey, are you two, like, dating now?' She has a lively sense of humour, which only emerges as you get to know her.

Frank transferred his arm to the small of her back, giving it an affectionate little rub. 'Yes, but only when you're safely tucked up at school. I'm a two-timing rat. It's our guilty secret, Wombat. Don't let on to Ellie, whatever you do.'

She couldn't seriously have thought I might mind them getting a dog from the pound. That really would have to give me pause.

~~

Oscar seems to have an intuitive grasp of what makes me tick. The new assignment is a case in point. Write a character sketch of an individual who has played a significant part in your life.

We were the full complement of six again, with bearded Greg back. Turned out he hadn't shot through, he'd only strained his back. Gilda the Dreaded was all over him, offering tea and sympathy and Bulgarian folk remedies for backs. Among other things, she offered to sit on it and bounce up and down. It always worked, she said. It was infallible. It was all in the way it was done.

I was sitting on his other side. With his beard and that mass of straggly hair you can't see much of his face, but it was obvious the poor fellow was struck dumb. Under no circumstances admit her over your threshold, I muttered into his ear, through the hair. Ring the police if you need help. Or ring me. He nodded with a strangled expression.

Oscar rapped his coffee mug with a teaspoon. 'Prepare for a surprise, ye troops. This week we are going to accentuate the positive. I've met someone new, and I've had a makeover in the seat of the affections. Yes, you see before you today an embodiment of sweetness and light. I've come over all warm and fuzzy inside.'

A muffled ripple of excitement from the group. Titillated murmurs. Was the somebody a he or a she? No one was prepared to ask. I heard Greg say, 'He means he's come over all queer inside.'

Oscar held up a cautionary hand. I hoped he hadn't heard this, but he seemed insouciant. That was all he was saying, dears, not another word. He was nothing if not discreet, as well as shy and retiring, as we must all know by now. We laughed on cue.

'But I felt I owed you some explanation for my momentary retreat from cynicism. While I'm still basking, I want you to think about an individual in your own life who has pushed *your* buttons. Write me a character sketch of someone who's engraved their initials on your heart. Someone you admire or even – shall we, should we, can we risk the word – *love*? Or perhaps, loved and lost?'

His eyes rested speculatively on our faces in turn, ending up, and I'm sure it was deliberate, on Gilda-lily's pudding-like countenance. If no one came to mind, he said, we could always resort to invention and he'd be none the wiser. It could even be a celebrity icon, think Marilyn or Garbo, or Diana. Think George Clooney or, if we really had to, Prince William.

'There, I can't be more inclusive than that, can I? Now go forth and multiply – the goodwill, I mean.'

Everyone left in rather a hurry and congregated in the pub I usually avoid. Even Greg and even me – I had no reason to stay behind today. Oscar had beaten a swift retreat himself, giving me a definite wink as he passed.

They buzzed with speculation. The majority view favoured a he. Greg was more forthright than the rest. Early on he'd thought it was a classic closet case (nice tongue-twister) but now? No way known was Oscar not gay, in his book. Look at the celebs he listed. There were noises of agreement and judicious nods.

I thought I was a lone voice in support of Oscar's hetero credentials (cred, I should say) but Gilda backed me up. I might have known. She has a vested interest in wanting Oscar to be straight because she has designs on him, absurd as it sounds.

I gave his assignment some thought. There have been significant individuals in my life, I can't deny that. My high school English teacher was an influence. Loved her work and conveyed it day after day in the classroom. Exposure to such unalloyed fulfilment influenced my decision to go into teaching in the first place. But if ever there was a mixed blessing that was one. If she'd known the outcome she would have regretted her unwitting part in it, would she not?

Matthew Rhode was one of the few members of staff I ever encountered who derived a similar satisfaction from teaching. Or seemed to. No, it is inconceivable that this was an act. There are limits to cynicism, even where Mr Rhode is concerned. By the time I appointed him I had almost forgotten how it might be. Seeing his exhilaration brought this back. It must have drawn me to him, I can see that now.

But the seminal influence on my choice of career wasn't a person at all. It was something much more prosaic: the existence of the bonded teacher-training scholarships. They helped hundreds, perhaps thousands of young people who wouldn't otherwise have been able to finance their studies, including me. Which implicates an enlightened government policy in my personal debacle.

Relatives? My mother was a strong-willed countrywoman, a natural feminist. That influenced me. She was a 'character', notably lacking in maternal instinct. I was not a loved child; she was far too angry and frustrated. Whereas my father was affectionate but an inhibited and rather colourless man. She ruled the roost, but it brought her no satisfaction because the roost was too confining.

They were both ardent churchgoers. It was a crutch; no matter how grim things were on the ground, it was all going to come good in the afterlife up in the sky. Probably the fairytale that turned me off religion in the first place.

Never be dependent on a mere male, my mother said to me. It was the only advice I can recall her giving me, and she gave it more than once. Make sure you earn your own living always and are self-sufficient economically. Then you will be free. Those words influenced me and do to this day. I became a self-sufficient woman, and I don't just mean economically.

I did take after her in one respect. I was similarly deficient in the maternal instinct department. Perhaps that's just as well. I've never lost sleep over being childless, unlike many women I've known. And not only women. Matthew Rhode wanted children. I recall a discussion on the subject one evening after dinner in my flat. The conversation was brief. He wanted several children, three or four.

You just want to perpetuate yourself with a tribe of little

Matthew clones, I teased him. But it wasn't that. I realised quite quickly that there was something else going on, something that was not subject to rational analysis or justification. He was unable to answer the question why, in any satisfactory manner. Why did he want children? He couldn't say. You simply do or you don't, I concluded.

Which leads me to something else. I haven't been conspicuously good at friendship, either. Some people have a talent for it, it's even their *raison d'être*, but not me. Which is not to say I do not have friends. Just that the friendships don't seem to develop beyond a certain point. None has crossed the invisible threshold between friendship and something deeper. Is it because the right person never came along? Is it a matter of luck, or – how shall I put this – is it to do with me?

Because it is true that I feel a disenchantment with my own species. I don't much like my own kind, quite apart from the ruination it has unleashed upon the world. I've liked some individuals, of course, but as a rule humans have been a disappointment. I think I have felt this all my life, but the feeling has grown on me, no question. It has become more firmly embedded.

What was it Kim said? 'Mr Fay must be a cool guy to have as a close friend.' Well, I wish, as she might also say, because I'm not convinced that I have any 'close friends'. Or, indeed, that I really want them. With the aforementioned exception, possibly.

Colleagues? Some I liked. One I liked very much, but I am not prepared to pursue that any further, not even on the non-judgemental privacy of this screen. Matthew was perhaps, for a while, the nearest to a close friend I ever had. And look where that led.

But I can't pretend it was that experience that put me off people. After all, I didn't cross paths with young Mr Rhode until I was in my late fifties. Fifty-nine, in point of hard fact. I was a bit of a misanthrope by then and a fairly well-ingrained one. We used to laugh about it together. He would take personal responsibility, I remember him saying, for divesting me of my disenchantment.

Disrobing me of it, he even said once. From this distance I can see that was a very suggestive remark for a younger male teacher to make to the principal. Out of order? It didn't occur to me to think so at the time. At the time, I recall, we were quaffing red wine in my flat on a cold winter's evening. He had brought it. Matthew was in the habit of bearing gifts of excellent vintages. He was an enthusiastic wine buff, which may well have contributed to the eventual outcome, when I think about it.

Yes, he was quite an accomplished *bon vivant*, as I became in his company. And as indeed I would remain, I suppose, if I had the chance. What was it we used to say? Make it one for my baby, and one more for the Rhode.

I must have been similarly accomplished at concealing my subversive opinions, otherwise they'd never have appointed me head of the school. Like Mr Rhode, I must have given the impression of being a together type of person at the interviews. When the board of governors declared their wish to take the school to another academic level, they obviously had no inkling that this competent woman with a distinguished teaching record not only didn't much like children as a species but had a jaundiced view of the majority of the human race.

Just as I had no idea what lurked beneath Matthew's friendly and convivial exterior.

Still, in spite of all this there is something to celebrate, as I should have told Kim. One individual of the male gender has engraved his initial on my heart. One who, with the sweetness of his nature, delightful company and uncritical devotion leaves all others in the shade.

And where did this train of thought come from? Kim initiated it herself. It was her observation − astute beyond her years − that Teddy, who never disagrees with me, must be a dream to live with. Like an ideal man, only with four legs.

So I might try a little experiment. See if I can describe Teddy's personality in some detail, but without telling any lies and without revealing that the subject is a dog, my red cattle x. I can truthfully say he happens to be the afore-mentioned bushwalking companion.

Wouldn't that give the group something juicy to think about? Never mind the queries swirling around Oscar's ambiguous love life, let them speculate about mine instead.

~~

They had friends visiting today. A couple their age, no kids. We saw them drive up at midday in a snazzy VW convertible, with the roof down. It was very hot. Soon afterwards, the two couples piled into the Subaru and didn't return until late in the day. They must have gone out for lunch. I didn't see Kim, although I looked over there, from time to time.

I embarked on my little composition. Like my previous piece of homework, the words flowed from the keyboard without effort. It must be because I know the subject so well. But how to portray him truthfully without letting on that he is a quadruped?

Difficult? Not a bit of it. It turned out to be a breeze. I decided to call him Ted. It sounds more plausible for a male my age or older. A legitimate little ploy, I think. No, Ted and I are not married. We live together by choice, I'll say candidly, if they ask. Bearing in mind none of them knows anything about me, outside the little we have revealed in the group. We don't socialise, or I don't. I've avoided it like the plague. Last week was the first time I've ever gone to the pub with the rest of them, and probably will be the last.

I began with a short dissertation on my special friend's character. The fact that Ted, unlike most people, is never ill-tempered, even when he is feeling under the weather. He has an exceptionally easygoing disposition. He doesn't go in for good and bad moods. He greets each day with enthusiasm in the same sunny frame of mind. And he responds to my darker humours with an unspoken empathy.

Moreover, unlike many men, I can truthfully say Ted makes no secret of his feelings. I don't want to boast but, even though it's nearly fourteen years since we first met, he is always delighted to see me. He has never suffered from a fashionable male malady such as commitment phobia. He makes it clear on a daily basis that he thinks I am the most important person in his life. This endears him to me in itself.

One of the reasons I find him so lovable is his loyal and straight-down-the-line character, which spills over into every part of his life. Deception, equivocation – these are quite foreign to Ted. He is direct and sincere. What you see is what you get. And, again unlike most men, he doesn't indulge in gamesmanship. He's not interested in messing with your mind, as the saying goes. On the contrary, he is almost entirely without guile.

I say almost. His sense of humour is the one area where he has been known to employ a touch of artfulness. Ted has a delightful sense of the ridiculous. It is most original, peculiar to himself and unlike that of most people I know. It can be quite subtle, like the changes of expression in his eyes. He likes to conceal things occasionally and play little practical jokes. He finds it amusing if I hide and jump out on him. In that respect he's quite childlike, I suppose.

I don't want to give the impression that we share

everything, I will say. We're not peas in a pod. In some ways we're polar opposites with widely divergent interests. I read a lot, write, listen to classical music. Ted has never read a book in his life and doesn't care what music I put on. He has no ear for it at all. He's an outdoorsy type, his interests are far more sporty.

He loves games, especially energetic, knockabout ones, although the wretched arthritis means he's not as athletic as he was. In his heyday he enjoyed swimming and running. He's still an enthusiastic swimmer, and I don't think I've ever come across a man with a better ball sense than Ted still has.

He likes rock climbing and has no fear of heights. He is my fellow explorer − it was Ted, of course, who was *we*. He was with me when we discovered the precipice I wrote about. We still walk a lot together every day. He's fun to go bushwalking with because he's so adventurous and curious, with a highly developed interest in the natural world, the scents and sounds of nature. Often he sees and hears things that I've completely missed.

He likes his creature comforts, loves his food. He's not a picky eater, doesn't have fads, has admirably catholic tastes. Indeed, I can't offhand think of anything he doesn't like except, as it happens, alcohol. Ted is not a drinker at all. He's not a teetotaler by philosophical conviction − he just doesn't share my taste for wine, which is a significant money saver for us.

He does have some funny little habits, however. He tends to drop off in front of the TV, almost as soon as it's turned on. He likes to lie on the floor. He's very tactile. He loves a good tummy rub, and to put his head in my lap.

Hang on a minute, better not say anything like that. Better steer clear of anything with potentially problematic and/or, good fictitious lord help us, erotic overtones. Apart from the bad taste, I wouldn't want to reignite the others' latent prurient tendencies. We saw too much of those at the last meeting.

Definitely better not say he likes to lick my feet.

At this point in the essay I realised I hadn't given any physical description of Ted. That turned out to be adroitly negotiated, too. I wrote: Ted has a finely modelled head with good bones. Not to everyone's taste, perhaps, but exceedingly handsome to my mind. He's of average height, stocky and well-built. He does have a tendency to put on weight, but who among us is exempt from that? He still has his full complement of hair, with the same fetching white streak he's always had. And all his own teeth, which are strong and white too. But his most striking feature is perhaps his eyes – they are an unusual shade of amber, most expressive and direct. And he breaks into a more infectious, purely generous grin than I have ever seen on the face of anyone else in my life.

I tinkered a bit and read it over again before emailing it to Oscar. I have become quite adept at this, after an initial resistance. It was a condition of joining Oscar's class that we had to be on email. Ollie Nugent set it up for me and printed out all the steps. After a couple of memory lapses I keep them stuck to the wall. Davy emails me most weeks, usually bad jokes. Apart from that I use it purely for our writing assignments. I doubt if Sandy has ever mastered it. La Harmonica handles the business side, and you need a tolerance for excruciating boredom to do that.

I was quietly pleased with the way the character sketch unfolded. I might even show it to Kim, if I see her tomorrow. I suspect it would appeal to her sense of humour. There was still no sign of her when Teddy and I walked past in the warmth of the late afternoon.

The ease of the exercise leads me to ask several questions of myself, rather thought-provoking questions. Have I, because of our close relationship over so many years, come to think of Teddy as a person? If he does function to some extent as an ideal man in my life, is this in any way a realistic ideal? Or is it the romantic fancy of a woman whose knowledge of such things is somewhat selective and incomplete? I have an affinity with Teddy that I never achieved in any human context. Could any man, indeed, have done what Teddy did for me?

Caring for a small puppy, training him, our long bush-walks, the discovery of our secret places, together with the planning and building of my house. These things enabled me to blot out the painful end of my career.

~~

I saw Frank and Ellice leave again, mid-morning. Kim was not in the car, although I thought there had been a strong possibility of going to the pound today. After a suitable interval Teddy and I went off and did the rock circuit. With no school, I half expected to see her reading up there in the crook of the sandstone, shaded by the scribbly gum. We saw the lizard instead.

That was a silly thing to expect. I made my disapproval quite clear. I would have been cross had I found her there again. Most annoyed.

When we got back, we walked closer to their house than usual and I spotted her on the deck in the sun. She was lying on her front with a bright orange straw hat over her head, so she didn't see us. There was an open book lying face down. I was tall enough to see that it was not one of the ones I gave her; it was a paperback. Also a glass of lurid green liquid – fizzy, most likely. I never liked those sorts of drinks when I was a girl.

She was probably asleep, although some kind of cater-wauling song was playing loudly – far too loudly – on a portable radio. Some children seem to be able to sleep through any raucous noise, I have found. Someone should warn her about the risks of hearing damage. Most young people these days have the ubiquitous I-pods, but listening to loud music through earphones is worse for you, I imagine.

Teddy and I sat on our verandah. It may have been my imagination, but I thought I could detect the screeching vocals from over there, polluting the atmosphere. I put on a CD of Bach's violin concertos to blot it out, at a higher volume than usual. There is nothing worse than other people's music, especially young people's. This is not something I ever used to have to bother about.

Teddy poked around in the garden and uncovered an old bone, a lamb shank. He hauled it up the steps and gnawed contentedly for the next couple of hours. I quite like the sound of Teddy's chewing, although I know it can be infuriating to some people. His propensity for burying bones is another thing I had to avoid in my composition. I must remember to mention that little detail when I show it to Kim.

I read and made some jottings in my notebook for a short story I'm thinking about. One about a girl who shows a talent for writing.

All in all, a typical Sunday afternoon for us. It might have been any Sunday in the thirteen years Teddy has been with me, except for the corner of an orange hat that was just visible. Now and then I glanced over at it. It remained in place for the next hour or so, for the entire duration of Teddy's rhythmic mastication, then disappeared from sight. She must have gone inside.

If we could see a trace of her, I suppose she could see us as well.

Then a disquieting thought occurred to me. Had she gone for a walk instead? Could she have ventured into the bush by herself again, in spite of my lecture? She did it once, after all. Or once that I know about.

I meant to raise the subject last week with Frank. I don't know if they have spoken to her about it at all, or whether they're even sufficiently aware of the dangers. They are intelligent young people, but they seem a trifle careless. They are not parents. They haven't brought her up. They have just acquired her in young adulthood, as Sandy might say.

Not that being a parent is any guarantee of a responsible attitude, as Kim herself would know only too well. I mustn't forget to stress to Frank when I see him tomorrow that it is essential to talk to her about these things. They seem to have a cavalier habit of leaving her alone, probably because they have been used to pleasing themselves. Rather like Teddy and me, I suppose.

I was on the point of going over to check on her when she materialised. The orange hat caught my eye first. And only a matter of minutes later the car returned in a cloud of dust. If they had left her alone for much longer, certainly if they had stayed away for the evening, I would have gone across and fetched her. They were driving too fast. Probably been drinking too.

A strong feeling of relief came over me when I saw the hat. Surprisingly overpowering. It had crossed my mind more than once that I could have made the move and offered her a cup of tea. It was up to me because it was my turn. She had made the first overture.

I suppose I could even have offered to take her to the pound myself.

I went to the blackboard and wrote out three times: I am too stubborn and set in my ways.

~

My Monday 'date' with Frank. There was a steady drizzle, which wouldn't have bothered me, but a minute before eleven he showed up at my door with an enormous golf umbrella. A thoughtful gesture. Big enough for two, he said, steering me by the elbow.

We had to rub Teddy down. Don't want nasty muddy paws spoiling your nice, pristine floors, do we? I said. Sanded and oiled timber floorboards, salvaged from a Mechanics' Institute circa 1900 (pulled down when the highway was widened) and looking less than pristine already. The words sounded more waspish than I'd intended.

Frank's coffee was excellent again, down to the professional impression of a heart he had created in the crema, if that is the right term. I told him he could morph into a barista after the revolution.

'Instead of a pumpkin? Thank Christ for that, Thea.'

Imaginary Christ, I corrected. He said he had a gut feeling I was not a religious nutter. We were sitting side by side rather cosily on one of the sofas. It seemed a lot more stable than last time, didn't skid all over the place when I sat down. Frank must have locked the wheels.

'You didn't go to the pound yesterday,' I said. It sounded overly accusing.

He looked guilty and fondled Teddy's ears. Yeah, well, the weekend got away from them. Drink, drugs and rock'n'roll, you know how it is, Thea. 'The bane of all our lives, huh? Actually, a friend's kid's birthday party. First birthday, the kind where the kid sleeps through and the grown-ups go on the rampage. It'll be a different story in a year's time.'

'Kim didn't want to go with you?' I said.

No, there was a strict 'no kids' rule in place. Well, apart from the one-year-old birthday girl. They were all their own mates, his and Ellie's. Anyhow, Kim claimed to prefer reading to social gatherings of any sort. She was a funny little thing, rather shy and retiring, he remarked, as if this might be news to me. I thought of the orange straw hat and the raucous music, and the paperback lying facedown on the deck.

'You left her behind on Saturday too.' I hadn't intended to mention that, it just emerged. 'Two days running,' I added.

She likes her own company, he said. Rather offhandedly, I thought. So, did I happen to have a word with her during the weekend?

'No, I didn't,' I said. The conflicting feelings I'd had yesterday on that matter returned in a rush. Next time they were planning to leave her alone for the whole day, I told him, they should let me know and I'd keep an eye on her.

Fine, they would do that in future, Frank said soothingly, no worries. He seemed unruffled. It raised my hackles a little.

Had they talked to her about the bush? She wasn't a country girl; they should always bear that in mind. Had they spoken to her at all about the dangers of getting lost?

Oh yeah they had, he said, they'd done that, they'd certainly aired the subject. But they didn't want to overdo it and make her paranoid. She was a sensible kid, she wouldn't just go off on her own.

'Oh yes she would,' I said. 'And she has, at least once.' I described how we had come across her while on one of our regular walks. I avoided any more supporting detail.

'Well, that *is* an interesting bit of info,' he said. 'She didn't tell us.' This corroborated Kim's account. I could see Frank was genuinely surprised. He didn't look especially alarmed, however.

Interesting was all well and good, I said, but it was something to be taken seriously. I'd given her a bit of a talking to but I didn't know how much had sunk in. At that age things had to be well and truly drummed in. Repetition was of the essence and you couldn't be too careful. It was like the thank-you reflex, I expanded. It's common knowledge among parents that in order to make children say thank you, you have to remind them at least two thousand times.

Then I wondered if I wasn't going overboard myself. Or nagging, even, which is a dreadful thought. I'm not usually a worry-wart, I'm not sure what got into me. I was discomfited to see that Frank was looking distinctly amused. He squeezed my hand. No sweat, they'd back me up on this. Maybe not quite two thousand times, but they'd drum it in.

'She won't take any notice of what we say, though. Much more likely to listen to you. The Wombat seems to have made a connection with you, Thea, a real connection.' He grinned. 'Hey. Don't look so appalled.'

But I wasn't appalled. And neither was I wholly displeased.

'She thinks so, anyhow. She likes hanging out with you, did you know that? Goes on about it. It's about the only thing she does talk about. I'm quite jealous.' He regarded me genially, flexing his spatulate fingers. 'I hope she hasn't been a pain in the bum. I know how you like your privacy. I'm not too worried, though. I reckon you're more than capable of telling her to make herself scarce if she gets in the way.'

I thought this over. Teddy was lying across my shoes. I pictured her toes burrowing into his fur. 'She hasn't got in the way yet,' I said. It was a surprise to hear myself say this.

'Well, monitor it, okay? If it's all the same to you, I'd rather it was you telling her to piss off than Ellie or me heavying her.'

'Heavying her?'

'You know, ordering her to leave you alone.'

That startled me. 'I'd certainly prefer you didn't give her any orders of that kind.'

'Fair enough. I'm cool with that.' He gave my arm a conciliatory little rub. 'We're feeling our way a bit at the moment, Thea, to be honest. I want to be friends with her, have a bit of fun. What I don't want to do is play the ogre grown-up, not just yet at any rate. Let's face it, I'm only an overgrown kid myself, right?'

You're in loco parentis, however, I thought.

'More than anything right now, she needs a lot of TLC, I'd say.' He looked at me to see if I'd picked up the reference. I knew that I knew it, I was just trying to retrieve it.

'Tender loving care. It's been in pretty short supply in her life to date.'

Well, she'd found a good home now, I said. I thought she felt happy here, and safe. That does seem to be the case and he seemed pleased to hear it, as he should be.

It turns out Frank met Kim for the first time only last year. Until then she'd lived interstate much of her life, he never knew where she was. So she'd been let down a lot by the family, and he was trying to make up for it now. Trying hard to get through her defences, he said, which were pretty rock solid.

He showed a certain defensiveness himself, not surprisingly. No doubt feeling guilty about his long absence from her life. I brought up the subject of his parents. They were Kim's grandparents, hadn't they had any contact with her?

Well, he said, they were not like me, put it that way. By this he meant they were gaga to all intents and purposes, I gathered. They'd been in a retirement village for years (they started planning for it and booked themselves in when they turned *forty-five* – oh yes, I told him, I've known people like that too) and couldn't even think of coping with an unconventional granddaughter.

Frank rolled his eyes. It wasn't only the mixed-race card. To give them their due, they'd had more than their fair share of a hard time with Kim's dad. His much older brother, the no-hoper sperm donor drug addict, Frank reminded me. Seventeen years older. No wonder Frank still thinks of himself as a kid brother.

'Considering all that stuff, the Wombat's majorly wary of families,' he said, 'but I'm working overtime on changing this flaky, isolationist mindset.'

'Don't bother trying to change it,' I said. 'It's an entirely rational mindset and I agree with it in its entirety. That's why she needs a dog in her life.' Nevertheless, I thought, you might consider spending more time with her instead of leaving her alone so much, even if that is her choice.

He laughed. 'You two have a lot in common, that's what I reckon. I can see why you've bonded. Okay, how about we do a raincheck on the pound expedition. How are you placed next weekend?'

Then he slapped his forehead with his hand. Shit no, he'd forgotten. They were buggered for a while. Next weekend was particularly buggered. Ellie was rostered on both days because they had this crazy staffing crisis at the café, and he was working with a guy who'd done this incredible low-budget movie. Working title: *Verminville*.

'*Verminville*? How very appetising.'

He grinned. There'd been a musical called *Urinetown*, so why not a movie called *Verminville*? But, seriously, it was a big break – his first feature. He was doing the music score. He looked at me mischievously. 'You wouldn't like it. The movie or the music.'

Piqued, I rose to the bait. Probably unwise. What made him so sure of that?

It was full of bad taste and a bit juvenile. 'And more than a bit, you know, lewd and crude.' I was aware of him monitoring my expression. 'But please don't think I'm accusing you of being diametrically opposed to lewd, Thea. I'm not suggesting that at all.'

Well, that's a relief, I said. But there was bad taste and bad taste, was there not?

'Yeah, exactly, there's gross and there's *gross*, I guess. This is mostly in the second category. Which is pretty fun to work with,' he gave me a frisky look, 'as you can imagine.'

He is quick on the uptake, Frank. Fly, as we used to say. Streetwise also comes to mind, a useful contemporary word to describe some people. His eyes are very direct. They are a subtle shade of hazel, clear and flecked with green. Rather hypnotic eyes, I imagine, although I have never been susceptible to hypnotism. They are two very different men, but I was put in mind of Oscar. Both are congenitally inclined to tease. As, indeed, was Matthew Rhode. Do I inadvertently invite teasing? Or even, subtly provoke it?

'I think I am a tolerably broad-minded specimen,' I said.

'Yeah, right.' He nodded with a sage expression. It reminded me of his niece, although they do not look at all alike on the face of it. 'I guess you've seen it all, Thea. Maybe more than once.'

'What goes around comes around,' I said. And we continued to sip our coffee in a decorous manner.

'I'll take her to the pound next weekend, if you like,' I said. 'We don't want to disappoint her yet again, do we?'

He seemed delighted. Would I? Really? Hey, that'd be great, if it wasn't too much trouble.

If you think she'll come with me, I said.

'Oh, she'll come all right. Know what? I reckon she'd rather go with you anyway.'

'And if we come back with a new puppy, you and Ellice are content to accept whatever we find?'

'We'll be fine with any furry critter that takes your fancy, I reckon, Thea.'

'It's going to be Kim's,' I told him, 'so it will be her choice of critter.'

Had he been angling for it? That did cross my mind. But my suspicious mind has a habit of seeing ulterior motives when they don't always exist. This is a habit of later life, a cynical habit. The result, I imagine, of having once been on the receiving end of a grievous lesson in moral dereliction and duplicity. And in the necessity of keeping one's eye on the ball.

Anyway, as they say, whatever.

Frank is very easy to get on with. I think he's one of those fortunate individuals who has no problems with social interactions in general. What they call these days a 'high people skills' person, which with my notoriously low tolerance of other people ought to mean that his personality is the antithesis to mine. We may be like chalk and cheese in this respect, but we seem to have made our own connection.

It is a common assumption that age differences create insuperable barriers between people, but I have not found this to be true, necessarily. There was a big age difference between Matthew and me, but we got on famously. My deputy head once observed that he and I got on better than she did with her own son. This was a disconcerting remark because I didn't see it in any way as a 'filial' relationship. I knew there was some bad feeling about our friendship in the staff room, but in my obtuseness I put it down to jealousy. Solely to that.

You'd think that Frank might have gravitated towards a more social type of occupation, instead of working in an isolated creative bubble. He says he enjoys bushwalking so he must have a reflective, solitary side. Perhaps this is the part of him that I instinctively respond to. It must be a point of contact with his niece too, I suppose. He is certainly fond of Kim, but I have a feeling he welcomes the chance to have her entertained off the premises for a few hours. It must be quite a responsibility for a young man who was hitherto unencumbered with any such thing.

If he is right and she would prefer to go to the pound with me, this may be because I am not part of the family she is majorly wary of becoming attached to, as Frank says.

Frank showed me where he writes and plays music, the end room he calls his studio. I had to steel myself. I tried to imagine I was visiting this house for the first time and being shown around by the owner. Tried to see it dispassionately. In this I was reasonably successful, I think.

On the way we passed Kim's bedroom. The den of the Wombat, he said. It would have been my guestroom. I'm not sure I needed a guestroom, or who I imagined was going to visit. The door was closed. He went to open it, but I put my hand on his arm to restrain him.

'We should wait until Kim is here to show me herself,' I said. 'A girl is very particular about her own room, it's her private domain.' I remembered that from the school boarding houses, which don't afford very much privacy at any time. And also from my own childhood. I never wanted anyone invading my sanctum.

Frank said, 'Oh, she's used to it. She doesn't care who barges in.'

I doubted that, and said so rather forcefully. It was all the more important as she'd almost certainly never had a room of her own before. He gave me a throwaway grin as if to say, have it your own way.

His workroom down at the far end would have been my study. This was the room in which I was going to do my writing, surrounded by bush on three sides. My inspirational room was unrecognisable to me now, full of baffling electronic gadgetry and switches, big speakers and a keyboard. There was a couch or day bed along one side, and a console of whizzbang controls, just like the dashboard of a Boeing 747.

I could see the need for extra power points in here. He was like a jet pilot in his cockpit, I told him.

He liked that. 'My cockpit? Cool.'

I nearly walked into a half-empty bottle of red wine and a half-full (to be even-handed) wine glass on the floor. Nearly knocked them both flying. I never drink a thing when I'm trying to write. Perhaps I should give it a whirl, it might improve my poems. Couldn't make them any worse, could it?

Frank played me one of his compositions on the synthesiser. It sounded like one of those discordant pieces I always find utterly pointless and alienating. I interrupted, with my hands over my ears, before he got to the end. It was too highbrow for me and far too avant-garde, I declared. I'm not afraid to say I like a nice tune. He looked comically crestfallen.

I added, 'But you never know. If I was locked in here and force-fed your music on pain of dismemberment, I might discover a liking for it.'

He laughed loudly and clapped me on the back. 'Good on you, Thea.' He took a disc from a shelf. 'Here's my new show reel to practice on. You've got a CD player, haven't you? Go on, force yourself.'

I might force myself, or then again I might not. He may even be absurdly talented. How would I know?

~~

It's been pouring with rain almost non-stop for three days. Unusual for this time of year, but the whole climate's out of whack as a result of the depredations of the species. Still, rain is to be welcomed for reducing the bushfire risk. I've hardly set eyes on them. Frank's been taking the other two

120

off in the morning, dropping Kim at school presumably and Ellice at the café. I've also seen him walking at a brisk clip in the rain. Then I've seen him go out later in the car to pick up Kim.

Two leaks in the kitchen from a blocked gutter. Water seeping under the windows. I got on the ladder and cleared most of the leaves, but still had to get Giorgio in. The TV conked out and I had to get Paul in as well. Not that there's ever anything on the box that any sensible person would want to watch.

At one point I even put on Frank's show reel. I lasted five minutes, maximum. Teddy couldn't stand it either and left the room.

Went to the library. I asked if a girl of Kim's description had joined recently. The dim little woman didn't know. This is a small community, not a teeming metropolis like Sydney or Saigon. She must be singularly unobservant as well as a halfwit.

You could say my piece about Ted was a washout too. Oscar said it was on the anodyne side. A little lacking in my usual astringency and bite. I'd thought it was quite clever, but of course he wasn't to know why I'd thought that.

'I dunno, Thea,' he said. 'The way you paint this saintly guy, he sounds almost too perfect by half. A goody-two-shoes. Almost too goody to be truey.'

'When can we meet this paragon of virtue?' Gilda-lily, of course. 'Can we come round for tea, seeing as how he doesn't drink? Will you introduce him at once so I can get my sticky paws on him?' Her paws? How creepily appropriate, had she only known.

Greg said he hated him already without needing to meet him.

Really, rather an extreme response. No one asked me if we lived together, so my preparatory work was not required.

121

I was left with the impression they all thought Ted was a figment of my imagination, and stopped short of saying so outright to spare my feelings. Galling is the least of it.

The others didn't fare much better. Mostly they had chosen influential people in their lives rather than love objects. Gilda had chosen Cary Grant. Enough said. I was sitting next to Greg again. The idea of Cary Grant pushing her buttons leaves a nasty taste in the mouth, I murmured in his ear. Or where I thought his ear was; he was having a particularly bad hair day. I don't do anything to mine, but at least it's short and straight. The longer Greg's gets the less he appears to wash it.

Oscar said it was his fault. 'I made like I wanted nice, when it was nice and nasty I was really after. Sweet and sour, the two sides of everybody's coin. Not to worry, we'll go there another time. And now,' he appeared to consider, 'for something completely different. Intercourse.'

There was an audible group intake of breath.

'Social *dis*course, you disreputable lot. Speech. Lofty diatribes, idle chatter. Write me an arresting page of dialogue between two people, about something. Doesn't have to be about something important, not even necessarily anything overt or spelt out. Think three things, troops. The three things are: subtext, subtext and subtext.'

He expanded on this theme, people talking about one thing and meaning another. I suppose people do this. I'm not sure that I do it. He says it happens all the time. If you doubt me, he said, go forth and eavesdrop. Shamelessly listen in to snatches of speak in buses and cafés. Especially snatches between life partners. You'll soon see what I mean.

I wondered how Oscar's amour was progressing. He seemed a little subdued and fretful today. His personality is very *fin de siècle*, Gilda said to Greg as we were leaving. *Un peu* Proustian, she added with a laborious moue.

Proustian? Good grief. She wouldn't have the faintest idea what that means. She probably thinks madeleine is the name of one of his characters.

~~

Sandy tells me Frank and Kim came in again after school. They bought three books, all for her. She was gobbling up his young adult stuff now, Sandy said. 'We went *Gone With the Wind, How Green Was My Valley* and *Jamaica Inn.*' Next stop, Jane Austen. And how had she gone with the two I'd given her?

I had to say I didn't know as I hadn't seen her, it had been so grim and wet lately. But I'd had coffee with Frank. We had a regular date on Mondays. And I was taking Kim to the dog pound on the weekend.

'An overflowing social calendar. You've struck up a friendship,' he said. 'That's good, I had a feeling you two would hit it off, even if she is only twelve years of age. Didn't I tell you she's your kind of person?'

And what would that be when it's at home, I inquired. A little on the unorthodox side, was all I could extract from him.

'Which covers a multitude of sins, and describes you too, what's more,' I said. How about Frank? Was he my kind of person as well?

Sandy gave me one of his playful looks. 'I'm sure he is. But I hardly know the man.'

I think he was just bantering about in the way we do together, but it did occur to me to wonder if there was a subtext in there. If so, what could he mean? I couldn't pursue this intriguing line of inquiry because the woman Monica came in and distracted him with a raft of dopey queries.

I'm sure he is. But I hardly know the man.

I juxtaposed the two sentences in my mind to see if they sounded any different.

I hardly know the man. But I'm sure he is.

Oscar, this is your doing. You have made me obsess over ten innocent words. Ten innocuous words, moreover, delivered by someone so constitutionally good-natured he is incapable of innuendo, even of ambiguity of any description. Or so I have always thought.

I was left wondering whether Sandy was implying something about me. I found myself asking quite what it was that he, of all people, was actually saying. And wondering if I was endowing it with an unwarranted significance?

If it means what I think it may mean, it is dismaying, not least in its inaccuracy. To suggest that I have an indiscriminate predilection for anything of the male gender is preposterous.

Of course, subtext is not the same as implication. Humdrum words and phrases can express different things depending on how you use them. This is a fundamental linguistic truth, yet it is something I feel am only just beginning to come to grips with. Is that curious fact enough, in itself, to explain why I became a teacher and not a writer in the first place?

I suspect Oscar may turn out to be correct, and writing conversational speech will have much, perhaps everything, to do with subtext. Is this because people incline by their nature to say one thing and mean another? What does this say about their nature? The idea that we are all devious, to a greater or lesser extent, should not surprise me, should it? And yet I feel an odd resistance to it.

And what about children? Is deviousness a learned behaviour, or is it instinctive? To be consistent with the belief that it is intrinsic to the species, one must incline to the latter position. And yet again, I seem obscurely disinclined.

~~

I felt I ought to consult Ellice before going to the pound. Establish that she has no eccentric dislike of any particular kind of dog. She doesn't appear to be a full-blown hysteric, but of that you can never be too sure. It wouldn't be the first time I've seen a relentlessly mirthful exterior on an inner loony. And it's strange, with her brain, that she seems content with waitressing.

I went to the café, only to find she wasn't there. 'She's off sick today,' the other girl said. I realised I still didn't have their phone number. The girl, who was a standard-issue simpleton, refused to give it to me. On what grounds? I demanded. On the grounds that I don't know who you are, do I? she responded with a bovine stare. You might be anyone, she added. Fools have never been known to shun the redundant observation, in my experience. I looked around the café, but on the one occasion I'd have been pleased to see somebody I knew, there wasn't such a one in sight. Always the way.

I considered throwing my weight around, heavying her, as Frank would say, but thought the better of it. The girl was too obtuse to respond to rational argument. Next thing I knew she'd be calling the police and accusing me of being a stalker. Of Ellice, of all people. The mind boggles. There's a stalker in the news; I saw some lurid headlines in a tabloid on one of the tables. Down in Sydney, of course. Luckily there are no celebrities (sic) worth hounding in this neck of the mountains.

I scheduled my visit for mid-afternoon, circa half an hour before Kim gets back from school. It was steamy and warm, the ground still muddy and churned up. I left Teddy behind in consideration for their floor. Ellice opened the door herself. As I suspected, she hadn't been in bed sick, she was fully dressed in ripped jeans (designer holes, a particularly

125

asinine fashion) and a red-and-yellow check shirt, with her hair in rollers. Looking in the pink of condition, too. She's well-covered, not scrawny like so many young women.

She greeted me with a beaming smile. A good-looking girl, certainly, in what people presumably mean when they say a high-impact way. She has a wide mouth and smiles with unnerving frequency. I would guess she is fairly highly strung. In contrast to me, I suppose, whose temperament is not outgoing and whose mouth is small and thin-lipped.

'I don't approve of dropping in on you like this,' I began, 'but I didn't have your number and that stupid girl in the café wouldn't give –'

'Oh, please come on in, Thea. I'm being a slack-arse and taking a sickie today. Got to work all weekend is my defence. Just washed my hair.' She pulled a clownish face. 'Have you come to see our Franko?'

'No, I didn't come to see our Franko, I came to see you,' I said. He didn't materialise, he must have been ensconced in his studio. I hadn't designed it with a cacophonous composer in mind, but was pleasantly surprised how soundproof the house seems to be.

Ellice does turn out to have some definite likes and dislikes where dogs are concerned. Lucky I checked them out. A relief too that they were mainly sensible: no yapping or snuffling, no miniature anything and nothing too small or too big.

'No mincing, no squashed-up faces, fancy poodles, chihuahuas or Great Danes, thank you very much,' she laughed. She's a vivacious young woman and laughs as much as she smiles. A live wire. Fizzing extroverts tend to provoke in me the opposite reaction, as with Newton's Laws of Motion. I become sour and surly, or more that way than usual.

No Mexican hairless dog? I inquired.

'Not on your nelly. It'll go straight back to Tijuana or Popocatepetl or wherever it came from.' A trill of laughter.

Age and sex? She agreed with me that these should be left open. Kim's pet, let her decide. See what was available. It was going to be the girl's responsibility, in the fullness of its canine being. I drank some tea and asked how she thought Kim was getting on at the new school.

To be honest, Ellice said, she wouldn't have a clue. When people use phrases like 'to be honest', I always think it means the reverse. She tossed her head.

'She doesn't confide in me much. Not at all, really – it's so depressing, I can't tell you. Keeps herself to herself. Talk about trying to get blood from a stone.' A curler had come loose on the side of her head. She rolled it up again expertly. 'Maybe it's too much to expect, you know, with all the upheavals in her life, being hauled around from pillar to post from a young age. Poor thing probably doesn't even know *how* to make friends.'

'Perhaps she doesn't want to,' I said.

This went over Ellice's head. I sensed she was hitting her stride. 'She's deeply psychologically detached as a result of her background, don't you think so, Thea? It's obvious – she's such a *loner*.' To be such a loner was inexplicable, the incredulous tone suggested. I refrained from pointing out that she and Frank had come up here to get away from the social whirl of Sydney. Or so they had told me.

She shook her head as another curler threatened to unravel. 'She's obviously been moved so often that she's developed an ingrained caution about getting attached to a new family. In case she gets whisked away again, right? This mindset makes it hard for her to settle down – that's obvious.'

What is more obvious is that the young woman fancies herself as a diagnostic psychologist. And as an amateur therapist, obviously. Still, it's an unobjectionable analysis and sound enough, I suppose, as far as it goes. I was carefully noncommittal.

A sigh. Frank was better at getting through to Kim, she thought. Being a guy helped, probably. Like with most things in life, right? I didn't respond, although she appeared to think this was a womanly moment. Another rueful laugh. 'I'll just keep on plugging on, I guess.'

Some film I didn't know was on the TV. She'd turned it down but not off. I caught her giving it a sideways glance, but I wasn't ready to go, not quite yet. We wrote down each other's phone numbers. Unnecessary, wasn't it, as we were so close, Ellice said, but I was insistent.

Then I said, 'You could always have a chat with Kim's teachers. Do they know about her background?'

She shook her head again, energetically. Kim didn't want her and Frank to say a word. 'That was one thing she's been really, really adamant about, so we went along with it. It was a bit weird, actually.'

'She just wants to be normal,' I said.

'Don't we all?' She heaved another dramatic sigh. 'I hope she makes some friends soon. I hope she does turn into a more normal girl, or at least a less introverted one, or at least not a deaf-mute – she'd be more fun to have around, that's for sure.' This was accompanied by a conspiratorial giggle, but it made me instantly uneasy.

I said I thought she was settling in well. As well as one could hope for.

'Oh, do you think so? Well, she seems to have taken to you, which is amazing, isn't it?' A peal of laughter and a hug. I recoiled but failed to avoid it. She's one of those people who hugs everybody; she should have been a luvvie like Davy.

'I'm trying to be a mum to her, or at least a big sister. I'm doing my best to bond, I really am, believe me, Thea, but she's such a self-contained little missy. And she's so bloody self-effacing I forget she's even here, half the time.' Another peal in which I did not join.

It might be more constructive to let Kim dictate the relationship and progress at her own pace, I said. Which showed admirable restraint. Perhaps you should back right off, was what I was thinking.

Frank said Ellice had been keener on the idea of taking Kim than him, initially. I can see that her fervent desire to be a sister and/or, worse still, a mother to Kim, while tolerably well-meaning in its way, might very well be misplaced. It would make Kim retreat further into herself at home, I suspect.

It's like approaching a bruised and wary young animal. You have to earn its trust, wait until it comes to you. And you have to be in it for the long haul. I am not sure that a young woman like Ellice, who I also suspect has money and is used to being handed everything on a plate, has either the patience or the intestinal fortitude for a long haul of any description.

~~

I was a bit done in when we got back from the pound. It was all I could do to give poor, patient Teddy his dinner.

The drive wasn't that long, but still the longest I've done for some time. I'd had the chariot serviced, to be on the safe side – it was a few months overdue – and curtailed my reading in bed the night before.

Kim came well prepared too, with a small backpack containing a notebook and pen, canvas hat, a bottle of water for each of us and a choice of chocolate bars to eat on the way. Her mobile phone was equipped with a camera in case of need, she said. And she brought a map with the exact location of the pound and detailed instructions on how to get there. She'd googled it off a net site, she said, and printed it out.

Before we left I asked her if she thought we should take Teddy with us. I had already made a decision on this, and was unsurprised when, without a moment's hesitation, she confirmed it. Seeing the pound, even if it was a different one, might stir some buried memories, she said. Bad ones, maybe. And it might even bring back some deep-seated terrors or fears of abandonment.

This didn't set off any alarm bells in my mind, although it probably should have.

'I'll be Teddy for today,' she said, getting into the front seat next to me. I realised that this was the first time I had driven with anyone other than Teddy sitting next to me for a very long time, and said as much to Kim.

So who was my last non-doggy passenger, she wanted to know. I searched my memory and had to concede I couldn't remember who it could possibly have been. She found this funny.

The journey took close to fifty minutes but seemed shorter because we chatted, fairly continuously. Soon after we set off, waiting to turn onto the highway, I warned her not to get too hopeful in case of disappointment.

'I'm trying to not get too, like, hyped up,' she said soberly. 'You can't afford to make a mistake, right? A puppy's not something like a perfume bottle that you can just take back if you decide you don't like it – that's if you haven't already opened it and then been stuck with it.'

Ellice's recent words came uncomfortably to mind, along with Oscar's subtexts. I glanced at Kim but couldn't see her eyes behind those awful mirrored sunglasses.

She said, 'I can't write funny poems like you, but I'm doing a thank-you drawing that I'm in the middle of. For my official birthday presents.' She does most of her reading in bed at night when they think she's asleep. She'd devoured the *Beau Geste* I gave her in a marathon session one rainy night, under the covers.

'I couldn't believe those brothers. It's so incredibly brave, right, to risk your life and take the blame for something you haven't done. I know it's a story but I so wish it was real life. Wouldn't it be amazing if people were like that now, Ms Farmer?'

They could be like that in real life at any time, I said. They just had to be the right people.

She looked unconvinced. Maybe in the olden days there might've been, but there were hardly any people like that nowadays, she reckoned.

There weren't many at any time, I agreed. But remnants did exist. What was important was to find them. All the people like that had to track each other down.

Immediately she asked, 'Have you? Have you ever managed to find any of the remnants?'

I drew a deep breath. I wasn't used to having a two-way conversation while driving – Teddy just sits and listens to my intermittent outbursts of road rage – let alone a probing conversation with a demanding subtext.

Finally I said, 'On occasion. But, you know, I think I have been at fault. I could have searched harder. When you don't find them in one place you have to look in others and not ever let yourself be discouraged.'

She nodded thoughtfully, lacing her fingers tightly in her lap. We drove on as she read out the instructions on the map. I wondered which of her foster carers had instilled in her the thank-you habit.

Her next question was: 'Did you always know what you wanted to be, or did it just happen?'

I told her that in a way it had just happened, although I'd had an influential English teacher in high school. And

I'd had an obligation to pay off a teaching scholarship. She wanted to know, as I'd already anticipated, and anticipated uneasily, if this had been the right decision. It was about half right, I said.

So what was the right half?

'I was a good teacher of English. A very good teacher. My students invariably got excellent results.'

And the wrong half? This came at me far too fast for any thought of caution. I didn't like children very much, I said.

She snorted, with a hand over her mouth. 'That's normal. Most teachers hate kids. They just hide it from you.'

This was news to me. Not reassuring news, exactly. I would have pondered it, to see whether I agreed, but she didn't allow me any respite.

It must've got better when I was a principal, right? Like, you know, being in charge of everything? Organising the school exactly how I wanted.

In theory, I said. Not having to take orders from fools on a daily basis was advantageous. But there was an interfering board, and there were other disadvantages. You had to appoint people to teaching positions. I found my judgement of people was unreliable.

I tried to concentrate on the driving. Why, on imaginary god's earth, was I telling this to a twelve-year-old?

'Yeah?' She looked surprised. She would've thought I was a good judge of people. A really good judge, she'd've thought.

'Not of everyone,' I said.

'Well, some kinds of people are just screwed-up. They're incredibly clever at hiding things, right? Like, their bad side, or their real nature?'

Before she could ask me if I had ever appointed such a screwed-up kind of person, I managed to get a question in first. 'Do you know what you want to be yet? You draw very well. Your drawings are much better than my silly verses.'

She didn't reply. Put her feet up on the edge of the seat and hugged her knees.

'Don't put your feet on the seat,' I said. 'We haven't got all day.'

'I thought we did.' The impish face. 'You don't want to know, Ms Farmer. It's really dumb. And far-fetched. Kind of like a secret ambition.' She started chewing her fingernails.

'Don't bite your nails. I don't mind how dumb and far-fetched it is. And I like secrets, as you know.' I took my eyes off the road. An enigmatic glance passed between us.

She frowned. 'Thought I might want to do acting once.'

Yes? I was surprised but concealed it. Well, that could be an interesting occupation.

This prompted an emphatic headshake. She made a face. 'Yuk.'

I stand corrected, I said mildly. All right then, out with the secret.

'Well, okay. I s'pose. Don't laugh, but.' In a rush: 'I'd like to write books. Fiction books.' She peered round at me under the distracting mirrored glasses in which I could see myself. 'Don't go off the road, will you?'

There was no chance of that. I was driving slowly and with even more care, if anything, than I exercise with Teddy as my passenger. I told her I thought it was an excellent ambition, to be an author of novels. Far better than teaching because you could do it on your own, without having to have any other bothersome people around.

'You're so right. No snotty-nosed brats,' she said.

She's already joined the library, needless to say. Frank had suggested she should get Sandy Fay to recommend authors, and then go to the library and take their books out. It would be a lot cheaper than buying them, even second-hand.

I agreed, but she confided that Mr Fay had told her she could pay for his books, and then return them and get all her money back.

That's Sandy all over, he's a hopeless businessman. Far too nice. No wonder he's never made a cracker. She's got in the habit of calling in on Sandy on the way home from school.

'You were so right about him, he's an awesome character.'

True enough, but did I really say that? I suppose she'd deduced my opinion from an earlier remark. From an earlier subtext, no doubt. Awesome is not a word, I can be fairly confident, that I have ever used in my life.

'Yeah, he always says things about books that make you want to read them. I think he's very insightful. As well as being the tallest human being I've ever met.' An intimate smile, more to herself. 'And he's read absolutely everything that's ever been written.' She swivelled round in her seatbelt. 'Hey. He's one of the *remnants*, right?'

'Now don't go getting a crush on Sandy,' I warned. I saw she was on the brink of asking me something back, then thought the better of it, which was just as well because I'm not at all sure what I would have replied.

A longish pause while she opened the snacks and handed me the Bounty bar I'd chosen.

'I thought you'd go for that, it's kind of more adult than a Mars bar.' Then, 'Did Mr Fay ever have any children?'

Didn't and doesn't, as far as I know, I said.

'But wouldn't you think you'd know?'

You'd think so, yes, but I'm not sure if I would. 'He's never mentioned any to me,' I said. 'Or any wife, for that matter.' I thought fairly dispassionately of Sandy and Monica Harmonica on their knees, sorting the books from the Monleigh estate.

'Hmm. Bit of a shame. He seems like he would've been

a really good father. It's kind of a waste.' Upward inflexion, coupled with a slight hesitation.

'Sandy is definitely not gay,' I said.

She nodded. 'I thought not, definitely. So he's available, right?'

'I suppose so. Technically.' We mulled this over while I negotiated a difficult convergence of roads.

Then she said, 'Yeah, technically, but the question is, whether he'd ever do anything about it, at this stage. That's the moot point.'

I agreed that was both the question and the moot point, at this juncture. Had she confided to Mr Fay that she wanted to become a writer? Or perhaps to Frank? Or Ellice?

The headshaking became more pronounced with each name. At Ellice's name it grew forceful. She combed the fringe of glossy black hair out of her eyes with her fingers. It is a lot longer now than when I first saw her. Her fingernails are ragged but she doesn't look as much like a street urchin.

'You're the first person I've ever told.'

'Then I'm privileged indeed,' I said. I found myself experiencing, rather absurdly, a feeling of gratification that I had been told ahead of Sandy. It was at that point that we arrived at the entrance of the pound.

It must have expanded, it was much bigger than I remembered. The car park was nearly full already. There were people doing the rounds of dozens of dog pens in a purposeful manner, mainly family groups. And it was noisy. It was nearly fourteen years ago, but I remembered the particularly upsetting quality of the noise – the barking and yowling of dozens of agitated caged animals.

There was a long desk in the front hall, for registrations and form-filling and exchange of money. We stood and watched. Attendants came in and out sporadically, bringing dogs on leads and delivering them to their eager new owners. Many of the dogs, you could see, were nervous. Teddy, I remembered, had seemed wary and almost downcast as I led him out. The way he had responded to me at first, in the pen, was far more indicative of his future happy, demonstrative character.

The bare, cramped enclosures were a sad reminder of an old-fashioned zoo, I said to Kim. She had fallen silent, almost from the moment we came in. We walked past the first of the cages. Most had a single occupant, on its feet in an energetic, often frantic attempt to attract the attention of the passers-by.

Kim said, 'It's like they know they're anonymous, and they think they might never get out of prison. And they desperately want us to know who they are.'

I could hardly hear her, with all the excited barking and hurling against the metal grids of the cages. I'd had the identical thought. Each one wanted to register the fact of its existence, and its predicament.

To begin with she stopped at each cage to gaze long and intensely at the animal inside. I began to think we were destined to stay here for hours.

She said, 'Even if it's not the kind you think you want, every dog is special in its own way, isn't it? Each one wagging its tail, despairingly hoping we'll turn out to be the ones who might love it. I can't bear to disappoint them. It's so sad.'

She walked with her arms folded tightly around her chest. Her posture had become more hunched, but I put it down to her natural empathy and wasn't overly concerned. We passed a thin, ten-year-old boxer, and then a squirming spaniel puppy who was being lifted out of its cage into the outstretched arms of a small boy.

Kim stood still, watching. 'Isn't it, you know, really, really *strange*? That people can just come by and look them over, and then just pick one out? That they think they like the look of? Almost like they weren't living things, like they were tins of food on a supermarket shelf, or something?' Her voice sounded strained, but I wasn't unduly alarmed, even then.

Nearly all the dogs were past the puppy stage. The majority were considerably older and had either been someone's discarded pet or had gone missing. You could see people casually assess and then dismiss those animals as they walked straight past.

Kim spoke to a young attendant who was cleaning out an empty cage. It looked like most of the dogs weren't ever going to be wanted by anyone, she said. What would happen to those left behind? I waited apprehensively as the boy, probably a university student, straightened up. I knew what he was going to say.

'We can't keep them for ever. No space, no money. If their owners don't reclaim them and nobody else wants them, after three months they get put down, mostly. All the older guys, and the ones that aren't too cute. After a bit you get to know the guys that aren't going to make it. All the losers.' He gave her a sympathetic look. 'A stray dog's life's a bummer, right?'

Kim nodded, her face taut. We walked on. The most distressing cases were the defeated ones who seemed to have given up already and were lying on the floor of their cages, inert and hopeless.

She said, 'I feel like we shouldn't pass by too fast, because it's so uncaring. But, we can't give them any false hope.' Her voice trembled. 'We don't want them to think that we're going to be their saviour when we're absolutely not.'

All of a sudden, although I knew instantly that I should have seen it coming, she seemed to crumple. She hit her head violently with an open hand and turned to me in a flood of tears.

'I'm really, really sorry, Ms Farmer, but I don't want to stay here any longer. I'm not going to be able to do it. I just can't. Choose one. It's too difficult.' She scrubbed at her eyes with her fists. I handed her a handkerchief. She blew her nose several times and stuffed it in her pocket.

I didn't attempt to argue. There were hardly any available puppies anyway. We hurried away from the barking, the clamour and the distress.

In the car park she began again, with a halting dignity, 'It's useless and pathetic of me, when you brought us all the way here just for me. I'm such a wuss. I'm totally sorry, Ms Farmer.' She wiped her nose with the back of her hand, then belatedly remembered my handkerchief. 'I forgot to bring any tissues.' There was a renewed burst of tears.

I said, 'Don't apologise about anything, because I share your feelings. And I'd rather you didn't call me Ms Farmer anymore. From now on, you must call me Thea.' It was all I could think of to say.

But as soon as we pulled up back home after a largely silent drive, I remembered something else that had been nagging at me. 'When I told you I didn't like children, Kim, I didn't mean all children.'

She was getting out of the car, about to run inside. She took off the mirrored glasses and gave me a shaky smile.

~~

Sunday. Distracted all day. Haven't set eyes on them, though someone's been out and about – the car disappeared early. Ellice, I expect, going to work. Another vehicle was there, an old Holden. Frank's movie collaborator, no doubt.

I sound like one of those dreadful women in English

detective stories. The cosy, old-fashioned sort that fly off Sandy's shelves. One of those village nosy parkers who spy on everyone through net curtains. Tea cosies, scones and prurient gossip: a lifestyle I abhor, and have strenuously avoided. Although scones and tea cosies have their place; one should never throw out the baby with the bathwater. I've had a tendency to do that, I suspect all my life.

I wanted to start on Oscar's page of dialogue but the muse absented herself. More accurately, the muse did not come within spitting distance. Why is the muse always portrayed as female? I would much prefer a male muse. A composite, perhaps, of Sandy, Teddy and Matthew Rhode.

That is, Mr Rhode as he was, or appeared to be, before he was unmasked. He appeared to be such a fresh-faced, inoffensive young man. He had a puppyish eagerness to please that was very appealing. It was an eagerness to please me; that was what made it so very easy to take. You wouldn't have suspected him of anything untoward. Or I would not, and therein lay the trouble.

I was on the verge of lifting the phone all day. But I thought she probably would not want me to do that. She wouldn't want to be on the receiving end of concern, especially in front of Frank and his friend. She wouldn't want anything out of the ordinary. I could have dropped by with Teddy, of course – it would have been the most ordinary thing in the world – but something held me back.

I think I may have an inkling of what that thing was. My innate 'inhibitions', if that is what they are. These constraints that, despite my best efforts, still exert an unhealthy influence on my life. They unleash themselves and I find myself boxed up. Imprisoned in a straitjacket of pride.

Pride leads to a fall, one of my more ignorant teachers used to parrot to her classes. Ha – not a bit of it. It leads to something much worse. Pride leads to paralysis. A paralysis of the will.

Wasn't it the central factor in my refusal to believe what was being whispered behind the net curtains, or to be more pertinent in the prefects' study and the staff room, about Matthew Rhode? Having always despised gossips, I refused to listen to unsubstantiated rumours.

I trusted my own judgements. I was too proud to call in the evidence. And as I attempted to tell Kim yesterday, my judgement of one person in the drama, the pivotal player, was compromised.

~~

Frank said she seemed all right. He hardly saw her yesterday. She was as terminally unobtrusive as she was on any other day, according to him. He was working all day with the movie director, busier than a builder in Kabul, he said. The Wombat stayed in her den reading, as far as he knew.

So how far would he know? Not very far, I would think. Distracted young men are not renowned for empathising with unusually sensitive twelve-year-old girls. Especially, I should imagine, composers of dissonant music.

According to Frank she hardly mentioned the visit to the pound, didn't say much at all on the subject. Which was a bit surprising, now he came to think of it. Only said that she and I hadn't come to any decision. Hadn't she found one she took a fancy to? Just shook her head glumly, Frank said. It was as I expected: she hadn't said a word to them.

I'd already decided I wouldn't go into any details with Frank myself. I did not interrogate him. I kept my remarks deliberately vague. Casual, dropped in while he was making the coffee. I merely inquired if she'd been tired the next day, or had seemed at all disappointed.

I deserved a medal for taking her, he said. She wasn't too heavy-going, hopefully? Not in the least, I replied. I could see he didn't entirely believe me. Oh well, better luck next time, he said. I did not tell him that I didn't think there should be a next time.

He asked if I'd listened to his show reel. Not the whole hog, I replied, but I was gearing myself up. It might take a while, I'd have to get in the mood. And how, I inquired, had the weekend's project gone? That of the vulgar film music.

Fairly shithouse, actually, he said. He doesn't make any patronising attempt to modify his language in front of me. On balance I prefer that – it puts relationships on a more honest footing. He'd made a start, but it was a hell of a sweat for a hell of a little return. He'd never scored a full-length movie before, and this one was pretty demanding. It was go-go-go all the way: big ideas, low-budget, with no money left over for the score. The director had dropped him in the poo and said he wanted practically non-stop music from start to finish.

This didn't mean a whole lot to me, but the way he said it he might have been asked to create the world in a week. He said it was an ambitious take on a multi-genre movie. 'Kind of, you know, like a comic strip take. But edgy, Thea. Cutting edgy.'

No doubt I looked baffled.

Well, it was ultra-violence meets maniacal comedy, with some R-rated material thrown in. It was full of car chases and crashes, lashings of blood, lashings of stunts, a token zombie and some speeded-up farce – intercut with graphic, cartoony bedroom action.

He looked at me with an air of triumph. 'That's the short version. You know the kind of off-the-wall stuff. Fantasy for grown-ups.'

It sounded more like fantasy for retarded adolescent males to me, I said. Not a highbrow film, in short? He laughed and said he wouldn't go *that* far. Cult arthouse was what they were aiming for.

And not an improving film, just possibly?

He grinned. 'No way, Thea, sorry. Cheap and nasty filth. But all done in a good spirit. In a spirit of good, depraved fun, if you can imagine that.'

It might be cheap but it didn't sound cheap to make, I commented.

Frank said the director was a mate, recent film school graduate, and he'd roped in everyone he knew to act and crew for a shoestring.

'The talent get peanuts. I get fuck-all,' he grimaced, 'and the director gets zilch. Unless the picture goes into orbit and then we stand to make zillions. But we all reckon he's got a real shot at being a genius, this guy.' He advised me to make a mental note of this genius guy's name. It was a name of Croatian derivation I have forgotten already. Croatian or Bosnian. Or Polish. Marek something.

'We looked at the initial rough cut over the weekend,' Frank said. 'That's what I'll be working with. It's on DVD in the studio.' He glanced at me, eyebrows raised invitingly.

Was it suitable for general exhibition to old fogeys?

To old fogeys, nope. No way. A grin, a hesitation. 'But I could give *you* a taste, if you like.' A faint, flattering emphasis. 'But only if you promise to make allowances and don't hold it against me. You know what these blokey movies are like.'

I made no response to that but my curiosity was piqued, of course. What was a blokey movie like these days? I realised I hadn't seen anything approximating such a beast since Matthew Rhode and I used to watch videos in my flat on Sunday nights. Matthew liked sophisticated gangster and noir films – Humphrey Bogart, the Godfather trilogy, *Chinatown*. I developed quite a taste for them myself, although after his departure I never watched them again. I suppose I associated them too much with him. In my mind they were tarred with the same brush.

In the studio Frank steered me to a swivel chair in front of a wide-screen desktop computer. I noted a new bottle of tequila and several empty beer cans. He riffled through a box. There was a sequence he thought might give me a general idea. It was not *too* in my face, he hoped. 'Now, let's see, is this it?' He scrutinised two discs with scrawled labels. 'I'm not sure. Hang on.' He inserted one, brought up another chair and sat down beside me. 'Aagh, shit! Cover your eyes!'

Before he could eject the disc I had seen a male member viewed in extreme close-up. It was expanding, in a jerky, stop-start fashion, to epic proportions. The camera was closing in on it rapidly, with staccato movements. The image was on the point of filling the screen. It was probably an animation, but I couldn't tell. It happened too fast to be certain.

Frank said apologetically, 'Ouch. Do you want to avert your eyes while I make sure – yeah, this is the one.'

This, by contrast, was a fight scene at dusk. It took place high up on a skyscraper, on one of those long, suspended platforms used by window cleaners. It was filmed from dizzy angles and mainly in extreme close-up in the same jumpy style, made even more disconcerting for me by the lurching of the platform. Men who looked to be professional body builders lunged at each other, diving in and out of windows like human projectiles. A beautiful young woman darted recklessly between them.

The fight was extremely violent and bloody, with much savage eye-gouging and ripping of clothes. I wouldn't have wanted to watch, but it was filmed in a way that emphasised the artifice and made it less confronting. All the clothing was eventually torn off, floating away into the twilight in a succession of rather artistic and haunting images.

It ended with a wrestling sequence. Nude, since by now none of the participants had anything left on. This was filmed in slow motion, and I'd have said it was almost balletic, were it not for the undiminished, exaggerated ferocity. The naked, grappling men, now covered in blood and sweat, swept ever closer to the edge of the wildly swinging platform. Eventually, with the exception of the young woman and one other heroic survivor (far more well-endowed than Michelangelo's David, I observed), every one was shoved to his death, into the void.

Frank removed the disc. I knew it was not in any sense realistic, but I found myself, against my will, quite affected. If I was reeling a little Frank seemed to be adrift in a parallel universe. He shook his head as if to disengage himself and looked at me expectantly. 'Well, what do you think? Unbelievably well choreographed, isn't it?' He sounded intoxicated.

I tried to gather my wits. 'Rather breathtaking, yes. In its way. And quite arresting. Was that young man the male lead?'

'That's Marlon Grando. Not his real name. Marek had to force himself to watch a bunch of blue movies to find him. Tough job but someone had to do it, he said. Yeah, that guy Marlon's been a bit of a porn star. You can maybe see why? I reckon he's got a more mainstream future, though, if he wants one.'

He replaced the disc in the box. Didn't want to see any more right now, did I?

I did not. At least he hadn't asked if it was too much for me. I was keen to go home and make some notes. I might even be able to make use of it, I thought, for one of Oscar's exercises. They mightn't have taken Ted seriously, but this would give them something to chew over.

Frank rapped me on the arm. What did I think of Marlon as a leading man? Was he an attractive guy, in my opinion? He wanted the woman's view.

Attractive, I mused. You mean, his facial appearance? Speaking purely as a woman I don't recall. We laughed, freely. 'I thought he was rather charismatic,' I said.

'That's good. We reckon he's got wide appeal. Marek's counting on him becoming a big star. He'll have to change his name back, I guess, for the movie.'

'I don't see why he should.' I remembered Gilda-lily's adoring essay on Cary Grant. 'It was probably something like Archibald Leach.' Frank laughed again. He is one of those people who always brings a sense of humour to the table. I suppose he and Ellice have that in common, although his laugh is more infectious and doesn't provoke the same negative response in me.

It was only then, as I was still sitting in the chair, that a thunderbolt hit me. 'Frank, what about all this?' I gestured at the screen and the box of jumbled discs. I saw he hadn't the faintest clue what I was talking about. 'Where are you going to keep this film?'

He still seemed to have not the slightest idea what I meant.

'This is adult material, Frank. You can't just leave it lying around. Kim might stumble across it, and it's not suitable for her to see. Not suitable at all.'

Oh, he scoffed, not to worry, she never came in there. He patted my hand soothingly.

I snatched it away and said, much more urgently, 'No, it is a worry and children do come poking around, you'd be surprised. Look how you go into her room and think nothing of it. You must keep the film locked up. I absolutely insist on this, Frank.'

I wasn't sure where that came from. It was not my place, strictly speaking, to insist. But he could see how strongly I felt. There was no mistaking it; I heard a quiver in my own voice.

'Okay, I give in.' He held his hands out in a gesture of surrender. 'I'll put it under lock and key. I'll sally forth this arvo and procure a strongbox. Only for you, Thea.'

I felt he wasn't taking this seriously. He must get hold of a lockable box, I insisted. And make sure everything was safely put away before Kim came home from school.

Something else struck me. Schools finish in the mid-afternoon. Frank didn't stop work then, did he, not that early? In fact, knowing what musicians are supposed to be like he probably worked into the night, more often than not. And to plan the music he must have to watch sections of the film over and over again. What if Kim came in?

'You must keep your door shut when you're working. You'll have to tell her she must always knock. Then you'll have time to turn it off,' I said. I was quite agitated. 'She's at a very impressionable age, you know.'

Instead of responding he stepped behind me and I felt his cool hands on my shoulders. I gave an involuntary start, but instead of removing his hands he exerted a firm downward pressure on my shoulder blades. Then I felt his strong, double-jointed thumbs kneading into the stiffness at the base of my neck.

'Thea, please don't get your knickers in a twist. I'll keep my door firmly shut from now on. Cross my heart and hope to die.'

The sensation of physical relief in my neck and shoulders was immediate. It was palpable. I felt the tight muscles relaxing under his hands, and a sense of wellbeing that overrode the concerns I'd just voiced. So much so, in fact, that I did not want him to stop.

He did, of course, after what might have been several minutes. 'You were very bunched up and knotted in there. How's that now? Any better?' I nodded. I think I was in a mild trancelike state. He stood back with a slight smile and let me precede him out of the room. He is well-mannered, something I find most important.

I should have a regular neck and shoulder massage, he said, and a good back rub. It's a great stress-buster. But I'm not stressed, I thought, generally speaking. Or not unduly. Teddy's calm presence helps me unwind. I told Frank I'd never gone in for massages. Never liked the idea and I'd always resisted them.

'Is that right?' He sounded amazed. 'Why would you do that? I thought everyone liked them.'

'The idea of some stranger's hands on my −' I caught myself flinching. I regretted saying anything on the subject.

'Well, I'm not exactly a stranger now, I hope.' His hands were back, resting lightly on my shoulders. 'Doesn't that break down your resistance, just a little?'

I acknowledged there had been an inroad. Hey, that was progress then, he grinned. Not too torturous, was it? Not like being waterboarded? I shook my head. It was anything but torture, although I did not say that.

Frank said, 'We all need compensations for the hell of living, as Ellie's old man says whenever he sees me.' I made a mental note to ask about Ellice's father another time. The old man sounds a lot more perceptive than the daughter.

~~

Is living a hell? I used to think so, quite often. There have been times in my life when I have thought so continuously and for a long time. These days the strength of the feeling seems to be in retreat, fractionally, in a stop-start way, rather in the style of Frank's film. Perhaps I shouldn't think this, or write it. I'm not superstitious; all the same I don't want to release a jinx.

After leaving Frank I did some writing. I finally saw my way clear to having a stab at Oscar's dialogue. At my desk with Teddy at my feet I basked in a glow of relaxation for quite some time. A slightly perturbing experience. It was as if I'd never witnessed the scenes of mayhem from Frank's film. It must have been the unfamiliar feeling of someone's hands on me. The healing touch. The – ha! Yea, verily – the laying on of hands.

All my life I have avoided such trendy, New Age things as massages, as I told Frank. They were very popular with female members of staff, especially the younger ones, who were always going to spas for mud wraps and pedicures. But the very idea of someone you don't know touching your body has always struck me, I will say it here, as deeply repugnant. However professional and detached they may be. The difference is that I do know Frank. I feel as if I know him quite well. I might have stopped him, very easily, but I did not. This could only have been because I did not find him, or it, repugnant.

The muscles of my upper back, shoulders and neck feel lighter, somehow. As if released from a tension I didn't know I had. I'd never have imagined that a few minutes of manipulation could be so agreeable. The way Frank's fingers worked, his 'technique', must be very skilled. He has obviously done it before, probably practises on Ellice. Well, lucky old her.

I constructed an imaginary dialogue between an unnamed woman (my alter ego, I suppose) and a young girl, also unnamed. It was ostensibly about a house the woman had built and then sold to the girl's parents, but I tried to suggest that it was really about the house as the embodiment of a dream. A dream of a certain kind of earthly paradise that the woman knew could never be realised, because this was the inevitable destination of dreams.

Oscar is insistent that we limit ourselves to a page. Any longer and I won't read it, he says. You can't fit much dialogue on one page. Mine ends abruptly, with two staccato questions from the girl.

'Do you regret selling it?'

And then: *'Do you wish we weren't here?'*

It was the question Kim asked me.

Direct and to the point, just like that. The woman does not reply. She is prevented from doing so because we have reached the bottom of the page. Or, to look at it another way, she is prevented from doing so by me, just as I chose not to answer Kim's question. Some time has passed, there is water under the bridge. Would I make the same choice now? And if not, how should the question be answered?

Had the woman always known she would never achieve her dream? I thought I discovered a suggestion of that, buried in what I had written. Writing is a pathway to your subconscious mind, Oscar says. Might he really be saying something else? That through writing you give your subconscious the permission to dismantle your dreams?

I used to dream about sitting out on the deck with Teddy, sitting under the trees and watching the deep vermilion sun slowly slip away.

Now, instead, we sit side by side on the verandah in the same old places we have sat together over the years, and look across at the new house, and new life. Young life, for which my house was the catalyst.

~~

I'd left the door open, since we've returned to morning heat and light and cicadas. Teddy bounded from the kitchen and down the steps. I found Kim standing there, dressed for school, bulging backpack, bike propped up. She was chewing that awful gum again and seemed short of breath.

Without saying a word she handed me an open envelope. Inside, washed and ironed, was the handkerchief I'd given her. One corner had been carefully folded down to display the small embroidered wattle.

'Thank you,' I said. 'I don't know when I last had the luxury of an ironed handkerchief.'

'That's okay.' Very offhand. Then, hurriedly, 'Um, can you come for tea tonight? Sorry, I mean dinner. Sorry again, I mean, you know, would you like to come?'

Almost a return to the old awkwardness. I sensed she was nervous at seeing me again. Teddy was licking her outstretched hand.

'That would be very nice, Kim, but the thing is, I've got my class tonight.'

'Class? Are you teaching again?' She was still jittery, not quite meeting my eyes.

'No, I'm being taught.'

She hadn't expected that. 'But you know everything already, Ms Farmer.' A welcome if inadvertent return to humour. She has a nice line in it.

'At some things I'm a novice. It's a creative writing course.'

Now she did look at me. 'Creative *writing*? You mean, you're learning to be a writer too?' Her mouth had dropped open.

'I'd like to write short things better, put it that way. Not to write proper books, as I am sure you will.'

150

'Me? Do you think?' No longer on edge, she scratched her nose. 'What time does it go to, the class?'

'It goes from six thirty until eight, officially. It's a little elastic. Sometimes it stretches on, and then it becomes an eight-ish night.'

'An eight-ish night? But that's early. You could come after, right? No way do we eat till then anyway, almost not ever.'

I deliberated. I always like to eat first. Kim said, 'She hardly ever cooks, Ellie, but she made a chicken pie. Last night. We could absolutely be ready to start the moment you get there.' Her expression reminded me of Teddy waiting for his dinner. She added, 'Bring Teddy, of course. He can have the leftovers.'

'Free-range chicken, I hope,' I said. 'I simply won't eat anything else.'

'Nor will I, simply not. None of us will. Battery farming is like, disgusting. Totally.'

'That settles it, then. I'll come.'

Although she was noticeably calmer, she seemed to be lingering. Or malingering, I recognised the signs: jiggling, shifting from one leg to the other, scuffling her school shoes.

'Now listen to me,' I said. 'We're not going to talk about the pound tonight. We won't mention it. And you must try not to think any more about it. It doesn't matter a fig.'

'But Ms Farmer, it does matter a fig. It matters lots of figs, it so does. I was – I do really, really want to get an abandoned puppy –'

I interrupted firmly, fearing she was on the verge of tears again. 'There are plenty of alternatives. We'll find one. And let's not be so stuffy, shall we? I did invite you to call me Thea, remember? But,' I paused, 'only if you think you would like to.'

She nodded. 'I *know* I would. Like to. I'll try.' It sounded ominously tremulous. She added, 'I'll try very *hard*.' She was hovering over her bike, twisting the front wheel from side to side.

I looked at my watch. 'You don't really want to miss the bus, do you?'

'Well, yeah, I do really, but I better not.' She heaved a heavy sigh.

'Be careful you don't swallow that dreadful gum when you're riding the bike. Is it all right though, on the whole? School, I mean.'

She nodded again, biting her lip. 'Oh yeah, sure, it's quite all right. On the whole.' Then she added, 'Don't worry, I won't swallow the dreadful gum. I've got the hang of chewing and riding at the same time. And I can chew it in class. Invisibly, like a ventriloquist.'

'Well, fancy that. But is this school any worse than the others?'

A decisive shake of the head. She began to push the bike off slowly. There were still some muddy puddles after the rain.

'By the way,' I said, 'I was wondering if you might like to come along.'

She jerked her head round.

'The writing class. I thought you might like to come with me sometime.'

'Yeah?' The single syllable conveyed utter astonishment. I could see she was flabbergasted.

'You could just listen and observe, you wouldn't have to say anything. Anyway, you can think about it.'

Her face, which I used to think vacant and now see as unusually expressive, transformed in less than a second. 'Oh no, I don't need to think about it, no way. I would. I would like to.'

Teddy and I watched her ride off, wobbling a bit at first

on the rutted road, unbalanced by the laden backpack. These schools make them carry criminally heavy loads, in my opinion. There will be an epidemic of back problems well before they get to my age.

She braked dangerously, turned to look back at us and called out, loudly, '*Awesome*, Thea.' She pedalled another few metres, stopped again and yelled, 'See you later. And no worries if it's one of the eight-ish nights.'

It was rather impulsive of me. I hadn't meant to raise the idea without clearing it first with Oscar.

I'd been on the point of emailing him the page of dialogue between the woman and the young girl about the sale of the house. Now, prompted by some obscure internal urge, I went to the computer and began on an alternative. This time a conversation between two adult women, both (although I did not say so) in their early sixties. One is subordinate to the other.

Were we permitted to place the protagonists or give them an age? Oscar hadn't ruled this out, so I added a scene-setting line: a small, elegant sitting room in the principal's apartment of a girls' boarding school; afternoon tea laid out on a trolley. The speakers are the principal and her deputy.

They start with what appears to be a routine matter, how homework time is allocated in the senior school. The deputy head raises a concern that current arrangements might perhaps be a little too relaxed. Would it be a good idea to set formal limits on the time allowed for each subject?

The principal says the staff understand and adhere to the unwritten guidelines. There are enough ruddy rules and regulations without adding any more.

Still, the deputy counters, one wouldn't want to see a situation develop in which, say, certain teachers got in the habit of setting a disproportionate amount of work. In their own subjects, of course. Or even, she adds, got into the habit of taking up too much of the students' free time. Would one?

Disproportionate, asks the principal? No one has suggested this is happening. Not to her.

In the intensive English classes, for instance, the other woman goes on. 'Your own after-hours group has always been in place. No one argues with that. But now some students are being coached separately, after school. This has never happened before.'

An intensive tutorial on the Oxbridge model is the pinnacle for gifted students, the principal replies. Unquestionably. With a gifted teacher, of course.

The deputy head agrees that this can be most effective. Then she seems to segue down a different alley. There's been the odd rumble in the staff room, she says. To the effect that there's some – monopolising, going on. Some snitching of the best and brightest. Special privileges, and so on – the same old Aunt Sally. You know what they're like.

I know how the petty and peevish like to guard their patch, says the principal. I take my pleasures where they can be found, and thwarting the small-minded is a fertile area.

'Isn't it funny, though, how the brightest students can sometimes be the most excitable?' the other woman essays.

'Amongst the able, every temperament is represented, in my experience.'

Still, it must be easy for intensive tutorials to go overtime, every now and again, the other woman persists. You know, without anyone noticing. There's a suggestion some students, the most ambitious and talented ones, might be getting – overstretched.

The principal demurs. Overstretched? She hasn't heard anything to suggest this.

'But perhaps you wouldn't, you see. All the same, a word of caution might not go astray,' the other says, tentatively. 'Might it? An informal word. During one of your regular,' she looks round the room, 'one-on-one briefings.'

The principal tells her she is opposed to curbing the freedoms of individual teachers any more than they are curbed already. Unless it is absolutely unavoidable. Her best teachers, especially.

'But —' her deputy begins.

'I have another appointment,' the principal says, looking at her watch.

They didn't come easy, these words, although I knew them well. They felt painfully familiar. Excavating one's memory is like dredging through years of sludge. It's all down there, buried deep, but you have to work like a navvy to haul it out. The sludge would keep it buried, if it had its way.

I wonder what became of my nice, ineffectual deputy. Wasn't she the subtext queen? She tried more than once, I acknowledge that, but such delicate ambiguity was no match for a practised defence of stubbornness and pride. The poor woman should never have relied on it. She might have had more success with the sledgehammer approach.

Re-reading, I wonder if subtext may not simply be another word for evasion. And pride another word for arrogance?

Should I show it to Oscar? I think not — it is too close to the bone. I like to think I am a bit of a favourite of his. But I suspect Oscar wouldn't make any more of the possible consequences of favouritism than I did at the time.

Which is neither here nor there. Oscar has no need to decipher this subtext. I, on the other hand, had every need.

I don't like sleeping in the day, and I rarely do it. But after completing that writing exercise I slept this afternoon for two full hours. Sitting in the armchair on the verandah with Teddy stretched out in the sun, I went out like a light.

~~

And it was an eight-ish night, always the way. Everybody hung around, banging on about subtexts in songs and stories, and I knew I couldn't leave without having a private word with Oscar. By the time I got home and picked up Teddy I was quite faint with hunger.

Oscar had been fulsome about my little dialogue on the sale of the house. Called it both stimulating and satisfyingly cryptic. 'I'm not entirely sure I got your full underlying gist though, Thea. But that's not necessarily a bad thing. The important thing is to *have* a gist. That's what's so rewarding about well thought-out dialogue.'

He had started off by reading a scene from a Pinter play. Our own efforts fell somewhat flat in comparison. Not all the others had much of an underlying gist, it seemed to me, but perhaps I am not yet as adept at identifying subtexts as I might be. Or at deciphering them, but I'm certainly not alone there.

When they discussed my piece I was amazed at the interpretations. Someone thought the house was a symbol of permanence, which had been removed at a stroke from the woman's life. Another, that it represented the tawdriness of materialism. Mousy Mary, who usually hardly says a word – her theory was the most mind-boggling of all – saw the loss of the house as a metaphor for loss of mental faculties. This sounds mildly amusing when I write it down now, but she has never been known to exhibit a sense of humour. I mean mildly amusing in an offensive kind of way.

She did not ask me if I was the woman. Thanks, imaginary goddess up there, for small mercies. If she had done, it might have been cause for real alarm. Could it have been a veiled reference to her own state of mind? She has been looking increasingly dishevelled lately. She wears layers of unprepossessing garments like a bag lady.

No one, not even Oscar, interpreted the underlying theme as the loss of a dream that could never have been realised. Oscar came closest, perhaps. He did use the word dream, but he talked in otiose terms of selling one's dreams to the highest bidder. Not the same thing at all, not remotely. In fact, when I consider it, a desecration of the idea. It disturbs me, that someone who is normally acute could get it so wrong.

I'd have tackled him on this but I was raring to go. I asked him whether he would mind, as we were nearly at the end of the semester, if I brought a young girl along to class. Just as an observer. She was an aspiring writer, I said – a bright, bookish child who lived near me. I'd pay a pro rata contribution for her attendance, of course.

'By all means,' he said. He looked intrigued. 'We need more brains on the table, don't we?' He gave me a speaking glance. Sad but true, I said. That was a relief, anyway. I hadn't expected him to object, but you can't count on anything where teachers' whims are concerned. They can be a thin-skinned, territorial lot. What did I say? Petty and peevish, and they like to guard their patch. Good to see Oscar is not of that ilk.

She was a sensitive girl, I told him, rather diffident and shy, so it would be important not to make a song and dance about her being there. Okay, he said, so he wouldn't ask her to do the hokey-pokey. Don't pick on her in any way, I warned, don't single her out or ask any questions. What! he expostulated. Not even how to spell gonadotrophin? I am tempted to give you the finger, I said. Oh, please do, he begged.

Thought I'd better play safe and mention it to the others, with similar cautions. No one made any objection. Not that they could since Oscar had okayed it, but the last thing I wanted was any covert unpleasantness. Or jealousy; I suspect some of them already resent our special rapport. Gilda, of course, made a show of wilful misunderstanding. 'Young blood to show us up,' she cried. Not at all, she's only going to listen, I said repressively.

I cannot allow myself to turn into a fusspot, in the manner of dreadful, overanxious parents. I must be careful not to over-egg the pudding. I may have over-egged it already, with Frank.

I did, however, want to satisfy myself that he had indeed obtained a box with a lock. Does that mean I do not trust him? I wanted to set eyes on it. An opportunity should present itself, I thought.

We ate at the vast mahogany table that had belonged to Ellice's parents. It's a genuine antique, I was wrong about it being repro. A ridiculous size; the four of us were marooned down at one end. I asked why they hadn't removed some of the leaves. Guffaws ensued. They said they'd inflated it to its full size when they moved in, just to see the fit, and then they'd gone and lost the winder. Until this crucial gizmo turned up they were stuck with the elephant in the room.

It was the first time I had seen the three of them together for more than a few minutes since drinking champagne on the deck when they first arrived. Strange to think that was only weeks ago. It seems longer, really. Much longer.

I found the dynamics somewhat troubling. It's not unusual for a girl of Kim's age to be reticent among adults, but Frank and Ellice do so much of the talking I can see it's hard for her to get a word in. It's quite remarkable how affectionate he is towards Ellice, and how solicitous. There is frequent physical contact between them. Touching, brushing against each other, even hugging. Ellice must feel cherished. She should know she is a fortunate young woman.

I haven't observed this to a great extent among couples. Certainly not to such a marked degree. My experience might be considered limited by some, but in the course of my career I must have encountered many hundreds of families. I am probably more aware of how couples behave with each other than most people. And, generally speaking, it is not in the overtly affectionate way those two behave.

Well, you can't spend much time in Frank's company without being aware that he is an unusually tactile, demonstrative young man. He is casually affectionate with me, whom he doesn't know that well. But perhaps he thinks he does, rather as I feel about him? Of the three, inevitably, it is Kim who is the odd one out. Not that either of them ignores her, they involve her in the conversation, but I can't help but think she must feel excluded.

This cannot be good for her. It must seem like a repetition on a daily basis of what she has felt all her life, or just another version of it. It's always hard with a threesome. And she has not been with them for long, this is part of the problem. I should mention it, I think, to Frank.

'I came home from work on Saturday all fired up, only to find no adorable new puppy,' Ellice wailed as we sat down. 'What a let-down, you slackers!' It sounded boisterous and accusing. I was aware of Kim opposite me cringing in her seat.

'We'll find one in due course. There is no shortage of puppies in the world,' I said briskly. 'So you enjoy working at the café, do you?' Abrupt, and somewhat clumsy. But I had to change the subject. And I was curious about Ellice – who in her way seems quite high-powered – and the café.

She became animated at once. Enjoys talking about herself, like most people. She was on an extended bliss-out, she announced. 'Taking orders for eggs Florentine on sourdough, with sides of home-baked beans, sautéed spinach and field mushrooms with sage.' Such a glorious relief after torts and company law, she couldn't tell me.

So that's it. She's a lawyer. It came back to me when she said it.

She was sick of the years of slog, she only ever did law to please her father. Now, and she exchanged a meaningful glance with Frank, she was taking a sabbatical. 'You've earned it, baby,' Frank said. He actually got up out of his chair and planted a kiss on her head.

I said I could only assume this was a temporary glitch. But how would she pursue a career in law while living up here? It wouldn't be easy. They just smiled at each other in their intimate fashion. A complacent habit that shuts out other people.

One of them said, 'We'll deal with that when it comes.' Love will find a way was the subtext I picked up. Far too saccharine a subtext for Oscar's purposes.

The pie was good, but I was so famished I'd have eaten slug and lettuce soup. Ellice may have made it but Frank refused to let her do anything else. He did most of the chores, brought the food in and out while Kim cleared the plates. And he had made the dessert – a delicious baked cheesecake.

Ellice poked fun at my surprise. Franko was a very *today* guy, very metro, wasn't he, Kimmie? Blokes were way better round the house than they were in my day, not much doubt about that. I must have winced. My day? Frank winked at me.

'He cooks up a storm, most days of the week,' Ellice effused, which was just as well because she wasn't into it herself. She hated cooking, not to put too fine a point on it. She succumbed very rarely, and under sufferance.

Well, lucky old her. She must be the moneybags, there's not much doubt about that. Frank's immediate family is clearly wanting in that regard, as in others. He made it quite clear that he's not earning much at present. She's bankrolling the family, I shouldn't wonder, or her parents are. What's the betting they forked out for the house?

At one point they said they were thinking of taking down the wall between the kitchen and living area, to make it more open plan. I detest open plan. If I'd known they were considering doing that, I'd never have sold it to them, I said.

After the meal I declined a coffee or herbal tea. Herbal teas were a travesty, I said. I would ban them when I come to power, along with daft homeopathic remedies that were an insult to the intelligence. This made Kim giggle, and I took the opportunity to suggest she might like to show me her room. Then I had to deter Ellice from tagging along. 'You can sit down with your old pal Franko,' I said, a suggestion that produced the ubiquitous fond glances.

'Kim's such a fastidious little thing, Thea,' Ellice laughed. 'She's not a terminal slob like us two. You'll be gobsmacked when you see her room.' Us versus her. Another irritating comment.

I had already visited the guest bathroom, which doubles as Kim's en suite. I'd designed it with two doors so it could be accessed from the living area as well as the spare room. It was immaculate. Towels folded on the rail, clean bath, gleaming mirror, a few toiletries meticulously positioned. This would be Kim's doing, I now realised.

Most girls her age live in a pigsty and plaster their walls with posters of lame-brained actors and drug-addled pop singers. Kim's bedroom was sparse and almost excessively neat and tidy. The obligatory TV and laptop, but no posters or girly knick-knacks like lava lamps or souvenir snow domes. Nothing cutesy at all. Not a scented candle in sight.

Then I saw a squat little statue on the windowsill near the end of the bed. A grinning Buddha with chubby children draped around his shoulders and linking hands behind his head.

Kim was watching me. She said, 'The kids' Buddha. That's what it's called. They often get given to Vietnamese kids.'

She picked him up and rubbed his stomach in slow, circular movements with the flat of her hand. The area was so shiny, I guessed this was a frequent action.

'The dimples and the laughing face, they kind of give you a happy feeling. Even, you know, when you're not, especially.' The rubbing slowed to a halt. '*She* gave it to me.'

I let an interval pass. 'Your mother?'

'That, and this.' The jade bangle on her wrist. I'd seen her wearing it before. 'The two things I got from my mum before she went.' It was said in a meditative way, with a residue not so much of sadness as of resignation.

'They are your keepsakes,' I said.

She looked up. 'Yeah. That's what they are. Keepsakes, to keep by me. And remember her by.' She replaced the statue in the same position on the sill and patted the head, as one might pat a child. We were quiet for a moment.

Usually girls pile their beds with cuddly toys. There was just one on Kim's bed, a moth-eaten wombat scarcely holding together, with one eye and one leg. That would be the source of Frank's nickname. She saw me looking at it, picked it up and hugged it.

'He's my oldest buddy. He's on his last leg,' she said. 'He doesn't have a name. Well, he sort of does. Just the Dear Old Wombat. He looks like he's been through the mill, right? Or a whole bunch of mills.' Like you have, I thought.

There were no photos either, of friends or family – well, not surprising. Only one shelf of the bookcase contained actual books, which looked like school texts all arranged according to height, and there was a neat pile on the bedside table that included, I noted, my presents to her. Next to it stood a personal touch: a jam jar of gum leaves and wild flowers – old man banksia and sprigs of geebung and scarlet mountain devil.

I approved of the simple furniture, white painted wood probably bought together by Ellice as a girl's bedroom suite. The curtains were striped Indian cotton, white and an unusual shade of blue, with a matching bedspread. I was aware of Kim monitoring my inspection intently while pretending not to.

'I think this is a very elegant room,' I said.

'You do? Huh. *Elegant*.' She pronounced this with a careful emphasis in a way that suggested she had never imagined such a word being used in relation to herself. She was not displeased, I felt.

'I like the Buddha and wombat and the wildflowers. And that particular shade of blue.'

'I chose the material. She let me,' a pause while she reflected on this, 'which was nice of her, right? The colour's called teal. I chose it because it was kind of ambiguous, like the sea. A mixture of blue and green.'

'The room is very calming,' I said. 'A place for everything, and everything in its place.'

'Yeah, right.' She nodded, rather lugubriously. '*She* says I'm anal retentive. I need to know where things are. Otherwise I get, you know, kind of anxious.'

That follows. When you're constantly moving from place to place you need to keep tabs on your belongings because you may have to lay your hands on them at short notice. If you stay in one place for years on end this is not such a problem. No matter how untidy you are, you know what you want is there, somewhere in the rubble.

I said as much to her, adding, 'Don't take any notice of what anyone else thinks, no notice at all. It's the best policy, I've always found.'

She nodded. 'Absolutely the best. I've found that too.' She folded her arms across her chest. 'People don't like it much, but. Do they? If they know you don't give a stuff about what they think.'

'But if you don't give a stuff about what they think, then it doesn't matter a stuff either, does it?' I said.

We laughed. She promptly opened a drawer on the bedside table and pulled out a photo in a pink, heart-shaped frame. She handed it to me. I recognised a younger and longer haired Kim, aged about nine or ten. She was wearing dungarees and kneeling on grass, thin arms tightly locked around a golden Labrador.

'That's Pippi, the dog I told you about? I don't want to see it all the time, but I keep it in there so I always know where to find it.'

We looked at it in silence. Normally girls of her age are beaming happily at the camera in all their photographs, but the body language here told a different story. The girl hugging the dog with such desperate possessiveness was not looking at the camera. She was frowning, lips sucked in and clenched together, eyes half closed.

Eventually I said, 'It was a bad day.'

She drew a deep, sighing breath. 'It was, yeah. That's so right. A black-letter day, one of the worst. It was the day I had to leave there.' She almost snatched the photo from my hand and replaced it in the drawer. She leant on the windowsill, rocking backwards and forwards, staring out. Her hand rested on Teddy's head.

There are two big-framed windows in the room. The curtains were not pulled, and one window was thrown wide open. The room was permeated with the tang of eucalyptus. By now it was completely dark, and in the faint evening melancholy lay a strong sense of the encircling bush. The hypnotic hum of cicadas rose, unnaturally loud, then fell into a lull. I sat on the bed.

'This was going to be my spare room.'

Kim turned and gazed at me, disconcerted.

'I was very foolish, you see. I invested all my savings in a company that collapsed.'

'It went bust?'

'I was taken in by an investment offer. Which is as silly as being taken in by –' I cast around for a comparison.

'By horoscopes?'

'Exactly. I lost all my money and had to sell this house instead.'

She came and sat down next to me on the bed. 'Instead of what? *Oh.*' She closed her eyes. I saw it dawn on her in a rush. 'Of course. Instead of the cottage you loathe.'

'Instead of the hated hovel, yes.' Teddy heaved himself up from the floor by the window and flopped between us.

'You built this house, right?' she said slowly, sitting up straight. 'Not, like, built it with your own hands, but you created it. Out of nothing.'

'Out of nothing, yes.'

'And it was going to be your new home. You were going to live here. With Teddy. For, well, for –' She stumbled.

'For the rest of our lives.'

'Oh shit.' She exhaled. 'The day you had to sell it to them must've been really, really bad. A black-letter day.'

'It was, yes.'

'One of the worst.' We contemplated this together, silently. She drew the back of her hand slowly across her mouth. 'It's hard, right? Them and me being here? Living,' she stared at me, her eyes widening as she thought this through, 'in *your house.*' She shook her head slowly. 'Yeah, I knew it was. Like, you know, I just knew. I just didn't know why, exactly.'

I contemplated this too. 'It's not something I ever planned for. But that's the way life sometimes is.'

'That's the way the cookie crumbles. And you have to grin and bear it, right?' We exchanged a wry smile. Or perhaps it was a wan grin. 'Do *they* know?' she asked, gesturing at the door. 'I mean, um, about the – about the circumstances.'

'Frank and Ellice? I dare say they do, but I've never mentioned it and neither have they.'

'Oh. But people gossip, I dare say,' she said, with meaningful emphasis.

'That sounds like a wise woman talking.'

A grin. 'I won't tell 'em anyhow. In case they don't know.' She inspected the ceiling. There was something else in the offing.

'Thea.' She made it into two pensive syllables. She leant forward, elbows on knees, chin propped on cupped hands. With her cap of dark, shining hair she reminded me, for a second, of a rare flower. Of a black tulip.

'Yes?'

'Who did you have in mind? Like, you know, for here? To invite to stay in your spare room.' That unusually direct, unblinking gaze she has was fixed on me.

'Well, that's the funny thing, you see,' I said. 'I don't think I had anyone in mind.'

'No? That's good then. That's a relief.' She seemed to relax into herself a little. 'Because, you know, I wouldn't like to think I was sort of usurping anybody.'

'No. You're not usurping anyone at all.' I found myself struggling, trying to distil some conflicting thoughts into one. 'And it's better this way.'

'Better. Like, how? How could it be better?' She sat very still, cautious and attentive.

'It would have been an empty room. Now it has you living in it.'

I watched as she processed this. She scanned the room, carefully and observantly, every wall and corner, then darted a quick glance at me. Bright-eyed.

We got up and left without another word. Frank and Ellice were sitting together on a sofa watching something on

TV, her feet in his lap. He was stroking her hair. I told them under no circumstance to move.

'Teddy likes to take me home,' I told them. Of course he does, Kim said, it makes him feel manly.

He and I were halfway there, imbibing the moonlight, when I heard her running feet, as light as falling leaves.

'Thea. With all that stuff we were talking about, that important stuff, I totally forgot to ask. To ask you when I should come?'

The writing class, of course. There are only two more weeks of term. 'You can come when you like,' I said. 'You can come when you feel a class coming on.'

She said seriously, 'That's good, because, you know, I think I might. Feel one coming on. This week?'

It was only when I was on the point of sleep with my feet against Teddy's back that I realised all the important stuff we were talking about had caused me to forget something else important too. I had completely overlooked my intention to check on Frank's purchase of a lockable box.

~~

And he hadn't done it. I thought as much. Moreover, he seems quite blasé, worryingly careless about the whole matter.

It was the second time I'd broken my own golden rule by not ringing first. The front door was open, no one in sight but an abundance of noise. Crashing cymbals – over a deafening rhythmic beat that shuddered through me – invaded the whole house. Teddy had picked it up, tail held at horizontal for danger, the minute we exited the hovel.

In a too-brief interlude of a surprisingly refined harp melody I called Frank's name as loudly as I could, twice. No response. We advanced gingerly down the passage towards the renewed racket. His door was wide open, needless to say, and Frank was hunched in front of the screen with his back to me. I was struck by how dark the room was. The wide bank of windows had been curtained off with a swathe of blackout material. The music had deteriorated further, the mind-numbing, repetitive rhythm overlaid by an undecipherable chant. Rap music, to my ear the most detestable of mindless modern genres.

I stood in the doorway, hands over my ears, eyes adjusting to the gloom. Teddy, who has always hated loud noises, cowered behind me. The flickering screen was partially obscured by Frank's back, but I could see a sandy beach and what looked like branches stacked in a pyramid. It was hung with motifs – the camera closed in on towels and surf boards, bikinis, rubber thongs and goggles. I found myself thinking quite incongruously of Breughel's *Tower of Babel*.

The room was not only dark, it was hazy. As I came towards Frank I smelt an unmistakable odour, sickly and musty. Sure enough, I saw a column of smoke rising from a cannabis joint in his right hand.

I placed a handkerchief over my nose ostentatiously and approached the monitor. A conga line of gyrating dancers had arrived, bronzed lifesavers, male and female. They started stacking things round the base of the pyramid, what appeared to be mummified figures swathed in colourful cloth. The scene was festive and celebratory and reminded me, incongruously again, of a Busby Berkeley musical.

Frank's eyes were glued to the screen. I repeated his name in a peremptory voice but he was oblivious, as immobile as a painted ship. I tapped him on the arm. He jumped an inch in the air, spilt another inch of ash on the keyboard and swore.

'*Fucking hell!* Sorry, Thea – *bloody* fucking hell.' He reduced the sound to a moderately acceptable level. 'Hey,' a marked change of tone, 'what a nice surprise.' The greeting seemed genuine enough, with every appearance of pleasure and not a smidgin of guilt. He blew the ash away and scrubbed at the keys with his T-shirt.

'Anyone could walk in, Frank,' I said. 'And anyone has.'

He was quite unrepentant. I wasn't just anyone, and he was in the privacy of his own home, right? 'We've only got the Wombat to worry about, and she's safely at school. Anyhow, nothing wrong with this scene, is there?' He pointed the glowing tip of the joint at the screen. 'It's a family friendly beach barbecue. Dripping with wholesomeness. Just get a load of all that colour and movement.'

I peered round to right and left. 'So, where have you put it? I don't see it.'

'It?' He looked mystified. 'Am I missing something, Thea?'

You seem to be missing a lockable box, I said. The one you promised you were going to get, remember?

Ah, well, he hadn't quite got it yet. Hadn't had time, been flat out, please don't spank him. 'Besides, it's not necessary, because there's a fallback position. Plan B's in place.'

When I didn't respond he grabbed me friskily by the arm. 'Thea, lighten up, huh? Never fear, there will be no glimpses of debauchery or adult themes. See the new blockades on the windows? I've resolved to keep them pulled and the door firmly barred against impressionable persons. I've put in place, here in my *cockpit*,' with solemn emphasis, 'an *H* and an *F KP*.'

He lingered on the letters but I was aggrieved. I refrained from batting even one inquiring eyelid.

'A hard and a fast knocking protocol, Thea. Outside school hours, no admitting without submitting.'

169

I found myself stubbornly resistant to this. There was no point in putting in place a knocking protocol of any size, shape or form, I said, since with that infernal racket going on he would never hear a thing.

Nor was he listening now. 'Not the Wombat, not Ellie, not you Teddy, and,' sepulchral tone, 'not even classy dames like you, Thea. Y'all didn't knock? Waaall, y'all go haul your sorry asses outta here this minute!'

He stubbed out the joint. Then, without warning, he seized my hand, encircled my waist with his other arm and twirled me round and round in a waltz. When he released me after several spins I had a disorienting moment. It was a brief giddiness, due as much to surprise, I think, as to the whirling speed of the dance steps. He kept a steadying arm round me for a few seconds. With our similar height our heads had been close together. I smelt traces of alcohol mingled with marijuana on his breath.

I thought, Frank is stoned. That was a full-on, rather risky – the phrase popped into my mind from nowhere – charm offensive. And lo! Mentally, where it matters most, I am unmoved. What made me think of that? Charm offensive is an oxymoron, on the face of it, which is what gives it its potency.

I did, however, linger a moment longer while I got my breath back. The pyramid on the screen was computer-generated, Frank explained. It was a virtual structure. He invited me to listen to something he thought might be more my thing. He played the harp melody I'd heard earlier, in an extended version. It was quite captivating, I'll give him that. I have always been susceptible to the emollient virtues of the harp.

'And now get a load of this. It's the ending of the movie. I think the harp will background it, but I haven't joined up the dots yet.'

The pyramid was on the move. I realised it was sitting on what looked like a wide raft, and the raft was being pushed slowly into the sea. While we were talking one of the mummies had been strung up on a cross at the precarious-looking apex. There was a sudden close-up, rather unnerving, of his face under a surf lifesaver cap – I recognised Marlon, the handsome porn star who was the lead actor. The chanting mob is going to crucify him, I thought with an uneasy jolt, then it belatedly dawned on me that the pyramid was a giant bonfire about to be towed out to sea and torched. This too would be computer-generated, no doubt.

I ignored Frank's plea to wait for the sensational conflag-ration. Call me old-fashioned, I informed him, but watching people get incinerated is not particularly family friendly, not in my book. Even if we're only playing let's pretend. I had no desire to see it, and it was high time Teddy and I hauled our sorry asses out of there.

'Don't lose any beauty sleep over Marlon,' Frank called. 'The other guys get burnt to a crisp but he's miraculously snatched from the jaws of death. By guys in an incredible kind of homemade heli-plane. He gets away to fight another day. Hopefully in a sequel, if the movie goes gangbusters.'

'I don't intend to lose any sleep over Marlon,' I said grimly, 'beauty or otherwise. It's you I'm worried about. And hopefully there won't be any sequel.' I'll be right back, I added. You can expect me. He blew me a placatory kiss.

On top of his other skills – composer, chef, masseur – Frank is an accomplished dancer, that's clear. He has several strings to his bow, this young man. Being so tactile he is probably a very good lover, I imagine.

In addition to the dump there are a couple of outbuildings on my remaining little parcel of land. This is an extravagant term for two decrepit structures: a dunny (now the woodshed) and a shed. You can find almost anything in my shed. I was too young to remember the Depression, but its residual influence permeated my generation. I have always found it hard to throw anything away because a use might be found for it one day. That day hardly ever dawns, but the chief advantage of the practice is that instead of having to dispose of every damned thing, one can just bung it in the shed and forget about it.

I went in and poked around the conglomeration of junk, the accumulated flotsam and jetsam of half a century. The best part of a life, I suppose. No one else's life but mine, and Teddy's too of course. A sobering thought. I had in mind an old metal toolbox with a hasp fitting. I'd seen it the other day while chucking out a moth-eaten bed of Teddy's.

The toolbox contained a few screwdrivers, a length of picture wire and some rusty nails. It was fastened originally with a padlock. This was long gone, but it was a simple matter to get a replacement from the hardware store. I chose a good strong one with a combination lock, four rotating numbers to set. That way, there was no key to lose. And if you had a better idea you could alter the combination after opening it.

The house was wondrously silent when we returned an hour later with the booty. I rapped on the front door, which was closed for a change, and called out. No response. I pushed the door in an exploratory way, and it yielded. We found Frank slumbering in his cockpit, stretched out on the day bed. With the heavy blinds blocking the windows the room was uncomfortably dark and close. The cloying smell had intensified.

The film was still playing away, I noted, and the door was still open wide. On the screen a man appeared to be copulating with an inflatable doll. That's what it looked like anyway, a full-sized, pink plastic doll. They were crammed inside an old-fashioned telephone booth. I was relieved when the screen went blank without warning. My reaction had been a blend of distaste and morbid curiosity, an uncomfortable pair of bedfellows. Nor had I looked away. That's my upbringing showing: curious as well as prudish, as Matthew Rhode once proclaimed.

Frank was lying on his back in an attitude of abandon, his arms and legs flung wide. I pulled back the curtain behind his head, admitting a triangle of light across his sleeping face. He stirred but did not wake. His upper lip was bathed in a thin sheen of sweat. I once read that the longer the distance between the nose and the upper lip, the more sensual a person tends to be. This sounds preposterous but is often true, in my observation. Frank has an unusually long upper lip.

The thick auburn hair was curling over his neck. I put out a hand and touched it. A light brush with my fingertip. It wasn't wiry, it was surprisingly soft.

I studied him neutrally. I know him to be twenty-nine and physically quite powerful, but asleep he looked younger and oddly defenceless. This is partly that pale Scottish colouring – I always think of it as Scottish, whether it is or not. The alabaster skin already taking on the beginnings of ruddiness, the soft and crinkly ginger hair, the nearly colourless eyelashes.

And the dusting of freckles across the retroussé bridge of the nose. I have something of a predilection for freckles, a frivolous taste, admittedly. For some unknown reason I've always found them decorative on a man. Particularly when they are artlessly scattered, like confetti, across the bridge of a turned-up nose.

I record this thought with an unsettling feeling of déjà vu. Matthew Rhode had freckles, although he was brown-haired with a straight nose. I recall admitting to him once, in an incautious moment: I have a soft spot for freckles. He had a penchant for puns. Does the fact that he had a dusting of them explain my continuing soft spot for freckles? It shouldn't, should it? You'd think I should have been cured of this little weakness. You'd think I would find them hateful.

There is a surprising level of strength in Frank's compact and sinewy frame. That was obvious from his massaging hands, and the expert way he twirled me through the waltz steps. I haven't waltzed since – when, since teenage dancing classes? When I was sixteen or so. None of the gauche country boys at dancing class showed anything approaching his competence or flair.

Today he was wearing jeans and a black T-shirt. Oscar wouldn't be seen dead in such an outfit, but I haven't seen Frank in anything else. Young women can look good, of course, but unquestionably it is on young men that jeans reach their, so to speak, apotheosis. When they are as narrow and well cut as Frank's, tight around the hips and thighs, they are very – there is no other way to say it – revealing. Very sexy. They are a distinct improvement on the baggy trousers men wore in my youth. You can see why blue denim took over the world.

There's something intrinsically masculine about Frank. This may be self-evident but it is not, perhaps, quite as silly as it sounds. I have come to think that energy is an essential component of masculinity. Energy as well as testosterone. Davy would like you to think he is over-endowed with both, which makes me wonder if he is deficient. Sandy may not flaunt his, but I feel he has them in good measure all the same.

Frank certainly has these credentials in spades, even if he is nowhere near as conventionally good-looking as his wife. Ellice is cover-girl material if she slimmed down a bit, but no editor would put Frank's face on the cover of a magazine.

174

Still, there's no mystery as to what she sees in him, quite apart from his prowess in cooking and dancing. It is sexiness, plain and simple.

Or is it naive to think it can ever be simple?

I'd been wool-gathering for imaginary god knows how long. When I came round, I found Frank's eyes were open and fixed on me with something like a wild surmise.

'Thea, you're still here. What is it? Is something wrong, or were you just deciding to do away with me?' He thought I'd been staring at him, I realised. Well, I suppose I had, although if he imagined I'd been thinking only about him he was mistaken.

He stretched his arms above his head. The T-shirt rode up, exposing his navel and a narrow line of dense auburn hairs bisecting several inches of stark white torso. After an interval he rubbed his eyes and swung his legs over the side. 'I must've dropped off. Power nap. I thoroughly recommend them.' He appeared puzzled. 'Didn't you leave, or did I dream it and you were here all the time?'

I went, and then I came back again, I said evenly, perching on the edge of the couch. And something *is* wrong. He blinked as I flourished the toolbox close to his face. I'd removed the cobwebs and given it a rough wipe. I deposited it in his lap, rather too heavily. He winced. I'd forgotten it was a metal toolbox.

. 'This is a box for your R-rated film discs. And this,' I waved the padlock under his nose, 'is for locking the said box. You choose a combination of four numbers to lock it. Don't write them down in an obvious place, don't choose obvious numbers like your birthday, and don't get in a drug-induced haze and forget what they were.'

'No, Miss. Yes, Miss. Whatever you say, Miss.'

I felt a rising annoyance and agitation. He must have picked up on this because he abandoned the jokey – and slightly impudent – tone and suggested a coffee. Just a quickie, as he must get back to work, but he had something important to tell me.

Well, I was right after all. Ellice is pregnant. Four months along and scarcely showing, he said. What I had not expected to hear was that this is her third pregnancy. The others ended in miscarriage. She is what is known as a high-risk prima gravid, for various tedious medical reasons I did not listen to.

On top of this she is easily thrown off balance, apparently. That doesn't surprise me at all – I recognised the signs as soon as I had anything to do with her. Hyperactivity, excessive nervous energy. She got a good degree but couldn't stomach practising law for too long at a stretch after graduation, Frank said. It was partly why they came up here, in search of a lower stress lifestyle.

'So we have to take it easy, kind of tread on eggshells a bit. We've got our fingers crossed.'

'You want a baby, do you?' I asked. A reasonable query, although he seemed a little thrown by it. And very pertinent, I should have thought.

'I don't think I've been asked that question before, Thea. Or not quite in that way. Well, maybe I'd have waited a bit if it was only up to me, but it's Ellie's call and she's gagging for one. You know how women are about babies.'

He must have seen from my expression that I did not, and broke into a broad grin. 'Well anyhow, thank Christ her bloody parents are out of our hair.' They hadn't told the bloody parents, who were convalescing on an extended luxury cruise right now, her dad's reward for surviving a quadruple bypass. He was a type A personality and was probably having to be tied to the deck.

Hadn't they told Kim either? Not yet, they'd been waiting for the right time. Waiting for her to settle in properly. But they would have to broach the subject, of course, sooner or later.

'Well, can you please broach it sooner rather than later.' I made this into more of a demand than a polite request. 'This afternoon, for example.' I felt uncomfortable, I said, being in possession of such inflammatory information when Kim was in blissful ignorance. It didn't seem right at all.

Inflammatory information? He queried *Blissful* ignorance? Not the most tactful way of putting it, I suppose. Because of my equivocal attitude to most children I've never quite understood people's desire to have them. Never quite understood it? Poppycock – I was born with a quadruple procreational bypass. Fortunately Frank appeared more amused than offended. He seems distinctly laidback about most matters. Normally I would find this admirable, but there are limits.

I didn't know you smoked dope, I couldn't help remarking. He claimed he wasn't a pothead, he only indulged in the weed when bogged down in a creative hiatus. And only when Ellie wasn't looking. She was a bit uptight about drugs – about *grass*, he corrected hastily. And only during school hours, he added, with a weather eye on me.

I was glad to hear it, I said, because I was a bit uptight about drugs myself. And among children, I said, I took a no-prisoners attitude. I gave him the gimlet eye as I said that. Unused for many years, it seemed to have lost none of its potency, I was pleased to see. A glazed look came over his features, albeit only briefly.

Before leaving I asked him what numbers he had selected for the rotating lock. He was caught on the hop. Obviously hadn't given it any thought whatsoever. I'll be asking you again, Frank, I warned. Sooner rather than later.

'I thought the whole point was so you wouldn't be able to open it, Thea,' he said.

The pregnancy news explains a lot. Frank's excessively solicitous behaviour. Ellice's rather wearing vivacity, which is as much induced as innate, I expect. No doubt the consecutive miscarriages would have taken a toll. Perhaps they are waiting to see if this pregnancy sticks, if that is the term, before informing Kim. All the same, I would prefer not to have been told in advance of her.

And Frank's casual attitude to what is a serious matter, the whole business of this highly unpleasant film, is very vexing. And he drinks and smokes while he's working. Rather a lot of both, I suspect. And while it may have been a casual reference, I also wonder if he was not downplaying a wider experience. One shouldn't generalise, of course, but all the musicians the girls used to drool over were notorious for their indiscriminate drug use.

Seeing him smoking dope stirred some uncomfortable memories. I'd never seen it until Matthew Rhode smuggled some in. I only dabbled in it, and only occasionally, towards the end. Like Frank, I did so in the privacy of my own quarters, which unlike Frank's were self-contained. But when I think about this now it was an extraordinary thing to have done. And in the presence of a male member of staff, too. Reckless. I was the school principal, for imaginary god's sake. What was I thinking?

It must have been the frisson of excitement. The illicit allure of the illegal, as Matthew said. I didn't even like the stuff. It did nothing much for me and, what's more, it didn't agree with me. It made me feel queasy. Matthew maintained this was because I'd usually had some wine beforehand, but it wasn't that. Just a whiff of that sickly smell turns my stomach, even now.

I know they all do it and maintain it's no more harmful than booze. They may well be right. But booze is far more agreeable and aesthetically pleasing. Those soggy fag-ends they pass round would make you sick even if the smell didn't.

I knew nothing about the cocaine. He never brought cocaine to my rooms. Never.

~~

They've given me a present, which I'm not sure if I want. Their old DVD player. Frank carried it over. Works perfectly, he said. They've just replaced it with a multi-system model. Different countries have different operating systems, apparently. Although quite why you'd want to bother with them is hard to imagine.

The contraption sat quite tidily under the TV. He'd even brought a DVD, a drama about Churchill and the lead-up to World War II. He said it was very good, probably thought that was my formative period. He showed me how to put the thing on, not that I have much intention of using it. It was surprisingly straightforward but I insisted he write the steps down. 'I'll forget if you don't,' I said. I didn't go so far as to refuse it. Nothing gained by being churlish.

And it was a nice gesture, even if prompted by recent guilt. I suppose it might come in handy on long winter evenings in front of the fire. There are masterpieces in film, as well as in literature. I doubt whether Kim has seen many of them yet, if any at all.

~~

I wonder how she is going to react to this baby development. Will she resent it? The other two evidently want a child, both of them; I suspect Frank downplayed his attitude when I surprised him by bringing up the subject. So it will further cement their closeness as a couple. Kim is likely to feel even more of an outsider.

I told Sandy, in strict confidence. Sandy can be trusted with confidences. He shares my disdain for gossip. You can never predict his opinions, though, about anything on our mythical maker's earth, and he confirmed this by saying he imagined Kim would greet the news with pleasure. With *pleasure*, I exclaimed. Am I hearing aright?

Yes, Thea, you are. Pleasure, he repeated, with what I have come to classify as his patience-of-Job expression. Isn't that how people usually behave in this situation?

Well, is it? I countered. I wasn't at all sure of that, I said. And anyway, this wasn't a usual situation, not by any manner of means. Kim was already the odd one out, and Ellice and Frank having a baby would only intensify that feeling of not belonging.

Why should it do that, Sandy wanted to know. It was more likely to make her feel she was part of a family. Had she told me she felt excluded?

She doesn't need to tell me, I said. It's glaringly obvious.

I could see Sandy was not going to budge. He started to rhapsodise about what a good relationship Kim and Frank have. Unsurprising, he said, since he's a nice bloke and she's such a special girl, but it was unusual, really quite heartwarming to see an uncle and niece who got on so famously.

They'd left the shop with another heap of books for her only yesterday afternoon. *Pride and Prejudice* was on top of the pile. A good choice, didn't I agree? And what about this? She'd asked for some Vietnamese history and he had located just the thing. Wasn't that a turn-up for the books?

Not too dry, sound on the war, quite readable. She was part Vietnamese, did I know that?

I suppressed a sigh and butted in before he could get started on the rest of the pile. I outlined the problem of the graphic film Kim's nice uncle Frank – who drinks and smokes dope while he's working, by the way – is working on. Nice uncle Frank has a decidedly irresponsible streak, I said.

Hmm, they all smoke dope, I'm told, was Sandy's phlegmatic response, even when they're not working. A surprising comment, coming from him. Unexpectedly savvy. Who could have told him that? Not the arch square Monica Harmonica, surely. She wouldn't know a joint from a leg of pork.

I described the toolbox and my purchase of the combination lock.

Do you think he'll use it? Sandy asked. This is what worries me. We had to cut the conversation short because a nosy parker had marched in and was hovering at Sandy's elbow.

Well, at least he has finally worked out how Kim and Frank are related. Like most men, Sandy doesn't make a parade of his sentimental side, but now and again he gives himself away with a throwaway phrase. He is really quite tender-hearted.

Heartwarming was the word he used. A heartwarming relationship. If that is to be the case, Frank needs to get his act together.

~~

No car but someone home, doors unlocked as usual. Found Frank leaning back and wearing a filthy old cotton sun hat of indeterminate hue, tilted low over his forehead, legs propped on the desk. And in blessed quiet. Nothing on the screen for once. Blinds pulled back and light streaming in. Beside him: three empty mugs and an ashtray with two mangy butts. Looked like discarded joints to me. I saw a new bottle of tequila on the desk. Unopened, as yet.

I could tell he wasn't asleep and I coughed. He opened his eyes. He seemed quite sanguine.

'Good day, Mr Composer,' I said. 'Sorry to wake you from your beauty sleep, or should I say, befuddled stupor?'

No worries, he said cheerfully, he'd been contemplating his navel. 'Mulling over the background muzak for the orgy scene.' He winked. 'Can't you see I've got my thinking cap on?' He took it off, gave it and then me a smacking kiss. 'A trusty heirloom. Only use it in times of extreme crisis, and it always works.' He scribbled some crotchets and quavers on a pad ruled for musical notation. 'There. Time for another caffeine hit.' He insisted it wasn't an intrusion. I suspect he actively likes being interrupted.

How much coffee did he drink in one day? Whoops, no idea, he said airily. Masses. It was not beneficial in large quantities, I pointed out. And neither, I added en passant, was spirituous liquor. Or marijuana. There was another study in today's paper suggesting marijuana could have long-term effects on the brain. Deleterious effects. I had cut the article out, I said, and just happened to have it with me. I put it into his hand. 'There you go,' I said.

'Oh, everything's bad for you, Thea,' he said. And I shouldn't believe everything I read in the paper. There would be another study next week saying the opposite. Which was something I might have said myself, but in this context I found it provoking.

He saw me looking around for my toolbox and pointed to it. It was on the end of the bed. 'Two-four-six-eight,' he said. 'I've committed it to memory. Forget you ever heard it.'

I thought that was far too obvious a code and said so.

Anything more complicated, he said, and he wouldn't have a hope in hell of memorising it. And anyhow, although she might wonder why it was there, no way would Kim ever think of looking in a funny old toolbox.

I pointed out that she might look inside as a direct consequence of wondering why it was there.

He put his hands together in supplication. 'Let's not second-guess ourselves, Thea, please. Give me a break, huh?'

'You mentioned an orgy?' I said.

Poetic licence, he declared promptly. I doubted that, especially when he did not offer to show it to me. We took coffee out to the deck for ten minutes. It was cloudy but intermittently bright. They'd acquired some comfortable cane armchairs instead of the Queen Anne numbers.

I decided to raise another matter. 'You and Ellice are an unusually close couple,' I said. 'And Ellice is pregnant.'

He patted me on the knee. 'Yeah, well, the two sometimes go together. So?'

I said I couldn't help thinking this made it difficult for Kim.

'Difficult? You mean –' he seemed to find this puzzling.

'The two of you are such a tightly knit unit she's likely to feel excluded.' And the pregnancy news could well intensify her feelings of being the odd one out, rather as she had been all her life. It was always hard with three, I conceded, and the person who was not part of the couple was inevitably going to feel resentful. This was to be expected. It wasn't that he and Ellice had done anything wrong, exactly, but they needed to keep in mind the psychological side.

Frank put down his coffee. I could tell he was finding this hard to come to grips with. He opened his mouth, shut it, and then subjected me to a playfully helpless look.

'I'm not just any old fruitcake you know, Frank,' I said. 'I've had some contact with children who've been through the kinds of experiences she has.' There was no one-size-fits-all solution. But I felt it was as well to be aware of the problem, and to be sure to pay her special attention. In particular, to avoid too much cosying up with Ellice when Kim was around.

I'd been speaking fast, maybe rather too over-emphatically. He jumped to his feet and stepped behind my chair. 'Thea, baby – I'm thinking you need another dose of my patent stress-buster. That's what I'm thinking.'

Before I could object his hands were on my shoulders. I had the same feeling of instant relief as before. An identical surge of physical gratification. He chatted away as his fingers and thumbs kneaded into my stiff shoulder muscles. I tried to keep my mind on what he was saying.

There would be no more cosying up for a while anyhow, because Ellie was going away for a bit of a break, a spot of R and R. She was going down to Melbourne to stay with a friend, an old schoolmate, so he and Kim would be baching. They'd have a golden opportunity to connect a bit more, and I could relax, he said.

He stepped back before I was ready. 'Good?' he asked.

I nodded. If this is stress-busting I can endure more of it, I was thinking.

'Any time,' he said.

I didn't overdo the subject of Kim's marginalisation. I've made the point, I hope, and there is nothing to be gained by labouring it. I'd laboured it already, his actions seemed to be suggesting. His successful diversionary tactics. For the second time I basked in an inexplicable feeling of wellbeing. It persisted for a good hour afterwards. Was it a release of serotonin, the so-called 'pleasure' hormone? Or is it what they mean when they talk about endorphins, supposedly released after demanding exercise routines?

These inscrutable substances are all the rage. I have been properly sceptical about them in the past and remain so. But is it conceivable I was experiencing an irrational flood of endorphins? I find this idea rather disturbing.

They do say almost everyone is afflicted by stress these days, with the daily outpouring of grisly news from every direction. I suppose there is no good reason why I should be immune. Can you be stressed subliminally, without knowing? This is another bleak idea.

There are advertisements for massage practitioners in the local paper – plenty of them, but I do not feel inclined to try out anyone. I have the same ingrained resistance to the idea of a stranger touching me as I have had all my life. That is not going to change.

~~

How much time do I have left? Of quality, that is. I must be using up a fair ration of my remaining quality time on this journal. The writing muscles ought by rights to be mightily flexed. So much so that I didn't think enough about Oscar's assignment in advance. When I came to it after Frank's patent stress-busting treatment I was at a loss, initially. And only partly because I was in a dazed condition.

Last week Oscar made an announcement. Our Chairman Mao moment had arrived. We were about to take the Great Leap Forward. Before we began the course, we were given a short questionnaire. The questions boiled down to two, in effect: what did we hope to get out of this course, and which branch of creative writing – fiction, non-fiction, biography, memoir – was our principal interest? I was tempted to say poetry, but opted for fiction because it seemed more achievable.

We never saw each other's responses, but he told us the preferences were confined to two areas, memoir and fiction. Now it's approaching the end of term he thinks we've done enough preparatory donkey work and should get down to business. He wants to collect our best pieces for a boutique anthology.

We might get it published, he declared. Who knows? Madder miracles have come to pass. But piggywigs have not been known to take to the air, I murmured. Or, he went on, with a reproving glance at me, we can always make an e-book. What you might call a group blog.

Who on this godless earth would want to read our ramblings? I said. I was feeling bolshie. No one would read them in all probability, Oscar said, save our nearest and dearest, but that needn't stop us from aiming them into cyberspace. And on the plus side it wouldn't cost a sausage. Not even a gourmet snag.

I cast an involuntary glance left and right. Did anyone have such a thing as a nearest and dearest raring to read their work? Certainly not me – Teddy is illiterate. Gilda-lily is a divorcee. Twice over, someone insisted. That she found two men prepared to marry her beggars belief. Mousy Mary was also rumoured to be married once, but that has to be a furphy.

Not a child, spouse or *partner*, as the gruesome modern term would have it, has ever been mentioned by anyone. I think we have in common a spinsterish air of disconnectedness, Oscar and Greg included. Perhaps this is why I have found some kind of niche in the group. I don't especially care for any of them, Oscar excepted, but for the most part we rub along well enough.

The idea of a little collection caused a buzz. Oscar said he ruminated on it in the bath, where he chews the cud on a daily basis. He'd noticed that our best pieces were those with a strong sense of place. What did we think of *Where It Happened* as a working title?

'It's non-specific enough that you can pretty much write what you like, but it also has a subtle specificity,' he said. I thought this sentence was very characteristic of him.

Then he pulled out a folder from the satchel he always carries. His 'manbag', as he calls it. He extracted a framed photo in black and white of two people, very blurred and indistinct, seated at a table. Both were smoking, and the twin columns of smoke entwined above their heads with a clarity and definition they themselves lacked. The background was anonymous, might have been a house, café or bar.

This was made by a photographer friend, inspired by an Edward Hopper painting, Oscar said, passing it round. It was a personal favourite because it told you nothing about the subjects. 'We don't know who these characters are. We can't even tell what sex they are, if any. Or if they're talking to each other. They might be total strangers.'

They were just there, a pair of anonymous objects inhabiting the moment. Nevertheless, there was something elegiac about them, in Oscar's opinion. They were once in the world, and now they were figures in a landscape of the mind.

Oscar said he's had this photo for years. He keeps it on his desk as a talisman. When he is hit by writer's block, when he is blundering around like a bull in the china, he ponders it and then buggers off and takes a nap. Then, with a bit of blooming luck, the elusive words come cascading down like manna. We could try doing the same thing. Select something with a special meaning for us and confer upon it inspirational status.

'Couldn't we just say um or Om?' suggested Greg, rather wittily I thought.

Whatever moves your mojo, Oscar said. Sometimes these unlikely things connect with the psyche and move in mysterious ways. Or they do not connect with the psyche or move in any mysterious way, shape or form, I muttered, and there was a general titter. I did spare a thought, however, for Frank's filthy thinking cap. Maybe there's a grain of something in the theory.

I could see the others were a bit thrown by it, though. Is the big O going off his rocker at last? Greg demanded on the way out. Not at all, he's got a point, I told them. Graven images have a proven track record, do they not? A couple of them looked censorious, I was pleased to see.

In the questionnaire I had listed my principal interest as writing fiction. Now, as I look at my 'best' pieces, a mangy bunch, I see that this was misguided. Plain wrong. I have no talent for fiction, no mind for making things up. My imagination is ploddingly earthbound.

This journal has energised me over recent weeks. Could I cannibalise it, use parts of it in a new way? Kim is coming to the class tomorrow. Her presence would preclude the use of some material. In the longer term, if there is one, would it also be too inhibiting?

I might have tried, for example, to follow up that conversation with the deputy head. What was the word she used? Rumble. There had been the odd rumble in the staff room. Well, as principal you quickly become immune to the parochial little jealousies of the staff. Is it any wonder that you'd gravitate towards the odd person with whom you have something in common?

Matthew Rhode was an outstanding teacher and a first-rate mind, probably the finest I ever came across in my career. If I hadn't promoted him and created opportunities for him to work individually with my best students I'd have been derelict in my duty. If that is favouritism I plead guilty. Why would you allow mediocrities to take advanced tutorials and waste students' time?

As for her other concern, it was all double-dutch to me then. Students getting overextended and excitable? Those kinds of amorphous complaints are always floating round any school, and always traceable back to one disaffected teacher or another. The staff room of a girls' boarding school is a seedbed of neuroses and a hothouse of petulant plants, Matthew informed me once. He was telling me nothing I didn't know.

When did he say that? Could it have been directly after I gave him a rundown of that particular conversation with my deputy? Perhaps that is why I have such a seamless recall of the dialogue. He was particularly disparaging of her, and I may have enjoyed relaying her cadences. It is not easy to admit this, but I may well have taken a deplorable pleasure in it.

On balance, I don't think it would be wise to expand on this subject. Or desirable. Can't think why I imagined it would be a good idea.

I was feeling quite hot and bothered, and nearly jumped out of my skin when the phone rang. Davy – I might have known. None of my other friends uses the blower much, but Davy has a symbiotic relationship with it. His phone bill must be astronomical. He was full of the news that he'd just been in the café and drunk one of Ellice's excellent coffees. Had an intriguing chinwag, he said. What a comely wench I had living across the way, although he doubted if that would cut any ice with me. No ice at all, I said coldly. Her coffees were nowhere near as good as her husband's, I added.

What did you talk about, I asked. He was uncharacteristically vague. This and that. She had a most engaging personality, didn't she? Very amusing and vivacious. Too vivacious by half, I said. Doesn't leave much elbow room in the personality for anything else.

Oh, you are such an unreconstructed curmudgeon, he scolded. I should know that *she* found *me* entertaining, however. Regaled him with several of my bons mots, she did.

'And oh how you laughed,' I said uneasily. I should never have introduced them to Davy, never have asked him to the drinks. They had an intriguing chat, he said. Talked about me. Could he have talked about my past? I wouldn't put it past him.

I considered asking, but couldn't bring myself. Too demeaning. And any request for discretion would produce the exact opposite, I'm sure of that. I wonder if I might employ Sandy as a go-between? To ask Davy to keep his mouth shut? Davy respects Sandy, everyone does. Sandy has a kind of unconscious moral authority I clearly lack.

And yet I have been raking up the past myself. Why, and for what conceivable purpose?

I thought it might settle me down if I forced myself to work on a different subject. Was quite unprepared for what came into my mind: an account of the building of my house. Such an impulse is a departure in itself. Until now I'd never have entertained the idea of writing one word on such a topic.

I might even preface it with the page I already gave Oscar: the dialogue between a woman and a girl. The dialogue whose intended subtext, which no one grasped, was the impossibility of realising the woman's dream of an earthly paradise.

I retrieved that page and reread it. It ended with the girl's stark question: *do you wish we weren't here?* Kim's question, after I had discovered her trespassing in my landscape, reading in the cradle of the rock I have always thought of as my secret. Except that she was not trespassing, and it is not a secret, not really, and it is my property only in my imagination. Or, perhaps, in the stony landscape of my dreams.

After that initial awkward confrontation, Kim and I have not referred again to this painful incident. We have avoided, most scrupulously, making any mention of it. As an event it has become untouchable, and this is my doing. By avoiding it I have let the subject burgeon out of all proportion until it is a pariah topic between us.

The girl's question was the single line of written dialogue in which I could find no discernable subtext. It was a seminal question left unanswered, which made for a dramatic finale, I had thought.

We are no longer limited to just one page. Oscar has relaxed his strictures on length, in keeping with our more upwardly mobile literary status, as he calls it. Run away and polish your audition pieces, he said. Pirouette to the music of time – but preferably confine the dance to one volume instead of twelve. He couldn't promise to read everything.

Already I find myself speculating, thinking ahead. I envisage a set of linked pieces inspired by real-life experience. I do not intend to figure in them myself, not at this stage. Instead I will construct for myself a shadowy alter ego. I will make this character anonymous, a she who is never described. Rather like one of the amorphous figures in Oscar's photo, as it happens.

~~

I expected it to be more difficult to write about the building of my house than it turned out to be. It sounds grandiose but I recognised quite soon that there was a mythical dimension to the subject. The making of a dwelling place is a symbolic behaviour common to all cultures, I suppose, whether the dwelling happens to be a cardboard box or a palace. It can symbolise a range of things: respectability, a refuge, hope, among others. And worldly success. Not to mention delusions of grandeur and disappointment and making do.

And then there is the whole idea of home, with all the baggage that entails. Home, where the heart is. I skirted around this emotional minefield by avoiding the subject altogether. The construction of the house was enough. It was a bigger topic than I had anticipated and I didn't get very far.

The project, I wrote, was unlike anything the woman had done before. Yet she was quite confident, rather abnormally so when I think about it now. She knew exactly what she wanted because the final conception was already there, fully realised in her mind.

In no other area of my life can I recall ever having had such a degree of certainty. The architectural draughtsman who drew up the plans said he'd never come across a client with such a tight, specific brief. Never thought he'd get to meet the one woman in the world who never changed her mind, he said to me once.

Well, there was good reason for my certainty. I'd worked out every detail over a period of years. Dreamt about it often, although the sequence of different houses that appeared in my dreams never once resembled the one that was coming into being. At the time I thought nothing of that. Now I find it thought-provoking, this perverse activity on the part of my subconscious mind. Insidiously subversive.

I can see that in a sense the project was a rebound activity, a break from the past, and I threw myself into it as if it were my new career. I was fully engaged, physically and mentally, as never before. Passionately engaged, I think. They have a useful word for this now. They call it flow, the experience of being so absorbed in your work that you are unaware of time passing. I looked it up in my *Shorter Oxford* but it was so old it only listed the traditional meanings.

I did not expect to experience flow again in my life. But lo! It has made a miraculous reappearance. It came back when I was writing my account of the precipice. It is a short distance from flow to fall, two innocent letters. I think my wily subconscious may have been setting me up for a fall in the only way it knew how, with those dreams of non-existent houses. Preparing me for one of life's sobering truths.

'Truths life has taught me.' This was the title of a recent series in the paper, a Saturday column in which older people, some well known, some not, selected five aphorisms that meant something to them. They didn't have to be original, they could be tried and truisms. I was sorry when it ended. Most of the choices tended to be on the rueful side, which was why I liked them.

Nothing in life turns out the way you wanted, I recall, was one of the selections in the very week I sold my house to the Campbell-Carringtons. Had my subconscious sought to give me advance warning of this? Had it tried to alert me to the fact that the outcome of human passions is almost always a can of worms?

If so, it didn't work. I was too blinkered to decode the advance warnings. Still, something was gained. It has become a truth life has taught me, too. And what was the other one I recently came up with? Pride leads to paralysis. Maybe they could resurrect the series and I could be a contributor.

The multitude of other lives one might have led. Should I have become an architect? Could I have designed houses for other people? Ah, that I doubt. I may have lacked the essential willingness to adapt to their harebrained wishes.

I have a query. Do you choose your home? Can you impose yourself on it, or does it, when all is said and done, choose you?

Don't have too much afternoon tea after school, I said to Kim, because we're going out for dinner first, not after.

Really? To a *restaurant*?

I thought it might be fun, I said.

Fun? Oh *yeah*, it so would. She wouldn't have any arvo tea then, not a skerrick. Just as well I'd warned her in advance. Awesome, because eating out was so cool. It was one of her favourite things, actually. Then came an abrupt change of expression. Her face clouded over and she chewed her lip.

'Of course, it's my treat,' I said casually.

She shook her head. 'But I've got a bit of – I've got pocket money. They give –'

'We're not using your pocket money, don't even think of it.'

'But Thea – you lost all your savings when –'

'I have enough left over for a few treats,' I said in a firm voice.

'But –'

'For quite a few treats, in fact. We'll say no more about it. Now scarper, before you miss the bus.' She gave Teddy a series of jubilant hugs and rode off.

He is in fine fettle at the moment. The new pills seem to be working – touch wood, do not tempt fate – better than I dared hope they might. He has come with me on the morning walk four days of the last five. And bounded at times, to my joy.

She hasn't had the chance to eat out very much, I expect, so it will be a novelty for her. I haven't either, I suppose. There are several places around here where I haven't been. They are not overly expensive; I've read the menus outside.

In an idle moment I looked up the word custodian. A person who has responsibility for something, who looks after something. I am the custodian of the museum in miniature. Even if I can no longer see it, I am the one who knows it is there. I am the holder of the knowledge.

I may have sole possession of the secret, but it cannot be said that I own it. Furthermore, I have a responsibility to her, the unknown artist who, in bequeathing her images, left behind the proof of her existence.

A new conviction has come to me, it has descended like Oscar's manna, and I find myself in the grip of it. It would be wrong to keep this legacy to myself, without handing it on. Nor, I find again, somewhat to my surprise, do I wish to. That would be like a betrayal of a sacred trust.

It would be *sacrilegious*. This seems to be the only appropriate word. Have I used it before, in my life? Never, I think, in the right context. Never in terms of its true meaning. What I am contemplating doing is rather like passing on the baton in a relay race. In the relay of life, the race towards death in which no one wants to be the winner.

There is less sadness in this process than I thought. There is an element of relief. Even a trace of exhilaration. It is quite unexpected.

~~

Last week I was about to keel over from lack of sustenance. It must be the special concentration the writing class demands. You can get lazy, living with your compatible canine companion. It's not that you don't think. It's more that your random thoughts end up in arid wastelands, or worse. The writing class requires a different order of application.

Oscar is a vigilant taskmaster. He notices if his troops of advancing age drift off in a daydream and snaps them smartly out of it.

After thinking it over I decided to take Kim to the Asian restaurant round the corner from the writers' room. It's surprisingly good, cheap and quick, and the owners know me. Atmospheric too, which you wouldn't necessarily expect. Kim was charmed by the gold tablecloths, the red lanterns on the ceiling and the candlelight. I thought it would appeal to her.

For such a modest establishment it has an eclectic menu, including a number of Vietnamese specialities. She exclaimed when she saw them. I invited her to choose. She said she hadn't spent much time with Vietnamese people, not for years. But when she pored over the list I saw a spark of recognition. She read out the names of the dishes fluently.

'You haven't forgotten,' I said.

'I can sort of pronounce the words, but I only really remember a few. Only a handful of words,' she said pensively. I wondered if it might have been wiser to go to the Italian place nearby.

She said, 'It's so different-sounding, like it's a language from another planet, but it's kind of compelling. Don't you think, Thea?'

I thought it was a very compelling language indeed. It was both guttural and melodious, with a harsh music all of its own.

She nodded. 'A harsh music. That's what I think too.'

After some discussion we ordered a feast of hot and sour seafood soup, minced (free-range) chicken and bean-sprout crepes wrapped in lettuce, and soft vermicelli summer rolls filled with prawns, cucumber and spring onion. And a glass of wine for me. Normally I'd have two, but I was mindful of the need to drive Kim home later.

Had I noticed anything? Kim asked. We had steered clear of any pork, beef or lamb.

'I don't eat them,' I said.

Not since I was a kid?

'Not since I found Teddy, for some reason. He does, though, I'm afraid.'

'Bit late to change his habits now, I guess,' Kim said. She didn't eat them either. It was the whole business of raising the animals and then taking away their young and herding them into lorries, and killing them in horrible, scary abattoirs, wasn't it? I agreed that it was. Somewhat inconsistent to make an exception for chickens and fish, but at least it was a start.

'I can foresee going total eventually, like when I get to about twenty,' Kim said. I thought at my age I'd have to make do with going halfway.

We were the only customers at that hour. She surveyed the room, propping her elbows on the table. I suppressed my reflex objection to this habit. For all I know, it has long since ceased to be considered bad manners anyway. She said, 'This is so fun and I'm *so* starving. Even though it's really, really early. Just as well I didn't gobble all the usual stuff after school. Wouldn't want to waste this experience.'

I was relieved. 'This experience' had an aura of enchantment around it I'd not associated with the restaurant before.

'I've brought you something to read while we're waiting.' I pulled out my piece about Teddy disguised as Ted. We had to write about an important character in our life, I said. She caught on right away. She has an infectious giggle, like the ascending notes of a xylophone.

She laid the sheet of paper carefully on the table.

'D'you want to hear my verdict, Thea?' I gave the requisite nod.

'I totally love it.' She shook her head. 'Absolutely.'

'I had to leave a few things out, as you might imagine,' I said.

'Okay. Like for instance, how he's always lying on his back with his legs in the air. I noticed that was left out.'

'And his habit of burying bones in the garden.'

'And of vacuuming up spilt stuff off the floor and then licking your face. It's phenomenally amazing you found so much stuff to put in. Can I keep it so I can read it again?'

She folded the piece and put it in her bag. The others must've been jealous of my live-in man, she said. I didn't tell her they were sceptical about Ted's existence; I said under no circumstances to let on.

She asked about the rest of the class. 'Don't feel obliged to leave out any of *their* funny habits,' she prompted.

I gave a brief run-down. It sounded uncharitable, even to my ears. She ticked them off on her fingers. Gilda-lily was predatory, Mary was frumpy and mad, Greg was rustic and hairy and the other two, Margaret and Joy, were nonentities about whom you could say nothing of any interest.

Humpf. And what about the teacher? Was he normal? Like, at all? Ah, Oscar is in a league of his own, I said. You can make up your own mind. I think you might like him.

She was impressed to hear he had written two satirical novels. They'd had small print runs; Oscar said himself that they were rather peculiar and hadn't sold well. Unfortunately no one in the class has read either of them. I've had Sandy Fay keeping a look out for a stray copy for months, with no luck so far. They were very likely to be eccentric, I said, and esoteric. That is to say, they were probably a minority taste.

'A minority taste? But that's so in their *flavour*, isn't it?' said Kim. She enjoys puns. 'You approve of Oscar, then. What about Frank? Do you like him?'

This put me in a quandary. Frank has some attractive qualities, but I have issues with him, as they say. I decided to leave out the big issue of his irresponsibility. 'I find Frank likeable in many ways,' I said. 'And he is your uncle and very fond of you, which are two more things in his flavour.'

He is your only relative, I thought. Or the only one who cares enough to have any contact with you.

She beamed in an untrammelled way. 'Yeah, I think he is. Fond of me. That's a relief, you know. That you like him.'

When I didn't respond, she said, 'It's bad enough to have people sort of invading your own house, but if you hated them as well it'd be, like, just *total* shit.'

She didn't ask me what I thought of Ellice, I noticed. They still haven't mentioned the pregnancy, that's obvious. I had to suppress the urge to tell her about it. This is making me angry. It's not up to me to do it, I know that, but I am strongly tempted all the same.

Before we left she asked, 'Did you give the house a name?'

'Only in theory,' I said. 'I was always going to call it Halcyon. It never had a christening.'

Halcyon. It sounded like a word from another life. I'd almost forgotten it. I explained that it meant a time that was idyllically happy, usually in the past. It was a beguiling word, to my mind, that suited the house. To forestall the inevitable question, I said I had intended to give the word an extended meaning, to include the present instead, and the future. Which was the melancholy truth.

I could see her mulling over this as she looked round the room. She said, 'But you wouldn't've had to change the meaning. As soon as you'd lived there for more than one day you would've had a halcyon past, right?'

It took a moment to get my mind around this idea. But I think it explains a thought process that had been unconscious. Halcyon was to be a break from the past and a new beginning.

We went into the small anteroom where they keep the coats. As we were shrugging our arms into our jackets she suddenly said, 'Do you want to hear the words I remember?'

'Very much,' I said. I experienced a flicker of severe anxiety.

She recited several Vietnamese words in an inflected, up and down tone. 'They mean "my love" and "daughter of mine",' she said in a careful, unemotional voice. 'And "I have to leave you" and "I am sorry." That's all I remember. It's not very much, is it?'

She had her back to me so I couldn't see her face, but I could hear both of us breathing fast in the cramped space. She seemed to be struggling with the jacket. I guided her hand into the sleeve.

'It's enough to tell a story,' I said.

She stood motionless for a moment. Then she turned to me. 'That's true. Enough for that.'

We thanked the waiter as he held the door open for us. In the street she slowed down and then came to a halt. 'Um. Thea.'

'Yes?' I saw she was looking rattled.

'I'm allowed to be invisible, right? I won't have to, you know, *say* anything?'

Nothing at all, I assured her. She could be the invisible woman. But if she had changed her mind, if she didn't want to go, I didn't mind in the least. We could go back, right now. She pondered, then shook her head, decisively.

'Nuh, no way. I haven't. Changed my mind.'

The others welcomed her arrival in a low-key kind of way. They were quite generous, I have to concede, and tactful, Oscar included. He merely said, 'Tonight, Thea has brought along a young observer.' We ran through everyone's name, then it was business as usual.

I remember Frank saying Kim is more comfortable among adults. She has a tendency to slouch in the seat, but I was aware of that active brain ticking over, matching each name against my description. Her presence didn't change the conduct of the class in any way. She sat quietly next to me, giving me the occasional sideways glance, making the occasional note, taking everything in.

While Oscar has tended to do most of the reading because he does it with such panache, today we were each asked to read an extract from our new work in progress. I trust this practice doesn't become a fixture. Most of them are droning readers with a singsong delivery and no tonal variation, unlike a Vietnamese speaker. Gilda-lily is an exception. She enunciates as if she were gallivanting on stage in the West End, in what she fondly imagines is still the BBC accent.

I detected a stir of surprise from Kim when I began to read. She hadn't expected to hear anything to do with the house. Perhaps I was more critical because she was there, but I thought my effort sounded depressingly plodding. Pedantic, even, and weighed down with unnecessary detail. And my attempt to embrace the mythical dimension sounded laboured in the extreme, as well as borderline pretentious. Or well over the line.

Afterwards when we were discussing our work I was more negative than usual. About mine, that is. The others were less ambitious but the better for it, I thought. Although nearly everyone seemed a bit dejected about their endeavours today.

Oscar responded by saying he could see we all wanted to go up a notch and were feeling we'd slipped down the ladder instead. He told us to suspend judgement, not to even think about whether our writing was good or bad for the time being. Just do the thing, he said. And do the thing more than usual, to iron out the creases. To move forward, writing needed to become a habit we couldn't do without.

'You might think you have no control over habits,' he went on, 'but the opposite is the case. It's a brainwashing thing. We have to indoctrinate ourselves in order to develop the habits we want. If we have aspirations to live a writing life,' I was aware of Kim beside me, sitting up straighter, 'the writing sensibility must seep into our daily routines, into all the nooks and crannies. Every experience, no matter how unpromising it may appear, is grist to an author's mill.'

I looked round at the others. They seemed to be drinking this in. 'Even filling the pepper grinder?' I said.

'Especially filling the pepper grinder, Thea.' Oscar was unfazed. 'The writer's life is an examined life, and the only way to have an examined life is by living in the moment. Do the small things intensely, wring every drop of juice from them, and then the big things will look after themselves. Waste some time, because that is an important activity, but not too much, because time has a habit of running out. And before you know it, you may find you've got yourself a writing life.'

He gave Kim a challenging glance when he said that. She responded as if he'd thrown down a gauntlet, her eyes glowing. I had the feeling this barrage of New-Agey mantras was directed at her. It wasn't quite Oscar's usual style. But I didn't want to rain on her parade so I forbore to say anything.

Oscar asked her if she'd be back next week. Or was it, he added, with a nod in my direction, the chauffeur's call? It's Kim's call entirely, I said coolly. She looked at me, then at Oscar. Oh yeah, she would, if that was okay. Would like to. Heaps.

Nothing further was said until we arrived at the car, when she extended her arms above her head in a long, luxurious stretch. 'Wow. He's kind of an inspiring guy, isn't he, Thea? Sort of like a literary guru, or something.'

I turned the key in the ignition. Oscar a guru? 'It's unusual for him to be so soppy and wishy-washy,' I said. 'Those hackneyed exhortations to get a life and live it to the full, and so forth. He avoids platitudes as a rule; he's more astute. And sardonic.'

She wasn't having that. Soppy and wishy-washy? She didn't really think what he was saying was *soppy*, not totally. It was good advice, right, to make use of every experience? And live an examined life? It just made her want to go away and write something this minute.

'I hear what you're saying. Those slogans speak to you, right?' I said testily. She darted a keen sidelong glance at me.

'It must be really, really scary to read your stuff out. You know, in front of them? And then have to listen while they *say* things about it. *Urgh*. I'd be like, no way am I doing this.'

I was non-committal.

'It must sometimes make you think your stuff is crap even when it's not. Like, when it's not in the least crap.'

I was aware of myself feeling absurdly mollified. 'It's daunting at first, and difficult, but it can be surprisingly useful,' I conceded.

'That's a relief. You wouldn't want to go through that ordeal if it wasn't, right? But,' suddenly anxious, 'you do think Oscar's, you know, a good teacher?'

I agreed that he was a very good one, yes.

'One of the best you've known?'

'One of the best.' One of the two best, but I did not say this.

And it was good advice to live in the moment? 'Like, not to get stuck in the past or the future? Because the past's been, it's over, right, and the future might never happen. Or, you know, might not happen the way you think.'

'Well, that's self-evident, isn't it?' I said, then thought this was unduly harsh. Truisms such as these are probably not as self-evident when you're twelve. And are hard enough to act on whatever age you are. The future won't happen the way you think. One more truth life has taught me.

She gave me another disconcertingly shrewd look. She said she liked Oscar's bow tie and those cool red straps holding up his trousers.

'Braces,' I said.

Did he always come to class all dolled up like that, like he was about to open Parliament or something? He didn't look at all like what she'd imagined.

'How did you imagine him?'

She hesitated. 'I didn't expect he'd be quite so fancy. Or quite so, um, fat. I guess I thought he'd be a scrawny old hippie with wispy hair. And a beard, definitely. Sort of, you know, more like what's his name. Greg.'

Was that how she imagined a writer looked?

Well, she hadn't met a real live one before. 'But I guess they can look like anyone else on the outside, right? Even if they're a bit weird on the inside.' She reconsidered this, adding, 'Don't tell me. It's self-evident.'

'Oscar says all writers are a bit off their rocker,' I said. 'A degree of lunacy is a prerequisite, he thinks. Arguably.'

'Yeah? Is that what you think too?'

'It's an agreeable generalisation. I'd say it was a persuasive working hypothesis, wouldn't you?'

She grinned. 'Agreeable and persuasive. That's good, then. You and me are fairly weird, *arguably*, so maybe we've got an outside chance of getting to be writers.'

'You and I, not you and me,' I said. The correction was automatic, a reflex I thought I'd abandoned long ago. 'Oscar always wears a bow tie,' I said. 'He's a very dapper dresser, for these days.'

'Dapper. Oh yeah, certainly way dapperer than the run-of-the-mill people round here. Like *you and I*, right?'

'You and me, that time,' I corrected. I explained the

principle. It was clear she had never heard it before. They are supposed to be reintroducing grammar in schools, and not a moment too soon.

Until recently it was light when I drove home after class. The days are getting shorter. It's autumnal already. As we approached the dump the headlights picked up a motionless figure standing a few feet away from their house. It was Frank, I saw as we came closer. He was standing still with his back to the car.

'There's Frank peeing on the lemon tree,' Kim said. She seemed to find this rather hilarious. It was supposed to be very good for lemons, did I know this? Ellie had bought a tree in a pot and planted it. She had given Frank instructions to water it regularly.

I have heard that theory, yes, but this information gave me an uncomfortable feeling all the same. Frank looked over his shoulder and waved cheerily as he zipped up. He came bowling over and opened my door with a flourish. He was quite unabashed. Bashfulness doesn't seem to feature in his repertoire.

'The scribblers return.' He kissed me on the cheek and threw an arm round Kim's waist. 'So, how was it, Wombat?'

She was still buzzing, but concise. 'Great.' The class had left her on a high, it was nice to see.

'Thanks a lot, Thea,' Frank said. 'Now Wombat, your turn. Thank Thea a lot.'

'She already did,' I said curtly. I might come over tomorrow, I added. The small matter of some outstanding business. Would he be in?

The P words. Prim and proper, priggish, and – pretend god help us – pious. Puritanical, prudent, prude. Is that it? Am I becoming excessively prudish in my old age?

Or was it ever thus? My prudish streak was the second of two ingrained attitudes the confident young Mr Rhode identified, of which he wished to relieve me. The two were joined at the hip, he opined. A beneficial adjustment to one should have a corresponding effect on the other. He sought to divest me of my disenchantment with the human race, and purge me of my prudery.

I never knew what I'd done to convince him I was a prude. When I joked that I was on the contrary something of a libertine, he scoffed. I can see now that this was part of his strategy. He needed a lax environment in which to operate. And a permissive atmosphere. He wanted to goad me into a state of unwatchfulness.

In the event, of course, he achieved neither of his goals. Subsequently and by his own actions he validated the views he ridiculed and succeeded in entrenching both positions. By now, I should imagine, they are set in stone.

~~

Sandy likes a double-shot cappuccino with plenty of chocolate sprinkles on top. A retrograde taste, those chocolate sprinkles, I tell him, but he is adamant. I ordered two takeaways from the café next door, where aproned waitress Ellice greeted me like a long-lost friend. Hold the sprinkles on one, I demanded, and double them on the other.

Assessing her figure, I concluded she does look somewhat rounded under the apron. There was no one else in the café and I decided to confront her. It made me feel very awkward, I said, knowing about this pregnancy when the person it chiefly affected was in ignorance.

She emitted a shriek of outrage. 'Thea, per-lease! You are such a hoot. The persons most affected are me and Franko, and in that order, *if* you don't mind.'

I might well be a hoot, she could have it her own way, I said, but would she kindly address the issue. Frank had informed me she was about to go away. It was important, surely, that Kim be put in the picture before she left?

At which point she planted herself down at a table. Yes, she was off to Melbourne for a fortnight at the end of the week. She was going to stay with an old school friend who was also preggers. She and Franko had decided to hang fire and give Kim the good news on her return.

'Two whole weeks of decadent girlie stuff, Thea. Binge drinking, male strippers, Brazilians, daytime soaps. The last chance to let the old hair down, before the end of civilised life as we know it.' She lowered her voice a few decibels to her idea of a confiding whisper and nudged me. 'Just like the last weeks of freedom before getting married, all over again.'

I made no response to this but may have conveyed attitude, as they say, because she embarked on a further round of specious explanation. I was in the know about their *gyno* history, right? Don't squirm, she wasn't about to enlighten me in glorious technicolour, but Frank had sketched it in? She was paranoid about this pregnancy, just didn't want to let on to anyone about it until the last minute because it seemed too much like tempting fate.

This was all fine and dandy, I said, but Kim was not just anyone. It was wrong to tell me ahead of her.

She shrugged. 'That's Franko all over. I hate to say it, but he shouldn't have let the cat out of the bag. He can never keep his big mouth shut.' She saw my face and added, 'You'll just have to let us do this our own funny way, Thea. Humour us on this one, okay? If all goes well we'll tell her as soon as

I get back.' Would I do her a big favour and promise to keep all fingers and toes crossed?

I didn't feel like doing her a favour, big or otherwise. I paid for the coffees but refrained from making any such binding digital commitment.

Sandy, I found, already knew about Kim's visit to the writing class. Which should not have surprised me.

'They do say Lisa's Second-Hand Bookshop is the fount of all gossip,' I said. 'Not for nothing do they say that. Might your source be Oscar Corne?'

Sandy may disdain tittle-tattle himself, but Oscar is one of his regulars. It was on Sandy's free community notice board that I first perused Oscar's original announcement.

I remember it word for word: 'Creative Writing Class now taking applications from aspiring creators. Creationists need not apply. Age immaterial. Professional tutor Oscar Corne. Personal attention, limited numbers, experience unnecessary and undesirable.'

It was the reference to creationists that did it. That got me in, as well as the clauses covering age and experience.

The others must have seen the notice at Lisa's too, I expect. Doubtless in idle periods between combing the shop for self-help manuals. Sandy would have redirected them towards literature. You can get more help from the classics, as he says.

It is entirely typical of Sandy that he cared nothing for the fact that I hadn't troubled to canvass his opinion in advance. Sandy is not stained with the sin of personal pride – more P words – unlike one we can name. And he thought it was a fine idea of mine to take Kim along. She was young for that sort of thing, chronologically speaking, but Oscar was an experience in himself and it might introduce a bracing breath of sophistication into her life.

She's already getting the odd whiff of that from yours

truly, I remarked. And possibly even the odd sniff from you. Indeed, she probably is, said Sandy, but any opportunity to broaden her horizons should be taken up, shouldn't it? Since conventional school was likely to be lacking in that regard and with that kind of child.

He was probably right, I said. Schools did their damnedest to cancel out the original and the individual, to my mind. I had fought against this long and hard, I told him, but it was a losing battle.

I didn't care to analyse these two statements. Sandy said, 'I'm sure you did your level best, Thea.' I never know quite how to take it when he says things like that. At face value, I suppose. Sandy resembles no one else I know, apart from Teddy, in that he is without guile. Unlike Davy Messer.

And unlike Davy, Sandy has never alluded to my teaching career's explosive finale. I've always assumed he knows about it because of the press reports at the time, although anyone less titillated by scandal would be hard to find. But even if he hadn't accidentally come across a newspaper account, a prurient stickybeak like Davy would have enlightened him. Still, chances are he forgot about it years ago.

If I were to enlist him to urge discretion on Davy, I would have to remind Sandy exactly what it is that he wants Davy to be discreet about. I decided I couldn't stomach that right now. Perhaps it would be better to confront Davy myself after all. I'll think it over.

Sandy said he had given Kim his prized copy of *Lost Horizon* the other day. What ho, I exclaimed, the famous first ed?

'The 1939 Pocket Book,' Sandy said with pride. Allowable, I think, in his case. 'American. I wanted to be sure it was going to a good home so I showed it to her first.' His eyes crinkled. 'It was by way of being a little test. She'd never heard of a first edition before, or seen one, so I had to explain what this meant. She already respects books, and I could see she would value it from the way she held it in her hands.'

He demonstrated, taking down a flimsy old copy of Boswell's *Life of Johnson* and cradling it in his hands as if it were a wounded bird. Rare books, out-of-the-way books, they're like narcotics to Sandy. I accused him of seeking to inculcate a drug habit she would never be able to support. He said this notion was unworthy of me.

Which one? I queried. That it's a drug, or the aspersions cast on Kim's future earning capacity?

'The viewpoint itself, Thea,' he chided in his mild way. 'The thing is, surely, to introduce something in life that may become, like music, a source of great joy and pleasure.'

'All right, all right, I know when I'm beat,' I said. Sandy usually has music in the shop. Most commonly baroque, but today it was a contemporary piece I recognised by Ross Edwards. The way it suggests the textures of the Australian bush always induces a reverie in me.

I was out there in the vastness of the blue ravines, about to balance on the dizzy edge of the precipice, when Sandy's voice, one of the few sounds that is not an intrusion, broke in. Kim had confided her uncle Frank was writing music for a movie. She was quite excited about it.

'I told you that last week.' I was terse.

'So you did. Yes.' He had no memory of this, I could see.

'Sandy, did she say she had actually watched any of this film?'

He didn't think so. Obviously hadn't asked. Typical of a man. He seemed also to have forgotten what I'd told him about the problematic content of the film. I shouldn't worry too much about it, he advised. He doubted that a young girl like Kim would have any interest in seeing a movie like that.

'That's where you're wrong,' I told him. 'Girls of that age

are extremely interested in anything to do with violence and sex.'

Sandy peered down at me. He looked perplexed, his glasses slipping down his nose. 'Are they? I think that might be an overstatement. Probably not all of them, Thea. Kim seems to me to have an innate capacity for discrimination. She may be uneducated, but she has a natural refinement.'

'All of them, Sandy, believe me. It's possible that I may have rather more extensive knowledge of young girls than you.' He had taken his glasses off and was polishing them assiduously. 'Not,' I added, 'that I would ever presume to discount the breadth and scope of your experience.'

This produced a gentle smile. He sipped his coffee.

I intended to talk to Frank about this again, I said. I was going to see him about this matter, and that of the pregnancy, this very afternoon. The mention of a pregnancy bewildered Sandy briefly. I had to remind him. He was quite thrown. I realised that for an awful moment he must have thought I meant Kim.

'Frank pees in the garden, you know,' I said.

'In your garden?' Sandy looked genuinely surprised.

'Of course not. In *theirs*.' I nearly appended something withering. I do not often get exasperated with Sandy. This was one of the few times. 'Not that they have a garden, but outside the house. At night. I saw him.'

'Did you? Well,' Sandy gave this some considered attention, 'men do tend to do this, Thea. I don't think it's a cause for concern. Perhaps he didn't realise you were watching.'

'Of course I wasn't watching,' I snapped. 'Are you trying to be amusing? Kim and I were coming back in the car. She saw him too. It was very careless – he must have seen the headlights approaching.'

Oh. Was she alarmed? Not in the least, I said. She seemed to think it was a riot. Sandy seemed to think that was reassuring. Well, it doesn't reassure me, I said. He gave my shoulder a placatory pat. Really and truly, he said, I shouldn't get too upset over something like that.

He thinks it is trivial, that was obvious. I went off to pick up Teddy's meat from the butcher. For once I felt displeased with Sandy. Tolerance is all well and good, but you can have too much of a good thing.

Fortunately, neither of us is one to stew over minor disagreements, otherwise I would be seriously out of sorts.

~~

Drove home, mind on a thousand things, completely over-looked dentist appointment. Receptionist rang. Reminded me, dear, that she had remembered to remind me only yester-day, dear. The world is divided into those who use the word dear and those who do not. Scrambled back in car. By then, needless to say, I'd lost my slot and had to hang around the waiting room for another interminable hour. Hadn't brought a book, always a disaster, and was reduced to leafing through their stack of asinine celebrity (sic) weeklies.

The bulk of the ghastly so-called celebrities were unknown to me and, you'd think, of no conceivable interest to anyone with half a brain. Only famous because they had one or more of three classes of problem: drug and alcohol; weight loss or gain; or a noxious partner who had cheated on them or whom (a preferable class of problem?) they were cheating on. A dispiriting litany. Can't think why their legions of half-witted fans aren't in a permanent vegetative state. Or perhaps they are; it would explain a lot about youth suicide. Very worrying to think these trashy magazines are read, and read avidly, by Kim's age group.

Rounding the steep bend close to home, the spot where

Kim had come off her bike, I spotted a flash of blue gingham. There she was, sitting on the steps with Teddy. On hearing the car she performed several hasty actions that reminded me of some disreputable schoolyards of yore. The movements conveyed, even from a distance, guilt.

I conducted a rapid debate with myself as I drove up. There are well-worn arguments for and against. Disapprove, and risk making a big deal of something which might be fleeting, or ignore it, and risk appearing to sanction something you deplore.

The bike and backpack were lying on the ground. She stood up as Teddy bumped down the steps towards me, tail waving.

'How nice to see you,' I said. And then, in a casual manner worthy of Sandy, 'And did I imagine it, or did I just see you smoking?'

Hand to mouth. 'Oops. You didn't, actually. Imagine it. I don't do it much, but. Like, you know, rarely. Very rarely indeed.' A wry grin. 'Can't afford it.'

I needn't have wasted time on the internal debate. My gut reaction asserted itself, independent of accepted wisdom either way. Very rarely indeed was still too much, I said, especially for a young woman of her intelligence. Why bother? She should stop now while it was easy, before it became a habit. I surveyed the area where she'd been sitting. Sure enough, there was the telltale fag end that had been quickly ground into the soil.

'That unpalatable object down there belongs in the bin. You can pick it up and take it inside.'

She disinterred the butt, with a demeanour half sheepish, half stroppy. I was reminded she is only twelve, something I increasingly forget.

'You do know never to drop lighted cigarette ends in the bush,' I said conversationally.

'Yup. Sure do.' Performed in a sing-song voice. She wrapped it in a scrap of newspaper, which I thought considerate, and deposited it in the kitchen bin. Meanwhile, I put the kettle on.

'I bet you smoked once,' she said.

'Not at your age I didn't.'

'When, then? When you should've known better?'

I should've known I wouldn't escape unscathed. 'Be that red herring as it may, it's you who should know better now. There is any amount of information about the dangers, far more than we had. Or than we bothered to find out. To be fair.'

'So were you once, you know, addicted to nicotine? In the olden days?'

I was incensed. 'No, of course I wasn't.'

Why *of course*? she demanded.

'Because, while I may have other reprehensible characteristics, I am not an addictive person.' She looked at me with an expression that clearly said, well, bully for you. I was never particularly taken with it as something to do, I added, and so I gave it up altogether. Eventually. 'I came to think it was an expensive habit and rather a cretinous one to boot.'

I dismissed from my mind another related issue. That of my subsequent flirtation with an illegal substance under circumstances, as well as at an age, when I should certainly have known better.

'A lot of dudes chew gum to stop themselves from smoking,' she remarked. 'You don't like people chewing gum either, do you?'

'No, I do not. It's a revolting habit but unquestionably the lesser of two evils because it's less harmful to one's health.'

With a nonchalant air she positioned mugs, milk and sugar bowl on the kitchen table. She remembered I take honey in mine, and retrieved that as well. Neither of us spoke until the tea was on the table.

Then she demanded, rather challengingly, whether I thought what Oscar said was right. About brainwashing.

'You *know*, Thea,' seeing my blank expression, 'all that stuff about choosing the habits you want, and then sort of talking yourself into having them. You'd say it in a more elegant way than that,' she added in a more conciliatory tone, 'but it's kind of what he was on about, right?'

Brainwashing was rather an over the top, Oscar way of putting it, I suggested, but he did have a point. It was to do with identifying those aspects of life that were subject to our own control, such as smoking. 'After all, there are enough pesky things in the world one doesn't have any control over.'

'That's so right. More than enough pesky things,' she said perkily. Such as adult interference, was the implication.

I opened a packet of chocolate digestive biscuits. Until recently I have not tended to have biscuits in the house, but the butcher had a full box on the counter. Fundraising for childhood cancer. Kim took one with alacrity and watched me pour the tea.

She munched the biscuit. 'You said you've got others. Reprehensible characteristics.' Articulating the words with emphasis.

I said I was a member of the human race, regrettably enough, so I was subject to normal human failings. Like her or anyone else.

'And unlike Teddy.' About to give him half a second biscuit, she saw my face, and ate it herself instead. 'Uh huh. Well, just to make us even,' a sly glance, 'since you don't smoke anymore, right, can you maybe name *one* other failing? Doesn't have to be normal or human. And only one, no coercion, no torture. It's not like I'm the Gestapo.'

I'd lent her a biography of Nancy Wake, the Australian heroine of the French Resistance. She must have been reading it.

We had bounced back on a normal footing now. The P-words – prudery, pride – stampeded into my mind. Without pause, although I think I was aware in a corner of my mind that our little tiff had made me imprudent, I said I had certain unfortunate tendencies. To be somewhat thin-skinned and self-protective, for example.

The eyebrows shot up. 'Yeah?' Probably had expected me to say I was bossy and opinionated. 'But that's way better than being, like, a thick-skinned redneck. And we have to protect ourselves, right? Because no one else will, and that's for sure.'

'I wouldn't say that.' I found I had an unforeseen desire to deflect her from my well-worn path of pessimism. I have a mordant proclivity to look on the dark side, which I would not want to encourage.

'As you go through life you will generally find people are well-disposed to you. Many, if not most. And you will make friends who have your best interests at heart. True friends. This will come about. There is every chance of it.'

Though vigorous, the assertion sounded dubious to my ears. 'Every likelihood,' I repeated firmly. She muttered something under her breath. 'I didn't catch that,' I said.

She gave me a cheeky look. 'Sounded a bit wishy-washy to me. A bit like the *hackneyed* Oscar-speak you so disapproved of.'

'I am not plucking platitudes from the air at random. I am speaking because I have, I like to think, some knowledge of the kind of person you are.'

'Yep. You do. So?' And a small smile, for my benefit.

I felt some additional heft was required. 'We should protect ourselves, of course we should, but sensibly. Not at the expense of –'

I stopped short. I was in danger of wading into deep waters. Then knew immediately that such a reflex was a demonstration of precisely what I had in mind. It was self-protective, and dishonest through omission, when what was needed was Oscar's unambiguous directive to be brutally honest.

'Not at the expense of buckling oneself into a suit of armour. Or of being over-cautious, because that can be crippling, too. Or of being fearful,' I stopped, unsure if I was prepared to go any further with this.

'No way. I can't believe you're fearful of anyone,' she said.

'Not so much of humans, perhaps, but I have, sometimes, been reluctant to confront the serious problems they can unleash. First to accept that they exist, and then to address them.'

'Why? Because you wanted more proof? Because it might upset, you know, the apple cart?'

Bingo. Two bullseyes. 'Indeed. Because it might destroy the status quo.'

She wrinkled her nose. 'But that's not fear. That seems like totally sensible caution to me.'

I looked down. My hands were gripping the table. Teddy lay at my feet, ever tranquil, ever watchful. For some reason I felt driven to be more explicit. There was something reckless about the impulse, when I consider it.

'Occasionally in life, you see, you can find yourself in a position where you are faced with difficult decisions. Irrevocable, life-changing decisions that must be made in order to avoid worse things happening.'

She rested her chin on her hands earnestly, elbows planted on the table. Wasn't I being too hard on myself here? Most decisions were a bit of a bugger. She hadn't had to make any irrevocable, life-changing ones yet – they'd always been made for her. But they must be the pits, absolutely.

Sometimes there was an additional, critical dimension, I said. Sometimes there was a moral issue to contend with.

'D'you mean, a matter of right or wrong?'

Exactly. The stakes were much higher in such a case.

'But shouldn't that make it more clear-cut? Like, easier to make the decision in the first place?'

It should in theory, I said. But sometimes it was a matter of courage. Of being brave enough to weigh up the consequences. The consequences of doing nothing, as against those of acting decisively. This was the point at which it became a choice between a right and a wrong decision.

She was regarding me steadily, drumming her fingers on the table. I thought, Kim knows that I have alluded to something with deep significance in my life, but has no idea what it can be. In a moment she is going to ask me for an example I am not under any circumstances prepared to give.

I resorted to evasion, a tactic beloved of men of the cloth as well as politicians and teachers. It was always better to be bold, in the long run, I said. I should have stopped there. Instead, for some obscure reason, I felt the need to add, 'And, generally speaking, it is better to advance boldly than to stay huddled in one's comfort zone, taking refuge in the belief that other people aren't worth it and full participation in life is beneath one.'

That came charging – how do they put it? – out of left field. Or out of the top paddock, the one that is a few kangaroos short. From Kim's changing expressions I sensed confusion was getting the upper hand. As well it might.

'In other words, it is better than using the excuse that full participation in life is alien to one's temperament.' This was an escapee from the same paddock. Now it was said, I reviewed it dispassionately. 'And, for that matter, regarding one's temperament as irredeemably fixed.'

I found I was very tense. My neck was stiff and my shoulders were aching. I tried to rotate them.

'Irredeemably. That's a good word. What does it mean?'

I replied, '*I know that my redeemer liveth not.*
Alas and alack, 'tis all tommyrot.'

Kim shifted in her seat. She took another biscuit.

'When something is irredeemable, it means it can't be restored, or made good. I have a tendency to be inflexible, you see. Rather more than a tendency, I suspect.'

Rather more than a tendency? Poppycock, I'm as stubborn as hell. I saw a responsive gleam.

'That's enough pontification,' I said briskly. 'Now, you must forget all about my reprehensible characteristics. They were never mentioned. We never said a word on the subject. All right?'

'But it wasn't *pontification*, and we did say a word on the subject. Lots of – *thought-provoking* words.'

She looked dismayed and her shoulders slumped. Posture needs work, I'd have written on her report. Her expression told me I had ended this interestingly opaque, adult conversation in a cavalier fashion, and at my own convenience.

'Just remember to sit up straight and embrace life with both hands. In a nutshell,' I said.

'In a wishy-washy nutshell, you mean,' she muttered. No attempt to hide the fact that she felt short-changed. I had to admire that. She helped herself to two more biscuits without asking, and took off.

After she'd gone I went and lay down on the bed, something I rarely do in daylight but have been succumbing to recently, and closed my eyes for an hour. I felt quite done in. It must have been the unaccustomed unburdening, although I'm not sure how I imagined the burdens might be eased. Or what I thought I was doing at all. You can't presume to teach anyone how to live life, can you?

Even when I was head of a school I was averse to anything that might be filed under 'life guidance'. Most principals would see that as fundamental, a central part of the job description. But it was never my thing. I lacked the desire to go there, as they say. The desire or the gall. I left it to others who had no qualms on either score. I was quite at home in the intellectual sphere, on the other hand. I had no problems telling pupils what they should do academically.

And now, what have we here? I seem to be suddenly dispensing advice for living. Is my temperament becoming unstuck, by any chance? Has what was once so irredeemably fixed lost its moorings?

I should have taken the decision to act against Matthew Rhode much earlier than I did. They said it all began with Matthew poaching my star pupil, but he didn't poach her – it was my doing. I suppose it could even be said that I gave her away.

The girl was demanding in her brilliance, and highly competitive. It required a deal of work to keep up with her, let alone to stay one step ahead. I can't pretend Matthew was not involved in the decision, but I firmly believed that she would do better being coached by him. I thought it was in her academic interests to be under his auspices.

The Rhode to hell is paved with good intentions.

Unlike many teachers, I do not think I was ever guilty of having a possessive or proprietorial attitude to any of my students. If anything, I had a more proprietorial attitude towards Matthew himself. And if the truth be known I was happy to have the responsibility taken off my hands.

I gave him what he wanted. This is a hard confession to make.

I should have been more proactive. I should have weighed

up the consequences and had the courage to act, before the consequences of my inaction overwhelmed me.

~~

My mind was elsewhere, as is the default case at the moment. I bumped into Ellice. Quite literally, our cars were parked next to each other. I said I'd been musing about her holiday in Melbourne. Which is true, I have been preoccupied with the subject, among other things. How sweet of me to muse about her, she laughed.

Was it really such a good idea to go away at this stage? I said. I was wondering if it might be tempting fate. She made a face. Tempting *fate*, Thea? Ooh, please explain.

Might it not be unwise to fly, in her condition? Wouldn't it be more sensible to stay at home and rest up? Let Frank wait on her? And Kim too? 'Bearing in mind all the *gyno* problems you've had,' I said.

She beamed. I was a poppet to be so concerned, but there was no need to worry. Flying that little distance at this stage was immaterial. The doc said a change of scene was as good as a holiday, and she was getting both, right?

A poppet. First time I've been called one of those. I tried not to shrink back as she gave me a hug. I may or may not have had the grace to feel a smidgen of shame. Not enough to make any difference.

Then, as we turned the keys in our respective cars, she looked round. Delivered, had she known it, a parting shot across my bow. Franko had told her I was worried about Kimmie feeling left out. Well, I should give her top marks, because she was doing exactly what I ordered and getting out of their hair. Wouldn't this be a perfect opportunity for the two of them to do a bit of bonding? Heaven sent, Thea!

~~

These bursts of unexpected heat. We've always had them in autumn, but they seem more common now and longer lasting. Not a breath of wind. Couldn't face lunch, drank a large glass of lime squash and soda on the verandah. At least it's shady there; it was like an oven inside. I've always resisted them and made do with fans, but if this continues I might have to give in and invest in an air-conditioner for the bedroom. They say you can get good ones second-hand.

Teddy disposed of a full bowl of water. I emptied an entire tray of ice cubes into our drinks and then regretted it because the freezer is so iced up it takes forever to make them. The faithful old fridge is on its last legs. A new one – a new pre-loved one – is becoming an urgent necessity.

My peripheral eye was caught by something white emerging from their kitchen. Frank, I guessed, heading out to the deck. The deck that is so adroitly positioned as to be partly in the shade and partly in the sun at almost any time of day. The luxury of such wide-open space. The luxury of choice that money can buy.

I couldn't face a walk but I had to get out. It might wake me up a bit, and the library has an air-conditioned room. Teddy was still spread-eagled on his back in a somnolent stupor. His favourite position, which amuses Kim no end. As I proceeded slowly down the steps in the torrid heat I snatched another quick glance in Frank's direction, then looked away. I had no wish to appear inquisitive, but I was gripped by a strong suspicion.

Coming back later on I avoided driving any closer to the other house, or much closer than usual, but just enough to confirm it. Frank was lying on the deck in the shade, the ancient cotton hat – his grungy thinking cap – over his head. He was completely unclothed, there was not much doubt of it. I couldn't be sure if he was lying on his front or his back. Not without slowing down even more.

I looked at my watch. I'd purposely returned a good half hour before Kim was due home from school. I parked myself back on the verandah with the paper and the radio and tried to stay on the qui vive. It was hard to concentrate in the baking heat. Teddy hadn't moved a limb.

I thought idly of the old bird-watching binoculars I used to leave on the verandah and take with me on bushwalks. They're rather heavy and I've got out of the habit now. The unholy ghost alone knows where I put them last time. But more pertinently, the idea of peering through binoculars struck me as distinctly on the nose. Beneath one, I think, even if motivated by legitimate concerns.

A few minutes later there was a little flurry of activity on the deck. I thought at first Frank was getting up and going inside to fetch his clothes. Instead he'd gone and got the hose, and turned the sprinkler on himself. I knew that because I could see the lights sparkling in the arc of the spray. He was lying down again in the sun. Basking in it, presumably.

I was in a stew of indecision, aware of the minutes ticking by. Finally I went inside and picked up the phone. I resent being put in the position of a busybody, I was going to say lightly, or of a moral tutor. That was a term we had at college for certain senior figures in authority who were not of the church. After only two rings the answering machine came on: an interminable, effervescent message. Ellice, of course. They should have asked Kim to do it, she'd have been more succinct as well as wittier.

I put the phone down without leaving a message. There was no alternative; I resigned myself to paying Frank a personal call. I could hear jangling noises as I came nearer. It sounded like his music, with plangent nasal vocals by a person who couldn't sing. I repeated his name with as much force as I could muster. No response, although I kept calling out until I reached the corner of the deck, only a few yards from his inert, outstretched form.

He sat bolt upright. 'Hi there, Thea!' All the insouciance in the world. Uh, how was I going? Anything he could do for me? He'd been lying on a towel. On his back, as I'd thought. His torso, very white and lean, was drenched with spray from the hose. I was careful not to come any closer, or to appear to scrutinise anything too closely. I did not feign embarrassment, but neither did I feign any neighbourly bonhomie I was not feeling.

Yes, there was something he could do for me, and right away, I said. He could pull the towel out from under him and cover up his nether regions because this wasn't a nudist colony. His niece was only a schoolgirl, don't forget, and she was due home any moment now.

There was no response to this for several seconds and I thought he hadn't heard. Then he threw me an openly facetious look in which I detected no trace of an apology and scrambled to his feet, winding the wet towel dexterously around his middle. As he tucked the ends in I heard the vigorous ringing of a bicycle bell. Kim, riding up at speed. She dismounted next to me, out of breath and dripping with sweat. No helmet, I also noticed.

'Hey, you guys. Am I interrupting something?' Her wide eyes were fixed on Frank, I noticed.

'Thea's just giving me a lecture,' he said. 'Come and chill out under the hose, Wombat.'

I told him he should stop wasting precious resources and turn off the hose at once. There were water restrictions in place. And I told Kim to go inside and have a long, cold drink. A full glass at least. And she should always wear her bike helmet religiously, even in hot weather. Or rather, irreligiously.

There was a convincing report in the paper last week. The use of helmets definitely reduces head injuries in children.

I went and lay down with the fan a few inches from my face. My mind was in something of a turmoil. After twenty minutes, which they are saying is the optimum time for a power nap, I returned to the car. There was no one on the deck, I ascertained.

I needed to canvass a second opinion, and the only possible person was Sandy. When I got to Lisa's he and La Harmonica had their heads together over a large art book. I hung round, increasingly restive, not even pretending to look at the new young adult section or anywhere else. Finally I could stand it no longer and said I wanted to talk to him.

Sandy looked up, seemed to realise I was there for the first time. Come and look at this, Thea, he said with unconcealed enthusiasm, a monograph on le Sidaner. Have a look at the quality of these reproductions!

She butted in before I could say a thing. Henri le Sidaner, one of the lesser known French Impressionists. A later one, but a wonderful painter of moods, oh my goodness yes, so talented.

I know his work, I said to her. I thought he painted scenes, not moods. I don't recall him ever painting a mood, not in my book.

'It's not in the pink of condition,' Sandy was going on. 'Lots of loose pages, we'll have to get it rebound. Some spotting. But I really think it's rather a rarity. An exceptional find.'

Sandy, I said, I'm sorry to interrupt your scholarly *tête-à-tête*, but can I have a word?

Of course, Thea, he said, fire away. He was still leaning over the book. Bent double, no wonder he has back problems. A *private* word, I stressed, with a nod in her direction.

I saw them exchange a glance. 'Can you hold the fort, Monnie?' he said.

We went outside. If and only if he could spare the time away from the citadel, I said, I'd like to go to the café and sit down. It may not compete with the fortress in terms of excitement, but at least we might get a word in uninterrupted.

Monnie, are we? I wonder what she calls him. Mr Sandman? Her sandbag? Her sesquipedalian sausage?

It seemed to dawn on him then that I was in a bit of a state. He took my arm solicitously and steered me next door. When I realised where we were I turned to him in consternation.

'We can't go here,' I hissed. He looked baffled, but let me lead him back outside. I glanced over my shoulder. The other girl was behind the counter, the bovine one. No sign of Ellice. Sandy and I ended up in the old post office café, where they do special iced coffees, sitting outside in the shade on iron chairs.

After we'd both ordered the specials I said urgently, 'Sandy, listen. Tell me honestly, do you think it's all right for Kim to see Frank in the nude?'

He didn't reply immediately. Didn't seem to take it in.

'In the nude. In the altogether. Buck naked.' He's no fool, but sometimes Sandy takes forever to grasp an elementary concept.

He nodded with exasperating slowness. 'Yes, I know what you mean. Well, I —'

'Is it all right, or is it not all right, for a twelve-year-old girl to see her uncle naked?'

He ran a hand through his hair. Although it has been white for years, Sandy has never lost his thick hair and it's quite long at the moment, which suits him.

I was chafing at the bit. 'Is this how they behave in modern, with-it families, do you think? Or is it well and truly beyond the pale?'

'Thea, I think you'd better fill me in,' Sandy said. 'Can you tell me what's happened?'

I explained with as much brevity and calmness as I could muster. He listened intently. When I stopped he didn't reply straightaway. I was on tenterhooks, but I made myself wait.

At last he said, 'I believe some families do have an unusually relaxed attitude to nudity. Frank probably comes from one of those. And to things in general. It ties in with what you've said about him peeing in your garden.'

It wasn't my garden, but I put that aside. I relayed Frank's description of his stick-in-the-mud parents, now ensconced in a home for the prematurely senile. They didn't sound like naturists to me. What was much more likely, I said, was that he and Ellice had got in the habit of prancing about in the nude together and hadn't bothered to modify it when Kim arrived on the scene. Or Frank had not.

Then I remembered another thing. Ellice's trip to Melbourne. Come to think of it, Ellice wasn't working in the café. She may have left already.

'They're going to be alone in the house, Sandy. Together, the two of them. I think we should talk seriously to Frank about how to manage this.'

'We?' Sandy's brow was creased in deep furrows. He hadn't touched his drink and the vanilla ice-cream was melting.

'It has to be we, doesn't it? There's no one except us. Kim has no one else.' I turned this over in my mind, rapidly. 'No, I think you're right, it would be better coming from another man. An older man he respects. He's probably never had the benefit of a proper father figure. It would be much better coming from you, Sandy.'

'A father figure?' He took off his glasses.

'Because it's inappropriate behaviour. In front of a child. Surely you can see that, Sandy?'

He put his head in his hands. After a long silence, in which his fingers ploughed repeatedly into his hair until it was standing on end, he said he could not be entirely convinced that this was an appropriate matter for an outsider to interfere in. As far as he could make out, Frank had an ideal relationship with Kim. Very caring and affectionate.

I know you think that, I said. He put up a hand. 'Slow down, Thea. Let me finish.' He must have felt some emotional involvement, he's not usually as forthright.

'When you saw Frank just now he had been relaxing. Outside. On a hot day. In his own backyard.' Sandy held up one, two and then three fingers as he recited these points. Yes, I can count to three, I said. The hand came up again. This didn't mean Frank necessarily walked around the house naked in front of everyone. Sandy thought Frank's wife would have had a view on that.

He doesn't answer the door starkers, that's true enough, I said. But that's because he never bothers to lock it. Even when he's puffing pot and watching blue movies. Also, he knew Kim was about to return and he hadn't moved.

Well, perhaps it might be best, if I was seriously concerned about this, for me to have a quiet word with the wife? What was her name again?

Ellice, I replied wearily. And she had most likely already gone, as I said before. Sandy thought I meant Ellice had left Frank. He doesn't listen; tries to but doesn't. He's like most men in this respect.

I would have expected him to be more alarmed. To show more solicitude, more of a protective, paternal concern for Kim. Instead of which he seems more concerned to take the man's part. Frank's behaviour is increasingly inexcusable the more I think about it, but Sandy seems mainly interested in excusing it.

I went back to the café and forced myself to speak to the girl. To pre-empt her, I said I didn't want Ellice's phone number this time, I merely wished to confirm that she was on holidays. Was she rostered on tomorrow? I wasn't asking for classified information, I added. There was no risk of jihad, or not that I could discern.

The girl said, and I quote: 'She can't be on tomorrow.' Why not? 'Because she's away.'

As I seized the door handle she called out, 'Don't worry about it.'

'I beg your pardon?' I thought I must have misheard.

'It may never happen,' she said.

I must remember to ask Ellice when she comes back if the café has an altruistic policy of employing semi-retarded people. If so it is misguided, as nothing would persuade me to order anything from that girl, except her prompt dismissal.

~~

It's an unprecedented happening, but Sandy telephoned. At first I thought he had reconsidered, and was willing to speak to Frank. Not a bit of it. Monica – that was his priceless assistant, I knew Monica, didn't I? – had taken in a stray pup. He'd seen it. Dear little thing, a mutt with a lot of blue heeler input.

Why was he phoning to tell me this? Of course I know who *Monnie* is, I said. Priceless had two meanings. Which one did he have in mind? I hadn't noticed Monnie telling lots of uproarious jokes. Didn't recall seeing people convulsed on the floor of the shop. I must make a note to ask her to tell me a corker from her extensive repertoire.

Sandy can be hard to provoke. He did not respond to this. The thing was, he said stoically, Monica mentioned the stray dog again when she dropped by just now, and he remembered me telling him Kim wanted a puppy. Monica couldn't keep it herself; her husband refused to and they've already got two elderly poodles. The nervous small breed.

Monica said she was about to ring up the dog shelter. The words dog shelter triggered his memory and he suddenly thought of Kim. What about someone, the uncle or aunty, bringing her round to see it after school this arvo?

'The uncle or *aunty*? This very *arvo*? What's with this patois? You're coming over all colloquial in your dodderage,' I said. 'The aunty's away, as I already told you, so it would have to be the unsavoury uncle, or maybe just the dotty old crackpot, yours truly.'

I wasn't trying to hide the fact that I am aggrieved. I still feel strongly that Sandy has let me down. I feel a deep and pervasive anxiety about the whole situation *vis-à-vis* Frank.

Well, he was afraid it had to be this afternoon – Monica was adamant on that score. Her husband was making a fuss. 'Her husband is a little difficult at the best of times,' Sandy said.

'Difficult, is he?' I said. 'I wonder why that would be?' I've been giving Davy's theory about Sandy and Monica some thought. Davy's an inveterate gossip, but I think he may be right after all.

Sandy said he couldn't chat now, much as he'd like to, as there was someone delivering some books. Wasn't the pearl beyond price working today, then? I inquired. Not today, evidently. He gave me her address, in a tone of mild rebuke.

Two nervous elderly poodles? For 'old and nervous' read neurotic. That follows. It's no accident that people's dogs often take after them, as is frequently claimed.

•

No sign of the car. No sign of Frank either. The front door was locked, for once. If he has not turned up by the time Kim comes home I'll take her, if she likes. It has cooled down again, thank hypothetical heavens.

The prospect of visiting Harmonica Hostel is less than alluring, however. Would any puppy be indelibly tainted, I wonder? On the other hand, delivering it from a dismal existence chez the hapless Harmonica and her brace of hostile poodles could only be an act of philanthropy.

~~

I gave Kim my old Swiss Army knife. 'I don't have much use for it anymore,' I said, 'and I thought you might like it. It's always a good idea to have a penknife handy, living out in the bush.' She looked surprised, but pleased.

Frank had gone to the city for the day, Kim told me, taking his completed score to the director. Wasn't it awesome, him composing the music for an *entire movie*? She was tucking into cheese-and-tomato sandwiches. Two rounds, to be followed by a third of jam, and a glass of chocolate milk. I have a dim memory myself of being similarly ravenous after school.

She'd made a beeline for the kitchen and removed the sandwiches from a container in the fridge. Makes them herself every morning, she explained, so they're ready for later. Always way too starving to do it when she gets home. She had her own key on a key ring with several attachments, including a tiny wombat and the letter K.

The film must be a big opportunity for Frank, I agreed cautiously. Did she know what it was about?

A vigorous nod that tailed off. Second thoughts kicking in. She did a bit, yeah. It was kind of, um, funny. Kind of like an adult fairytale movie. She took a large bite of her sandwich and added, funny peculiar.

I was on the verge of asking a follow-up question, but decided to wait. I remember overhearing a conversation between two younger female staff members in which they said they always avoided discussing sex or anything touchy or tricky with their children until they were driving in the car. No one had to look at each other, they played music, and it was much more relaxed and less confrontational. They often elicited a surprising amount of sensitive information that way.

'Remember my advice about talking with your mouth full?' I said instead. 'Half-masticated food should be concealed considerately from the casual observer.'

An appreciative look, if satirical. 'Didn't realise it was advice. Thought it was an order.' She chewed the food at exaggerated speed and swallowed it in one go, with an effort. 'You better not say another word to me until I've finished *masticating,*' she said. 'Can I take the rest to eat in the car?' She'd been consumed with impatience since hearing about the abandoned puppy we were going to see.

Not *can* I take. *May* I take, I said. Crumbs and stale-food smells in cars are not a good combo, I said. I don't hold with picnics in the chariot.

She turned pleading eyes on me. 'D'you think you could hold with it for just this once? Make an exception? If I take a plastic bag and catch absolutely *every single* crumb?'

I relented, just for this once. Half the sandwiches had already been demolished, and the old chariot is not spick-and-span, not by a long chalk. I'd probably been thinking of my parents' car, which was scrubbed inside and out by my father before church every Sunday. You could have eaten crumbs off the floor without a qualm.

The Harmonica street turns out to be in a town about twenty minutes away. We don't have seriously rough districts up here, but there are postcodes with a predominance of transients, backpackers and rehab centres. I switched on the crackly car radio while Kim tore through the jam sandwich. I found what I thought might be acceptable to both of us, one of Bach's Brandenburg concertos. It was wholly serendipitous, but the Brandenburgs happened to be the first pieces of classical music I recall responding to as a child.

'That's kind of nice,' she said. I told her a little about it. Then I brought up the subject of Frank's movie, very casually. She'd seen it, I imagined?

Sort of, some of it. Well, not all the way through. She was looking away from me, out of the window.

'I haven't seen it all the way through either,' I said. 'Which bits have you seen, then?' I thought I had posed this in a negligent manner, but I was aware of a subtle shift in her attitude.

'Oh, just some fighting and stuff.'

I saw some of that too, I said. Did she happen to see the scene on the platform, up on the skyscraper? Rather remarkable, wasn't it?

This lured her into a burst of unguarded enthusiasm. Oh *yeah*, it was unbelievable, wasn't it? Beyond scary. Couldn't imagine how they'd filmed it. She thought Frank's music for that bit was really incredible as well. I wondered what she'd thought of the full-frontal nudity.

Did he show it to her with the music attached? Yes, he did, actually. He wanted to get her verdict. She thought the sounds of the triangle and the tambourine on top of the percussion added to the weirdness of the whole atmosphere. Like, it added a fourth dimension. How about the way the thumping beat kept time with the swaying of the platform? How clever was that?

I said I wasn't sure I'd seen it with the right music, although his music in general was hard to ignore. I particularly enjoyed the harp melody that accompanied one long section.

233

Had she seen that part, by any chance? The bonfire, wasn't it?

Oh *yeah*, the bonfire. The harp was so cool. She loved that beautiful, sort of sweet, lilting tune. It was sad, and somehow innocent.

Innocent was a good choice of word, I agreed. It was the fact that the tune was so different from what was going on in the scene that made it so effective, wasn't it? Energetic nods. That was called counterpoint, I said. You could hear the same principle going on in music. I pointed out a passage in the concerto now playing. She listened attentively. With a newfound appreciation, I think.

'So, what other bits of Frank's movie did you see?' I asked.

Not much else, she said, fiddling with her seatbelt. Can't remember, really. Just a chase or something. You know.

I refrained from flogging what was probably a dead horse. We were nearly on the Harmonica doorstep. I had obtained most of the information I wanted, although it was not what I wanted to hear.

Kim knew who Monica was: the nice woman who worked with Mr Fay, the pretty one with blonde, curly hair. I let this pass. The nice pretty woman turned out to live in one of those single-storey suburban houses made of liver-coloured brick. Didn't surprise me. I have never known a house or indeed any building constructed out of that material to have anything to recommend it. They are eyesores disfiguring towns and landscape, and specially incongruous out here. At least some attempt had been made to hide the ugliness by training roses and wisteria over the front of the house.

Kim told me she was taking deep, slow, relaxing breaths. As we drew up she said, 'Thea.'

'Yes?'

'I'm becoming weak with anticipation. At the knees. Might have to be carried out of the chariot. Supposing it doesn't –' She ground to a halt. I waited. 'Supposing it doesn't *like* me. Or supposing it was stolen from someone else. It might have to go back. Or –'

'It will like you because puppies always do. It's possible it was stolen but unlikely because it hasn't been reported missing. Let's not get ahead of ourselves,' I said.

There was, predictably, one of those awful fifties ding-dong door bells. The silence was short-lived, immediately supplanted by shrill and frenzied barking. La Harmonica materialised in an unflattering tracksuit, with a rabid poodle under each arm. Before putting them down she issued a warning: on no account should we try to interact with them or pay them any attention at all.

'They're besotted with me, you see, to the exclusion of anyone else, and I'm afraid Roxy *will* bite. She broke the skin on Sandy's shin once.' A winsome smile directed at me, to which I did not respond. 'They go into attack mode. They think they are protecting me against marauders.'

An unnecessary warning in my case, as I had not the slightest desire to interact with Sandy's nemesis, but Kim was challenged and enchanted. Before Monica or I could stop her she had bent down with hand outstretched. She shrieked and snatched it away from the snarling jaws in the nick of time, as one of the poodles launched into attack mode at breathtaking speed.

'See what I mean, Kim, dear?' was her owner's feeble response. 'If you ignore them they'll be fine. Roxy may not have any teeth left, but she can still inflict quite a painful injury. Rupert is a different kettle of fish. He's all bark and no bite.'

Kim had a fit of the giggles. The close encounter with Roxy's toothless jaws had disarmed her. Then her face fell a mile as we were taken into the lounge room and offered tea and scones set out on an old-fashioned trolley – dainty cups and saucers, doilies and all. She gave me an eloquent glance.

How kind, Monica, but we've already had afternoon tea, I said firmly. The room was crammed with photos of the Harmonica progeny of varying ages. She must have raised a menagerie, I said. Near enough – five, she said apologetically. Invariably, it is those who should reproduce themselves least who show no restraint. The most unpleasant children always had a tribe of equally dreadful siblings.

Harmonica said she would wheel out the puppy in a minute, as soon as she had shut the poodles safely in another room. They were very jealous of the poor baby. Not at all nice to it. She couldn't have all three in the same room or there'd be blood on the carpet – it was the main reason the baby had to go. I told her it was not at all surprising they were jealous. They felt marginalised by the newcomer. I wished Sandy had been there to hear this. Why should humans be any different from dogs, where a new baby is concerned?

The puppy had been found in the street. It wasn't the first time they had picked up a stray. 'We've had some problems round here with drunks and druggies and hoons,' Harmonica proclaimed, as if this was some kind of achievement. 'Probably unconnected, but dumping does go on.' Mainly unwanted dogs and kittens, but last year a lame pony was left in their neighbour's front yard and had to be put down.

Kim looked distressed. Fortunately this never happens in our area. We're too far off the beaten track. Thanks be to our fantasy father for my foresight in buying up all that cheap land, so many years ago.

It goes without saying that baby animals of all sorts are charming – with the sole exception of the human product, I've always thought, which is not charming and irritates with its demanding helplessness. One assumes this cannot be a widespread view or the species would have died out instead of being a virus on the face of the earth. But puppies are especially endearing, and this one was no exception. I knew Kim was hopelessly in thrall the moment she saw it rush into the room at the end of a cheap plastic lead.

It was a little larger than Teddy had been, and far more lively than he was when I first saw him. The characteristic blue heeler coat was dominant, but there was evidence of another mystery antecedent in the muzzle, body shape and longer than usual tail. It raced around to inspect each of us in turn, long tail wagging – like a windmill, Kim exclaimed, before scooping it up with an inarticulate cry of delight. A second later she was being licked all over.

La Harmonica was relatively sane, I'll give her that. Deterred Kim from going straight to the pet shop. Better wait a couple more days before buying anything except food, in case any claimants came forward. If any claimants were emboldened to come forward I would personally disembowel them, I vowed privately.

In the car on the way back Kim's mobile rang. She had to struggle to retrieve it while hanging on to the wriggling puppy on her lap. Teddy had been much calmer. He lay quietly on a towel on the passenger seat, I remember, all the way home. He was still shell-shocked after his ordeal.

The call was from Frank in the city. He was going to be late, I gathered from Kim's end of the quick-fire exchange. Then I revised this: he wouldn't make it back tonight. She'd be okay, wouldn't she? Kim's response involved me but was cut short.

She listened as he said something else and gave a muted 'really?' followed by an 'awesome'. On the scale I am now familiar with, and on which I can claim some expertise, the latter sounded somewhat perfunctory.

Then he rang off. 'He's in a *movie* meeting,' she said, 'so I couldn't tell him. It'll have to be a surprise.' She cuddled the small bundle and made soft cooing noises.

'What else did he say?'

She was evasive. Nothing much. Just some guys who might be coming up at the weekend.

Anyone she knew?

Not really. Well, she knew them a bit.

I let an estimated thirty seconds pass. So, who were they then, I inquired, in as uninterested a way as I could manage.

Oh, only a couple of Frank's friends. She shrugged dismissively and kissed the puppy's head. Nothing mattered in comparison to this, she seemed to be implying.

Male guys, I supposed. From the movie. I said this with studied neutrality. I always have to remind myself that 'guys' includes women as well. My instincts were on high alert.

Uh huh.

The director? I guessed Frank would have things to discuss with him, I said brightly. Kim nodded. With reluctance, I thought.

And what about that other one, the leading actor. The very good-looking one. Marlon, wasn't it?

Another shrug. Maybe him too, she wasn't sure.

My instincts were right. Marek and Marlon. But probably only for one night, she said.

The next few hours were a bit of a blur. I'd not forgotten the delights of a small puppy, but had some memory loss in other areas: the desire to chew everything in sight, the need for regular feeding, the toilet-training rituals. Kim's instinctive competence in all these areas was impressive. She was quite sure it was half trained already.

I went to the bathroom library and dug out several useful books on training and caring for puppies. They were appropriately dog-eared, as Kim observed. It came flooding back to me, how ignorant I'd been. Not only that but consumed with anxiety about my lack of experience. My attitude was the complete opposite of Kim's, when I think about it. It crossed my mind, suddenly, that she would probably be a good mother. What's more, that she would enjoy being one.

Teddy's attitude was easy to read. He was tolerant of this small, high-energy power house that cavorted around his legs like a clockwork toy and charged back and forth at him in mock aggression. But where he was mildly diverted, it found him irresistible. When its attentions became too much for him he emitted a deep warning growl and flopped down on the floor near my feet.

With provisions sourced from both houses, we cobbled together a surprisingly good dinner. Spaghetti with a sauce of tinned tuna and tomatoes, grated cheese on top, and salad. Kim urged me to finish an opened bottle of white wine in their fridge. I saw she was expecting some so I poured her a glass. It's probably wise for children to be introduced to sensible drinking habits early on. The French and Italians have always done this, and their drinking cultures are more civilised than ours. And far more so than the British. Afterwards we stacked the dishwasher I'd taken such anticipatory pleasure in choosing. I'll never have one now.

I stayed the night in the house. She resisted – she'd be perfectly fine – but I was adamant. When she was a teenager it would be perfectly fine, I said, and when her dog was trained and a bit older. Anyway, it was the law that anyone under thirteen should not be left alone. I was not a hundred per cent certain I was right about this, but I stated it with authority. I think Kim was relieved by my insistence, although she tried to hide it.

We stripped off my sheets and brought them over. She suggested I sleep in her bed while she bunked down on the day bed in Frank's music room. There was no need for that, I said at once. The obvious place was their bedroom.

She took a step back. 'But I've got a really comfy bed.'

'No. I'd prefer that room.'

'Yeah? It's a train wreck, but. You *sure* you want to go in there?' About to bite her thumbnail, she snatched her hand away.

'Why do you say that?' I queried, although the subtext was crystal clear.

'Well, you know. Because it's, like – it would've been your bedroom.'

'That's why I want to sleep in there.'

She digested this idea. 'Yeah, I can sort of understand that. I can. Definitely. But –' A pause. 'Do you think you ought to?'

Well, that was a question I was not prepared to deconstruct. 'Just this once,' I said.

'Wouldn't it be very *hard*?'

'It would. But not too hard.'

'But wouldn't it be, like, a different place? Not yours? With another, you know, atmosphere, kind of written all over it?'

An occupying presence polluting the atmosphere, I thought. It would be a distortion of my original, yes. But I found I had a compulsion to do it all the same.

A train wreck was to the point. Male clothing was scattered all over the floor. I saw jeans, T-shirts and underwear. Papers, a couple of used ashtrays, a vase of dead flowers, several DVDs. Kim surveyed it all with distaste. It's clear she finds squalor disturbing; I've caught myself reviewing my own habits a little in response. Fortunately puppy detritus seems to bother her not a whit.

She started kicking the clothes to one side. I stopped her.

'It's best if we leave it as it is.' I sensed a touch of constraint between us, then thought I was imagining it.

The puppy came hurtling in and made a beeline for the undershorts. Kim prized first one pair and then another from its jaws and draped them over the bedstead, alongside two grimy towels already flung there. It was an enormous iron bed, raised high off the ground. King size – that's the biggest bed you can get, she muttered. An odd remark, I thought.

We made it up by putting my sheets over theirs. Mine were far too small to tuck in, and the bed was far too high for Teddy. We had to put his blanket on the floor, over one of the large lounge room cushions.

Kim wrinkled her nose. 'The bathroom's in a dire state, too. I could clean the bath, if you like.'

'It doesn't matter.' I wondered how she knew this. Must have wandered in, I suppose, after Frank left this morning. I remembered how I'd told Frank that children are constitutionally inquisitive. How I'd insisted on it.

Teddy and I were ready to hit the hay, I said. The puppy had done us in.

'She's done me in too. Totally.' Kim lifted her up tenderly and yawned, rotating her shoulders. 'I know what I'd really like right now.' Still holding the squirming puppy, she lifted her arms above her head in a prolonged stretch. 'One of Frank's massages, that's what I'd really like. A good back rub. Wouldn't you, Thea?'

I shouldn't have been so jolted, I suppose, but I was. And shaken. Do you have them often, I wondered. An impossible question, like a chat-up line from a bad comedy. Frank had told her about my liking for them, that was clear too. I found this disquieting also, in some way that was not so obvious.

'I could give you a shoulder massage,' she offered. 'Wouldn't be as good as his, no way. Might be better than nothing, though. Then you could follow it up with a relaxing bath.'

I shook my head. Thanks but no.

She gave me a prolonged, probing look. Was I totally sure I'd be all right in there? Totally, I said, with more confidence than I felt. Did I need a box to get up on the bed, she worried? I shooed her away and closed the bedroom door on the puppy. From the passage she called out, 'I'll've thought of a good name for her by morning.'

~~

I felt as if I hadn't slept. Fuzzy-headed and faintly nauseous. Kim by contrast was full of beans, spilling over with energy and joie de vivre. The puppy had slept like an angel in a cardboard carton on the end of her bed. Peed last thing at night and again first thing when Kim took her outside, having set the alarm for five-thirty. She was going to be a dream to train, like Teddy had been, she could tell.

And she had thought of a name for her: Andie. A girl Andie, spelt with an 'ie' at the end. What did I think? Didn't it suit her, like, amazingly well? It was lively, kind of *effervescent*, like her nature. Tomboyish. It went well with Teddy too, didn't it? Teddy and Andie. She was sure they would be friends.

Teddy did in fact show a little more interest in Andie this morning, sniffing her as she frolicked around him. He even gave her a lick or two. But his patience with her antics was short-lived, and he kept her under control with cautionary, rumbling growls that were alarming and very effective. I had the impression he rather enjoyed this.

Kim, eating muesli, striving not to talk at the same time and more or less managing, said she wished it was the weekend. She hated having to leave Andie for a whole entire day after just getting her. I watched as it dawned on her what day it actually was. Her body slumped. The spoon dropped from chest height, clattering into the bowl.

'Thea.' Her face was a study in consternation.

'It's quite all right,' I said. 'Don't even think about it.' I'd planned to take her to the new Thai restaurant, but had already ditched that plan.

'You're *certain*? Totally?'

'Do you really think I would have gone out gallivanting and left Teddy so soon?'

She flashed me a look of fervent relief. 'I couldn't have kept my mind on gallivanting,' she said. 'Even on Oscar talking about writing, which is pretty amazing when you think about it. When it's my deepest and most serious interest.'

'Of course you couldn't.'

She scraped up the last of the muesli. Then she said soberly, 'I suppose, you know, it's the difference between your feelings for a living thing with its own personality, and something that's an imanin – an inaminate –'

'In*an*imate.'

'An in*an*imate object. You think you're completely taken up with something, like it could be your life's obsession, your number one. But when you put it up against something that you also care deeply about that is alive, like for instance this darling little creature –' She swooped on Andie. 'You just don't hesitate. The *in*animate thing is demoted to number two. No contest, right?'

No contest. Then I said, 'By the way, I've been thinking.'

'No. For a change?' she said.

'Would you like to come on a picnic tomorrow? I thought we might take the two dogs on a little excursion. A bushwalk.'

A picnic? A bushwalk? *Awesome*. High on the enthusiasm scale, I was pleased to see. 'Where?' she asked.

'Oh, I have somewhere in mind.' Her eyes flickered.

'I think Teddy is up to it. He can help keep Andie under control.' She nodded, dark head bobbing like one of those fairground clowns.

'Because, you see, I have something I've been wanting to show you,' I said. I watched her face. 'Something very important.'

It was not an impulse suggestion. It is time for it. High time.

We took Andie to the hovel with us after Kim went off to school. It seemed like a good idea, as Kim said, that she get used to homes in both houses. An anxious, interrogatory glance as she said this. Was I really, *utterly* sure I didn't mind? I don't mind at all, I said. Teddy could be in charge, it would do him good to have some responsibility. Kim added that she was deliberately not thinking about the possibility that anyone might call and claim Andie. If she stopped to think about that she would have a terminal collapse.

It was a temperate day, I think we've had the last gasp of summer, and my secure little garden makes puppy-minding easy enough. Belated thanks to the previous owner in the sky, a finicky old biddy who put in wire fencing on three sides and a picket fence in front. The dump was more of a cottage then, with a well-maintained vegetable garden; that and everything else has decomposed under my watch. I didn't touch the fence, although I always thought it was pointless out here, and Teddy was never a dog to wander off. Now it has a use. All puppies are not like Teddy.

Besides, who could say when Frank would show up – if ever? He hadn't even rung to check on her this morning, I noted.

After she'd covered Andie with kisses and ridden off, helmeted, wobbling as she waved, I had a shower. My decrepit old bathroom had never looked so inviting.

I'd been far too tired last night, as well as deterred. Their en suite, spotless when I'd last set eyes on it, when in another life I had watched it come into being, was in as dire a state as Kim suggested. Dirty ring around the bath. Frank's dirt, this would be. Toothpaste trails in the basin. The lavatory hadn't been flushed, and the seat was up. That follows – a gentleman always puts the seat down, we were taught.

Is this how all young men behave when their wives are away, or is Frank an unusually slovenly example? Slovenly and decadent, both physically and mentally. This belief has been growing on me for some time, but it is now more than a belief. It is a conviction. I now know I am right.

Last night I employed the dressing-table chair to climb up on the bed. I lay there, sleepless, as Teddy snored away on the floor. There were no blinds or curtains to keep out the moonlight. Or to keep anyone from peering into the room through the wide windows. But they would have to walk along the north side of the house, the side facing the dense, unpopulated bush. I'd deliberately given the two bedrooms a northerly aspect, for two reasons. They would be cool in summer and invisible from across the access road. Long years in the hovel made me do that. The years without end, amen.

I recalled the day I went into the house just before Kim, Frank and Ellice moved in, wanting to experience it as mine for the last time. I'd had a feeling of bereavement then, almost as if the house was repudiating me. This time, although I was lying in darkness in Frank and Ellice's bed, I felt none of that. The house seemed to welcome me back, even to embrace me. And yet I was restless.

Things come to you, lying in bed at night. Especially lying wide awake in an unfamiliar bed. It's a long time since I've spent a night away from the dump, more than a decade.

I reviewed the situation, the sequence of events that had brought me to this singular point. I'd never occupied a bed that was anything like this size – I seemed to be swimming in it. There was a TV attached to the opposite wall. It had a built-in DVD player, but I had no desire to watch moving pictures.

The downy mattress was unusually seductive, softer than mine, but not soft enough to subdue my unease. If anything, the comfort contributed to my pervasive misgivings about one member of the duo whose bed I was appropriating. Young and vigorous, both of them. Highly sexed, in Frank's case, and doubtless in Ellice's too.

Had the baby been conceived here? No, from what Frank said it predated their arrival. I think, in a way I do not care to analyse, this came as a relief. My house was not a catalyst for that, in any way. Let not my heart be troubled more than it is troubled already, O long-forsaken lord.

I got up at two am, carefully lowering my legs onto the seat of the chair. A sturdy one, fortunately. I had put in a door to connect the bedroom with what would have been my study. And why, I wonder, did I do that? Did I envisage inspiration striking like lightning in the dead of night? Eureka moments in which I got out of bed and rushed to the computer? Unlikely, surely. I was always a sound sleeper, like Teddy.

Now, of course, my study is Frank's music room. I ventured in. It was as dark as pitch with all the heavy blinds pulled, but I remembered the location of the light switches. Lingering over everything was a subtle odour, sour and stale. I had no trouble identifying the ingredients: tobacco, beer, dope and spirituous liquor. Unless steps are taken this will be a fixture. It will pollute the room with the contagion of Frank himself.

I surveyed the clutter, the mind-blowing bank of electronic gadgetry. The toolbox was behind the computer screen, my padlock dutifully attached. I had no difficulty calling to mind his ridiculous code: two, four, six, eight. In all probability he had never used it because there was nothing inside. I guessed he'd taken all the discs with him.

Not a bit of it. I located several in minutes. He had made not the slightest attempt to conceal them from anyone. They were scattered around the work area, and two more on the day bed, easily identified with scene names in thick black letters and the title of the movie in heavy capitals: VERMINVILLE. Copies, I assumed. It was tempting to try to put one on, but I feared the technology would defeat me. Or worse, the puppy might bark and alert Kim. I stacked them in the toolbox and punched in the code.

I was on the point of leaving when something, some atavistic lesson dredged from past experiences, prompted me to lift the foam mattress on the day bed. Underneath, pushed to the back, were three magazines. I am not an expert but there was no need to open them. The covers were informative enough.

I say I am no expert and it is years since I have confiscated such things, but some fairly sickening material passed through my hands. A high percentage of teenage boys went through a stage of looking at hardcore porn. Yet another effing bloody boy thing, the teachers used to say, and not always confined to the most effing bloody boys either. I understand they watch pornography on the internet nowadays, more commonly, because it leaves no incriminating paper trail. Frank would do this too and in that room at night, I have not the shadow of a doubt. Or in the daytime, without locking his door.

I appropriated the magazines. Then I reopened the toolbox and retrieved two discs, the ones that had been on the bed. I locked it up again, only this time, to cock a snoot at Frank, I changed the combination. The four numbers I chose are significant only to me: the year after I left teaching for good. The year after my disgrace. A thumb on the nose to you, Frank, should you ever try to undo the padlock.

The two discs were marked, indelibly, MISTER WOLF, 1/2. Seeing the two words had triggered a memory, caused me to recall something Kim said yesterday about the film. It struck me as curious at the time, but I had not remarked on it. She said it was like an adult fairytale movie. Or, well – kind of like that.

I rolled up the magazines and put them and the two discs into the canvas tote bag I'd brought over for the night. In the hovel this morning, having confirmed their contents, I tore the magazines to shreds and shoved them well down in the rubbish. They weren't the worst I'd seen, but they were bad enough. A passing adolescent phase is forgivable at a pinch, but grown men who use porn are beneath contempt.

The discs are safe for the moment. They remain zipped up inside the old tote bag under my bed. I cannot bring myself to examine them. Nor am I altogether sure I can operate the DVD machine. The one, ironically, that Frank gave me.

Did I get any sleep at all? It didn't feel like it, although my mind is uncommonly active. Seething, almost. Writing group tonight, and I have as yet done no preparation. The last meeting of the semester, term, whatever you want to call it. Once a week, one-third of a year of our lives gone. No one has been game to ask Oscar if he is prepared to continue.

He has talked about going overseas, waxing lyrical over the beneficial vibes of a change of scene. But he has also talked about the vital necessity of routine in a writer's life. Is he advocating schizophrenia? Would he favour a life at odds with itself? I must remember to ask him.

Most successful writers lead boring lives, he says. That is, on the outside. In their heads it's a different story. I would go along with this, although I could wish for less of the different story.

For the moment, however, I shall take a power nap and then sit down at the computer.

~~

Mindful of Oscar's remarks about a talisman, I hunt around the place for something that might inspire me. There are no photos in the dump, something that people have found odd. I did have one of myself with Matthew, taken by my star student after he begun tutoring her, but I burnt it.

There are two of Kim's drawings on the mantelpiece, both looking a bit dog-eared. I've been meaning to put them between perspex sheets. I take the second one, the thank-you drawing for her official birthday present. She and Teddy, round-eyed, reading the two books I gave her. I stand it between the salt and pepper shakers and place it in front of me on the little wicker table on the verandah.

I've never done this kind of thing before. It feels like a new departure, and slightly peculiar. Like all new things, it will take a bit of getting used to.

Polish the pieces you are best pleased with, Oscar had suggested. Don't feel you have to produce anything new to knock my socks off. So I look over the account I wrote of the way Teddy and I discovered the precipice. My report: promising effort, room for improvement. I'd been pleased with it originally. Complacent, verging on smug. Now I see the flaws. Over-writing, clumsy transitions. There are only three ways of improving one's work, Oscar says, and they are all foolproof: rewrite, rewrite, rewrite. He enjoys grouping things in threes, it's one of his little quirks.

It is always interesting to reread one's past work. Sometimes it stands up, sometimes you can't fathom what you saw in it. Just like people. You can start off liking and end up despising. No need to look very far to ascertain the truth of that, just look at the divorce statistics. Just look at Mr Matthew Rhode. And at Mr Frank Campbell.

Matthew got on well with people to begin with. He was like Frank in that respect. The fact that he was also so unassuming was an effective smokescreen. It allowed him certain privileged practices. It allowed him to tutor individual girls in his private apartment.

It allowed him? What am I saying? *I* allowed him. He was my favourite. I encouraged him. It was my decisions, unbeknown to me, that enabled Matthew to refine his ideas of tutoring.

His coaching sessions transformed very slowly, over an extended period, we discovered afterwards. They evolved over several semesters and began with imperceptible changes. Nothing untoward, just a few minutes overtime at first. He and his pupil were so absorbed in discussions they lost track of the time. Gradually the sessions extended. Music was introduced, sophisticated Berlin cabaret songs from the 1930s, flattering to the impressionable mind. Later, sitting on the sofa, they began to watch films. Cosmopolitan foreign movies with subtitles. Wine was brought out, and later still, dope.

Afterwards the police found a cache of cocaine in his flat. Wrapped in plastic in the lavatory cistern. The traditional hiding place of such things, they said.

It was Matthew's charismatic teaching style rather than his appearance that made him popular with the girls. My star pupil was thrilled to be the first of those selected for advanced tuition. In addition to being intellectually brilliant, she was blessed with good looks. She was an exceptionally attractive girl. Rather beautiful.

Why did I not mention that before? Why was I not alert to it?

I took Kim's drawing of herself and Teddy and put it over the computer screen. The words I had just made myself write were successfully concealed. I took a moment to collect myself. Then I replaced the drawing on the table and began a new page.

The mild weather was conducive to writing. So was the company: I worked on the verandah all afternoon with Teddy and Andie. Little Andie is already toning down her exuberance with Teddy, of her own volition, I told Kim. She realises she can provoke him so far and no further. And she knows her name already. I think she is going to turn out to be unusually intelligent and responsive. On hearing this, Kim glowed like the parent of a clever pupil.

Frank hadn't returned, and did not show up until just before I was due to leave for the class. Someone was pleased to see his car. Kim had been bursting to show off the new arrival. I watched her race out to greet him with Andie pulling on the lead. I was using the binoculars. I'd located them after a short search; they were under some books in the kitchen.

Frank was alone. I am unsure whether this is cause for relief or the opposite. My mind is ringed by a minefield and I hardly know where to tread. There was no sign of Marek or Marlon. I watched Frank hoist the puppy in the air.

I made a Spanish omelette for myself. Cancelled the early booking at the Thai restaurant. Much better for the two of us to go out in a week or two, when Kim has settled down with Andie, always assuming she can keep her. The alternative doesn't bear thinking about. We should pay a visit to the vet next week. There will be puppy business – registration, vaccinations and desexing – to schedule. Although she may not want Andie to be desexed. She may decide she would like her to have one litter. I wonder – Teddy was never desexed because there were never any dogs in the vicinity.

When she is older, and being of mixed race, Kim is going to look exotic. In certain lights I can see this already. As I drove off the girl and her dog were frolicking together on the deck, burnished by the fading, early evening sun. It was a timeless picture of a childhood idyll. I am holding fast to this in my mind, as if to safeguard it against the encroaching dark.

I have heard it said that once one has a child, one is never truly at ease unless that child is safely asleep upstairs. I assumed this was hyperbole. I realise now that I hadn't an inkling of what was meant.

~~

The class had an end-of-term feel. Normally I might have quite enjoyed it. At the end of the session Greg slipped outside and Gilda-lily, flushed with self-importance, made an announcement. We were all to stay put, because we were going to *party*, double exclamation marks!! I quelled the impulse to leave. It might take my mind off things, briefly.

Greg returned carrying an esky. The group mood, already frothy, nearly frothed over at the sight of mixed nuts, stuffed olives and two bottles of prosecco. Gilda and Greg had apparently hatched this little plan in tandem, and were mightily pleased with themselves.

The wind was taken out their sails somewhat when Oscar unveiled a bottle of Veuve Clicquot from a cooler bag, along with proper champagne flutes. A birthday bottle from his mama, he said. He hadn't felt like drinking it all up in solitary confinement. Which must mean that his little amour has fallen through. I think we were all disappointed for him, although it had been a not inconsiderable stretch to see Oscar in a relationship of any kind.

He is going on a writing retreat to Laos courtesy of our kind financial contributions, he announced, leaving next week for two months. Solo, not with other writers; he'll be staying in a crumbling old guesthouse in Vientiane on the banks of the Mekong – nearly falling into it, from the photograph. Very romantic, less than twenty-five dollars a night for a room with balcony and river view.

We were all envious. Sounds like my hovel minus romance and river, I said. What was he going to write? A new book, he said, and it was going to be all about us. Only very thinly disguised. Hair colour and a few sex changes to protect the guilty.

'But you don't know anything about us,' Gilda-lily protested.

Oh yes he did – we would be surprised what pickings he had gleaned. This, he disclosed, had been his ulterior motive all along. Not only an ingenious method of coping with writer's block but a cash cow and a rich supply of source material to boot. By then we were well into the second bottle and there was a minor eruption. No one knew quite what to make of it. It was immoral, Greg chose to declare, and illegal.

'But you will come back in two months' time for more of the same?' Oscar inquired, all serene. This came as a relief all round. No one wanted the classes to end. He asked me about Kim. Might she enrol for the winter term? I am putting her name down right now, I said.

Was there a grain of truth in Oscar's story? Had the rapacious Gilda-lily succeeded in getting her claws into Greg?

These questions, worthy of the celebrity (sic) rags, were in the forefront of our collective mind for the duration of the party. I speculated with the worst of them; I am sinking to new depths. Another pertinent question was the amount we had all drunk. Three bottles divided by seven? No, by five, because Mary and Margaret, predictably, were abstainers. Lucky there were no police on the road. Could I have relied on Frank to bail me out if I was thrown in the clink for the night?

A medicinal dose of champagne is supposed to drown out your worries. Instead I found the opposite: the tempo of mine increased as the evening wore on. I thought I was doing a good job of concealing my agitation but both wowsers, Margaret and Mary, came and asked me separately if I was feeling all right or if I needed a lie-down. The other boozers, Greg, Joy, Gilda and Oscar, noticed nothing amiss.

By the time things were winding down I'd made a decision. Plainly it is no use trying to talk to Sandy anymore – he thinks I am making mountains out of molehills. And Davy would be worse than useless. I felt it was essential to seek a second objective opinion. I contrived to snatch a moment to ask Oscar if I might consult him on an intimate personal matter.

He was very jovial, which did not bode well. 'Consult me, Thea? On an intimate personal matter? I'm not sure this lies within my limited area of expertise.'

I badly needed a man's advice, I told him, and he was a man.

I had to wait for the others to take their interminable time departing. They weren't amenable to polite pressure; it was tempting to resort to brute force, I said to Oscar. Gilda-lily and Greg, the last to leave, urged us to party on in the pub. They waltzed out singing the Marseillaise. Arm in arm.

Eventually they clattered down the stairs and we were alone. I moved my chair opposite Oscar so I could make eye contact and command his attention. I began to summarise the situation. It wasn't an easy matter, the magnitude was too great. To protect Kim I took the utmost care to name no names and disguise anything identifiable.

But I soon saw it was a lost cause. Like Sandy, but in a different way, he was incapable of discerning the gravity of the problem. He thought I was discussing bad behaviour. He could not see that I was identifying a threat. He could not see the subtext.

'*Men*,' he said. 'They're a different species, Thea. I hear exactly what you're saying about their deplorable habits and aggravation. I find I'm on the outer myself, and I *am* one, as you so perspicaciously point out. Nominally, at least.' He patted my knee. I was reminded, and it outraged me further, of Frank.

'You are not hearing what I'm saying at all. You're hearing nothing, Oscar.' Consumed with impatience I went to stand, then realised I was already out of my chair and was pacing the floor. 'You have no conception how duplicitous some men can be. How unscrupulous.'

'Oh, but I think I do,' he said with benign reproof. 'You should try chastising him about his depravity, not me, Thea. I'm sure that will make him pull his horns in.'

I left soon afterwards, marching ahead of him. 'Take it easy down those stairs and drive very carefully now,' he called.

Decent men do not understand what other men are capable of. Bewildering for a novelist such as Oscar to be so lacking in imagination. He says he is a satirical novelist; perhaps this explains it.

I was musing along these lines when I passed their house and pulled up outside the dump. It was quite late. Through the south wall of glass windows I could see Kim and Frank seated in close proximity on the modular sofa. They were watching something on the big TV. From the verandah I was surprised how clearly I could see them through the gaps in the trees. I was using the binoculars. I am no longer concerned about peeping Tomism. Sometimes there are valid reasons.

I went to write up the journal. They were still sitting there by the time I was ready for bed. Must have been a long film they were watching. I couldn't make out what kind. I suppose Kim is allowed to stay up later on Fridays and Saturdays, although the words 'Frank' and 'rules of any sort' would be mutually exclusive. I saw him get up and go into the bathroom, the one that connects with Kim's bedroom. Why wasn't he peeing outside on the lemon tree?

Next time I looked, the lights had gone out on that side and everything was in darkness.

And then – I am not sure how to say this – I had an urge, my madwoman in the attic moment, Oscar would have said, to walk over there in the dark. I toyed seriously with the idea of circling the perimeter of the house to the far side, where the two bedrooms look out on to the empty bush. The urge was very nearly irresistible.

How long before reality, as they say, kicked in? Because I have talked myself out of it. Even in this extremity, I cannot quite come at it. The whole sordid business of snooping and spying, the possibility of the puppy barking. There is the contributing factor of the champagne. Oscar thought I was affected, that was clear.

Not least, there is Sandy's certain conviction that I am becoming paranoid.

~~

I would not ask her if she had ever returned, I decided. Some things are best left alone.

I put a torch into the rucksack, along with water and a thermos of tea. Then I started on the sandwiches. Cheddar with avocado, lettuce and mayonnaise. Teddy knew something was in the offing. He kept getting up and walking from the kitchen to the verandah and back again.

When he barked I looked through the open door. A car had pulled up opposite and two tall young men were getting out. The *guys* who were coming for the night, the director and the actor. Marek and Marlon. I watched long enough to see Frank come out to greet them. Kim was not with him. Then I went back to the kitchen, wrapped up the sandwiches and added apples and two wedges of chocolate mud cake from the deli.

When Kim ran up the steps with Andie not long afterwards, I was startled. I'd been in a cocoon of abstraction.

'I'm ready,' she said breathlessly. 'Can we go? I mean, *may* we go?'

I felt the malaise lift. 'Shall we go, in this case. It sounds more natural, I think.'

I looked closely at her for any signs of reluctance as Andie jumped all over me. I found none, only a bubbling excitement she wasn't bothering to hide.

'I brought my army knife,' she said, brandishing it. 'Might come in handy to repel wild beasts.'

'The guys arrived, did they?' I enquired lightly.

'Yup, they did.' Non-committal. The presence of three young men in the house seemed to be neither here nor there.

She took the rucksack, full of admiration for my organisation. It was amazing I had such a knack of picnics, she'd thought she was going to have to do it all, not that she'd've minded. I was relieved to find I hadn't lost the knack of them, I said. It had been a while.

It was no surprise to me that she was fully alive to the significance of this expedition. When we plunged into the dense bush behind the hovel I saw she knew immediately where we were going. I felt she had anticipated it.

Teddy led the way, walking fairly freely today without stiffness. He knows this route backwards because it remains a central part of our lives. We were in single file, the puppy on the lead for safety, although I now think Andie will be like Teddy; she shows no inclination to run off. She is extremely playful but she seems to want to follow Teddy's example in everything, which is most encouraging.

Kim and I said almost nothing on the way. Now and then I glanced round. When we reached the rock after a half hour of brisk trekking we stopped. It is still a marvel to come upon it, even after all these years.

She said, 'It's so suddenly there. It kind of makes the hairs on your neck stand up in wonderment, doesn't it? And yet it makes you smile at the same time.'

We contemplated it. It did bring on a smile. I wondered if I had reacted to it that way on other occasions, unknowingly.

'This is Andie's first real walk. I'm so stoked to bring her here.' She lifted Andie in the air. 'It's a very special thing for both of us, Thea.'

She put the puppy's nose up against the surface. 'Andie, you must sniff this.' She held Andie there, enthralled by the smooth, golden sandstone. Very focused, living in the moment. Following Oscar's instruction.

I stood back. The girl and puppy were immobile in front of me, engraved on the air like a hologram. Then she put Andie down and turned a meditative gaze on me.

'I've reached a conclusion. This is my favourite place in the world.'

'I thought it might be,' I said. 'It's one of mine, too.'

'Not that I've seen much of the world,' she went on, 'but when I have seen more, I can imagine thinking about this from far away. And then coming back again and again, like a homing pigeon, and knowing it's still my number one.' It was the longest speech I've heard her give without the unnecessary use of like, or you know.

And I can imagine her in years to come, returning to these magic places from far away, like a homing pigeon. Though in all likelihood I shall not be here. Except perhaps in spirit.

I said, 'There is something hidden in this rock. It is just possible that no one else in the world knows it exists.'

She stared, open-mouthed. I motioned her and Andie forward.

In an expectant silence we climbed what I think of as the foothills. A moderate climb, not too steep, even for Andie's short legs. We dodged the scribbly gum, with a nod to each other, and ascended a little further. Then Teddy veered round a hairpin bend and a slope of indented rock into the shallow channel that was once a cascading watercourse. We followed it towards the source as it wound its way up towards a wider, scooped-out area.

'There is a little cave just behind here,' I said. 'Give me the lead and put down the rucksack so you can go inside.' I took out the torch.

Teddy had already gone in and Andie was tugging at the leash. Kim could hardly contain herself. In the bleaching sunlight, her eyes shone like dark moons.

'You have to crawl in on your stomach,' I said. 'Then when you're inside you can stand up and look round. Shine the torch on the walls and tell me what you see.' In the blink of my pale eye she had vanished.

She was much younger and more observant than I had been. She spotted all three marks at once. I had wondered if she might be blasé, if they might seem trivial, but when she emerged she seemed lost for words. They weren't – were they – not – *cave paintings*? I told her my theory of the left-handed female artist.

259

She accepted this without hesitation. Of course it was a woman. Definitely. She'd never have made such a small print with her left hand otherwise. It was like, her sign. It was her signature, right?

Just how I had thought of it.

'I laid my hand against it,' she said. 'It was pretty much the same size.' The hand and the wallaby were obvious. But what was the third painting, the one with the squiggly lines inside the kind of picture frame?

I had to admit I had never managed to get to the bottom of this conundrum. It was like a TV, I'd thought when I first saw it. An old-style television with wavy lines of electrical interference across the screen. 'A bit like mine,' I said.

She found that amusing. Well, she was going to solve the mystery. 'I'm determined. To get to the bottom of it. If it's the last thing I do.'

If anyone could, she would, I said. There was a pause. I saw her retreat abruptly into an interior mood – into what used to be called a brown study.

After an interval she said, 'Thea.'

'Yes?'

'Are you really, really the only person in the entire world who *knows*? What am I saying? – I mean, are *we*, now, the only ones? You and –' a marked hesitation. 'You and *I*?'

'You and I is the correct form, yes. And yes, I think the likelihood is that we are the only human beings who know about the existence of these particular paintings.'

I have passed on the knowledge, I thought. And eventually you will be the custodian.

She breathed out slowly. 'You mean, you haven't actually shown them to anyone else? Before?'

'No. Because before there wasn't anyone else I wanted to show them to,' I said.

She said nothing. We found a flat area of rock and spread

out the picnic. I watched her thinking intensely about this. The profound seriousness of it, the responsibility.

Finally she said, 'This is beyond awesome, Thea. I shouldn't have touched the handprint, right? It might infect it.'

I had done the very same thing when I first saw it, I said. I explained how I had come to think of the cave as a tiny museum and myself as the sole curator.

'The guardian,' she said.

'And if, as guardian, you come to think that something should be done about it, you will be able to do as you think fit. With no interference from me.'

She turned sombre eyes on my face. 'If I come to –'

'In the fullness of time,' I said.

We enjoyed the picnic greatly, in a mood of gentle contemplation. I had thought to bring along some dried meaty chews for the dogs. Teddy would be no problem, but where exposed food was concerned a puppy was another matter. I also carried my water dispenser for dogs, a nifty plastic gadget clipped to my belt.

You make the best sandwiches, I was told. Not a sentence I'd expected I would ever hear. I unwrapped the two slices of cake. They were warm and squashed, but it didn't affect the taste.

'Thea?'

'Yes?'

She took a small, pensive bite. I had an intuition about what was coming next.

'This cake is the best.' A short pause. 'You don't believe in God, do you?'

I had anticipated this question, some time ago, and given it careful consideration. No getting round it, I'd concluded. No honest way of sugaring the pill.

'No, I don't.'

'Not of any, you know, kind? Like Zeus or Athena? Or Jesus, or Mohammed, or Krishna, or Allah or, um, any weirdos like that?'

'Not of any kind. Although, of the various competing candidates, the holy ghost has a spooky appeal.'

A grin. 'Not even my fat smiley Buddha? Not that any of the candidates are any weirder than the others, right?'

'All religions are as weird as each other, yes.'

She looked towards the cave. 'How about the spirit of the rainbow serpent? That's a bit different. Like, way more cool for a start. And colourful.'

'Not even the rainbow serpent. It's part of an appealing explanation of things, though.' It was part of a web of storytelling that was more enthralling to me than the mythology of ancient Greece or Rome, I said.

'But did you ever believe in anything?' she asked. 'In any supreme sort of being? Something that would, you know, explain things?'

Until I was a little older than you I did, I said. Probably because I'd been forced to go to church as a child. Then I had an epiphany, of a non-religious variety. There was no supreme being in the room, I concluded. No indication of one, not a smidgin of proof. Not even a handprint in a cave. A somewhat reluctant conclusion, but there it is.

'However, don't pay any attention to what I think. There are any number of opposing views – even otherwise intelligent people end up on the other side of the fence. You must make up your own mind.'

She said earnestly, 'I'm doing that. Still making it up. But I'm not gigantically optimistic about the other side of the fence, not at this stage. Although, it'd be ever so nice – heaven and stuff. To believe in happily ever after.'

Happily ever after would be very nice, I agreed. Everlasting life might be pushing it, however. She looked unconvinced by that.

'But you still believe in right and wrong. Don't you, Thea?'

Civilisation depends on it, I replied. It depends on individual deeds just as much as the decisions of our rulers. If not more.

My judgement may once have been sadly awry, I thought, but there is another truth life has taught me. That is the value of pre-emptive action.

A cool breeze was springing up. I thought of my own quasi-spiritual moments, standing on the rim of the precipice.

'I said that this was one of my favourite places in the world. But I have two favourites,' I said. There was another destination. The other face of the secret.

I had no fear of the effect being overshadowed by what we had just seen. The two complement each other in a way I cannot begin to define. The artistic and the ineffable, I suppose it is. The tension between the limitations of human endeavour and the sublime achievements of nature. An eternal tension, as I see it.

We gazed through the gap in the arch to the far ridges and escarpments that roll away to the horizon. It was hazy, accentuating the blue. We hadn't spoken for a while.

'You can see the curvature of the world,' I said.

Kim said that after the cave she'd have thought anything else would be an anti-climax. 'But this —' she sought to articulate, 'this is unearthly. Like being on the far side of the moon. Maybe you won't like this, Thea, but I think it's kind of *heavenly*.'

'Maybe the nearest to heaven we are likely to get,' I said.

With that I was slugged by a bolt of primal fear. 'Keep a tight hold on Andie's lead,' I told her. 'Be careful not to go anywhere near that sheer drop. It is slippery, very treacherous just there, where the waters tumble down.'

I did not tell her that I stand there almost routinely. That this rush of danger is my fix.

Instead I heard myself saying, 'You must promise me, Kim, that you won't ever go near the edge.'

I should have predicted the response.

'I can't promise that I won't *ever*.' Lightly, 'You wouldn't have promised when you were my age, right?' I had to acknowledge the truth of this. She added, 'And I bet you wouldn't at any age.'

I observed her looking at Teddy. He strolled, with a sangfroid borne of years of familiarity, towards the edge in question, the tipping point where the foaming waters disappeared. I called him back, but I had a feeling she drew her own conclusions.

She pondered, then repeated that whatever happened in the future, she knew she would always come home, to these two places. 'It's like they'll be my *spiritual* homes, Thea,' she said with a mischievous look.

I told her I thought she had stumbled on something. Perhaps our true homes are not the houses we build or buy or save up for. Unlike those products of bricks and mortar, our spiritual homes can never be taken away from us. They lie in a different realm, in the realm of the imagination, and when we find them we have them for life.

Is this a consolation of any kind? Only if ideas can ever be comforting. And about that I am ambivalent.

As we pushed through the thickets close to home, separated by bushes, I judged it reasonable to bring up the subject of the two guys, Marek and Marlon. I was only going to touch on it, I wasn't intending to have an interrogation. We'd been together for some four hours, and I thought it was safe.

Did they have any plans for the evening?

'I dunno.' Refractory, but I ignored the signs. I'd almost forgotten how children of that age can have quicksilver changes of mood.

'How well do you know them?' I queried. I realise this was incautious.

'You asked me that before. A bit, I said.'

And were they nice, did she think?

'Why? Would you like to have a *drink* with them, or something? Watch the movie? Is that what you'd like?' It was an energetic response, not rude exactly but with an edge that took me by surprise.

'No, I wouldn't like,' I said at once, without thinking. 'I don't like what I've seen of Marek's film and I don't think Marlon is a particularly admirable character. I doubt very much if either of them is.'

'But you've never met either of them,' she said defensively.

'By their deeds ye shall know them.' Elevated eyebrows. 'It's a biblical quotation.'

'*Biblical?* I never heard you quote from the *Bible* before.'

'No? Well, it has some uses. It's a good doorstop. It's a reliable source of aphorisms. And much of the language in the King James version is very fine.'

She shrugged. She and Andie overtook me, pushing through the scrub.

I remembered that the director, Marek, had been to their house once before to work with Frank. She must have met him then. The actor had not visited however, to my knowledge.

'Where did you say you met Marlon?' I couldn't help myself. He had been a porn star. A discomfiting vision of Marlon's nakedness rose in front of me. Awesomely well hung is how he would be described by the uninhibited young women of today. Young women and not by children, one hoped.

A fractional pause. 'I didn't say.' She strode forward.

'Well, can you say now?' She had moved further ahead of me with Andie. No reply. She wants me to assume she hasn't heard the question, I thought. I quickened my pace. 'What did you and Frank do last night?' I asked.

'Watched an amazing science fiction movie,' she replied promptly. '*Blade Runner*, the director's cut. It's very famous.' The information conveyed nothing much to me.

'Did it have subtitles?'

'*Subtitles?*' She looked round. 'No, of course it didn't. It's in English.'

Where were the visitors going to sleep tonight?

Another shrug. They'd probably doss down somewhere. There was tons of space. 'Like there is out here,' she said, gesturing. We had emerged from the scrub behind the hovel.

I knew how she didn't like mess, I said. Three guys were likely to create havoc. If she needed to escape from them, just come to my place. At any time. We could make up a bed. We could rent a DVD, or she might like to bring one over.

She had my phone number, didn't she?

I don't care if this is overdoing it, whatever Sandy may think. I don't give a fig. As I said to him, she has no one else.

~~

I'd just turned the computer off when Frank appeared. I was having a restorative cup of tea on the verandah. He wanted to warn me that he was having a bit of a party tonight. Apologies in advance for the noise. He hoped I wouldn't mind. A small gig, only about a dozen or so.

I motioned him to a chair. He sat on the edge, with discernible reluctance.

'When the cat's away,' I said. I didn't offer him any tea.

He crossed his legs.

'Who's coming?' I asked.

Well, Marlon and Marek were here already. Their girl-friends were coming up. The usual suspects. He did not suggest an introduction, I noticed, and just as well. I have no desire to meet any of your grubby friends, I thought. He was watching me with a quizzical expression.

'What is Kim going to do, Frank?'

'Kim? She can pass things round.'

'She doesn't like parties.'

'Oh, she'll be fine. As long as she's got a book, and now Andie, the Wombat's happy as Larry. Or Harriet.' He obviously hadn't given her any thought. 'That puppy's a great success, Thea. A real cutie, in spite of the fact she chews up everything in sight. Thanks for your role in that.' The thanks sounded perfunctory.

'Kim should come over here tonight,' I told him. 'It's an adult party. And I strongly feel she should not be around people like actors in porn films, Frank.'

He rolled his eyes. 'Oh, she's cool with that. Marlon's quite harmless, Thea.'

I felt my blood pressure rise. It wasn't a matter of her being cool with it, I said, or of him being harmless. That was not the point.

'Okay, *okay*, Thea, relax,' with exaggerated, humorous annoyance. 'Chill, huh? I'll tell her. We could use her bedroom tonight. Some of them might stay over. Hey, she said you took the dogs on a bushwalk today. Wouldn't tell me a thing about it, where you went or anything, she's such a secretive kid. Said it was awesome, though.'

An upward inflexion and an inviting look. I did not respond.

'I was quite jealous. Got no info even after I tried to bribe her with a back rub. That usually works a treat. Not this time.'

'Furthermore, Frank, you must stop giving her massages. It's completely inappropriate.'

He gave a loud theatrical groan and jumped up, planting a quick kiss on my forehead as he left. I had no chance to take evasive action. I know this is automatic, an unthinking habit of his, but I no longer want to be on the receiving end of any of his habits.

What I once found endearing and affectionate in Frank I now see as seedy. Queasily so. He should not be giving her back rubs, that is beyond doubt.

Nothing was said about the toolbox or the missing discs. He probably hasn't even noticed.

Several cars arrived in the early evening, disgorging loud, casually dressed occupants. Initially crowding in to the kitchen, they gravitated to the deck. He was right about the noise. It blasted in our direction, upsetting Teddy. Making me even more troubled in my mind, if that is possible. I picked up the binoculars and swivelled among the guests. I located Kim. She was talking to a tall young man with his back to me. It could have been Marlon or Marek. She had a glass in her hand.

It had clouded over without my noticing and began to pour with rain. This put paid to the deck. They all scurried inside. You'd think that might have decreased the decibels, but there wasn't much difference. The French doors remained wide open.

I made a small supper and turned on the TV, for once, in the hope of distraction. Sat in front of it for some considerable time before realising I had no idea what programme it was.

I was only partially relieved when Kim did, surprisingly,

show up, carrying a toothbrush and Andie's bed. Frank said he needed her room for the friends staying the night, she explained, rather off-handedly I thought. No idea what time I went to bed. Thought she better get over here by ten-thirty. But the party would go on for ages, she added. I detected a touch of asperity.

'I thought you didn't enjoy parties,' I said.

'My age group I don't. I don't mind hanging out some-times, with adults. Like, if I know some people *a bit*.' She gave me a sidelong glance as she said this.

And she knew several people there, as it turned out. Very vague about where she had met them. So, were they film people? Sort of, yeah. Musicians and stuff. People who'd worked with Frank. I judged it counterproductive to single out Marlon again. I suspected she had met all of them.

She spotted the binoculars. Struck by what you could see in the front room, she quickly picked out Frank with Marek's fiancée. Wiser not to say anything, I decided. I had a look. They were dancing, if you can call it that. Jiggling on the spot and flinging their arms in the air.

I was surprised that Marek would have anything as conventional as a fiancée, I remarked. Kim seemed to regard this as disparaging. She had become rather uncommunicative, with a heightened demeanour. I could tell she'd had some-thing to drink. More, unquestionably, than a single glass.

'How much did you drink?' I inquired.

A pointed shrug. Not much. Some punch.

Some strong punch, I thought. I held my tongue about this also.

We made up a makeshift bed on the couch. A little two-seater, not a big sofa like theirs, but she said she could sleep anywhere. I told her to look at something on TV if she felt like it.

'I don't. Might look through the binoculars, but,' she said.

She is aware that I disapprove of putting prepositions last, and had been eliminating this practice.

She is in the first flush of adolescence, I reflected. This is the period when girls are at their most impressionable. More susceptible to influences, perhaps, than at any other time in their lives. And consequently more vulnerable.

It was not only the noise that kept me awake into the small hours.

What am I going to do? What options do I have?

~~

This morning she was more or less back to normal. I left a packet of Aspro on the bathroom basin. Two tablets went, I noted. We had a quiet tea and toast on the verandah with the dogs. Teddy is more at ease with Andie, who has toned down her boisterousness somewhat. His outbursts of snarling growls, which can be quite terrifying, have reduced in frequency and in force. At one point the two of them were lying alongside each other. Kim entwined their tails. A pity there was no camera handy. She said she could always borrow Frank's.

I've never owned a camera since taking those pictures of the cave paintings, and that was a throwaway. I might invest in one. Or even in a digital. They've become much cheaper and easier to use, apparently, and you can take as many pictures as you like.

It was cool but the sun was out. Everything was as quiet as the grave opposite. Some of the cars had gone, but there were still four parked at the side.

Kim was engaged in the task of spreading peanut butter thickly on her toast, very slowly and deliberately; she appeared mesmerised by the process. Finally she put down the knife.

'Thea.'

'Yes?'

'I've decided something.'

'Ah.'

'It's something I really, really want to happen.' Still seemingly riveted by the glistening grooves of peanut butter.

'Hurry up, for imaginary god's sake.'

She sat bolt upright and transferred her gaze to me. 'I want to have a writing life, Thea. Starting from this moment in time, sitting here at this little cane table. Shall we have another tea?'

She poured tea from the teapot into the two mugs, staring at the amber stream with a powerful intensity. She was going to do what Oscar said. You *know*, Thea, what he said about developing the correct sensibility? Sort of squeezing every drop of juice from every small experience? And she was going to start writing every day. Like he said, just do it until it became a habit she couldn't do without. A journal, to begin with.

She looked at me searchingly. Did I think those were the right essential ingredients? For an ordinary existence to evolve into a writing life?

'Writing a journal every day sounds good. Obsessively looking at everything might have value, if you can overlook the mind-numbing tedium,' I said. 'A love of reading is important, and you have that. But I also think the desire itself must be there. A desire that comprises wish, intention and – most crucial of all – the fierce drive to write.'

'Oh, yeah, I have that all right,' she said. 'I do definitely have a true, fierce desire and intention. A *ferocious* desire.'

I was no expert, I said, but I thought those were the essential ingredients.

Where that ferocious desire comes from in anyone remains a mystery. Must be a gift from the gods. Or the goddesses.

I showed her the photographs I had taken of the cave paintings. They had sat in a drawer away from the light for thirteen years. This had the advantage of keeping the colour from fading. We pored over them for some time, no closer to solving the identity of the third set of marks.

It was noon before there was any sign of life from across the way. Kim took her toothbrush and gathered up Andie and departed. She was going off to write an account of the party, she said. She assured me she would get her bed back tonight. All the gang were going home today.

This is not reassuring to me. There is a certain safety in numbers. The cars departed at intervals during the afternoon. By nightfall, Frank's was the only one left.

~~

It was colder tonight, and I lit my first fire of the year. I always leave the fireplace set at the end of winter. The supply of firewood will be well dried out in the woodshed, and we have collected a big heap of pine cones. Teddy and I have always enjoyed bringing kindling back from our walks. He carries a few sticks in his mouth and I take a basket.

Lately I haven't been very hungry at mealtimes. I have lost my appetite. But I know it is important to eat. I made myself some baked beans on toast with a grilled tomato and poached egg on top. Comfort food, I suppose, dating back to childhood. Then I succumbed to the urge that had been niggling at me for the past few days. From under the bed I took out the DVDs labelled MISTER WOLF, 1/2.

Something prescient and methodical had made me

tape Frank's instructions to the DVD player and keep the remote control on top of my TV. I inserted the first disc tentatively and pressed play, without much confidence. To my considerable surprise, a picture came on.

A whole series of pictures. It took a while before I realised these were disconnected phrases, a collection of unedited takes from different camera angles of the same scene. A rocking chair, then an animal's head. A wolf's head, under bedclothes. Shots of a cottage not unlike mine but considerably more charming. Huge daisies and other flowers in garish colours. Some full-screen close-ups of body parts – it took me some time before I realised what these were. They were entangled limbs. Then the rocking chair on the verandah with a motionless occupant seen from the back. A wolf's snarling jaws. Various shots of a skipping figure among trees, distant, sometimes in silhouette, sometimes blurry and overexposed.

After a while I tired of the disjointed nature of this. I removed the disc and put in number 2.

Taking up the whole screen was the rocking chair in close-up, on the verandah of a timber cottage. Big, obviously artificial flowers curled over the verandah posts. The chair made a loud rhythmic squeak as it rocked. Then a pair of dirty old sneakers attached to legs in jeans. The long legs belonged to someone unseen who was lounging in the chair.

The scene switched to sparse bushland in blinding sunlight. On the soundtrack was the traditional children's nursery rhyme, 'Girls and Boys Come Out to Play', only it crackled, as if it was on a radio but not quite on the station. In the distance you could just see a figure, very bleached out and indistinct, skipping towards the camera.

Then a startling change. One after the other, coloured drawings of Australian animals, kangaroos, koalas, wombats, possums, sugar gliders. They occupied the whole screen.

They looked like exuberant kindergarten pictures made by small children using thick crayons. And then a crudely drawn black snake in the grass. I thought of Frank.

Back to the rocking chair. The abrupt buzz of cicadas. Swooping cockatoos and parrots. The camera panned slowly upwards from the narrow blue jeans to a toned, muscular chest. A brawny young man seen from the front, his face obscured. The camera reached the head, which suddenly spun round. I jumped. It was the head of a real wolf, an actual animal superimposed on the young man's torso. It echoed the famous scene in the old *Psycho* film of the 1950s, when you suddenly see the head of an old woman in a rocking chair and it is revealed to be a skull. I had watched that film on TV with Matthew Rhode.

The skipping figure. Now you could just see it was a girl. A little closer, a little less fuzzy but still very washed out. I supposed this was deliberate. As she advanced you began to make out white ankle socks and black patent leather bar shoes, and a very short pinafore dress.

The wolfman was climbing into a narrow bed, pulling up the covers. Now the wolf head was an obvious model. It was set on the neck at an awkward angle, with a grandmother's bonnet tied under the chin and large, round spectacles.

The girl approached the house. A slender girl in bright light. No music, but in the background a children's chant – 'What's the Time, Mister Wolf?' – repeated hypnotically and increasing in volume. The girl, skipping lightly up the steps of the verandah. An alice band over cropped dark hair. The glint of a jade bangle on her wrist.

I lean forward, nearly hitting my forehead on my small TV screen, unable to believe the evidence of my eyes. Is it? I cannot be sure. The hair is very short, as it was when I first saw her. The camera moves behind her back as the chant intensifies.

She enters the bedroom. The bedclothes are humped over a long, lumpy shape, with only the bonnet visible.

In a sudden, nightmarish cut, the wolf's head rears up with bared fangs and a blood-freezing roar. The girl screams, an ear-splitting scream that slices through the drone of the sinister chant. In agonising slow motion the wolf pulls her down on top of him. A close-up of the girl's terrified eyes. They are Kim's eyes, without question. My heart is racing. The children's chant rises to a deafening pitch. He pushes her under him and leans down. As the wolf's head touches Kim's face, it becomes that of a dashingly handsome young man – Marlon. Marlon kisses her.

It is a prolonged, adult kiss that sends shockwaves through me.

And now it is no longer Kim on screen but a young woman, the stunning girl I remember seeing once before in the fight on the lurching platform. She is naked. The image has switched at some point, without my being aware of it, and a sweet, lilting harp melody has replaced the chant. I saw her again last night, I realise, through the binoculars – it is Marek's fiancée. A love scene ensues between her and Marlon. If it were not so explicit it would almost qualify as lyrical. I've read that some sex in films these days is the real thing. Were they acting? The screen goes black.

I know this shock, although I had suppressed its full, evil force. I know it because I have felt it once before, when Matthew's activities finally came to light, when a deputation of girls finally came to me and I could no longer close my ears to the whispers and the rumours. Those girls were courageous enough not to be evasive. There was no subtext to ignore. I could not refuse to act.

But by then the damage had been done. Irreparable damage to several lives. Principally, of course, to the bright, promising thirteen-year-old who was such a prodigiously talented student.

The delegation came too late to save her. Mr Rhode was dismissed from the school and charged with drug offences and sexual assault of minors. The girl hanged herself.

They say if you confront the full force of your transgressions you may gain some form of redemption in return. But I have found no catharsis in writing this down.

I watch the film through again, to be certain of what I have seen. How many options do I have? How many options do I need?

Only one. One of each, and it is the same one.

~~

Monday morning, eleven o'clock. Sunlight and – hosanna in the highest – no rain. Teddy and I stroll across for coffee with Frank as if nothing has happened. The front door is closed today, however. There is a bell that I have not seen before. I press it.

I know Frank is inside because the car is here. He goes for walks, but never this early. I give the bell another long, insistent press. And after a couple more minutes he materialises. Rumpled, in a dressing gown, a stripy seersucker number, only knee-high. Bare feet. No pyjamas, I see.

Andie hurtles out, a mini-projectile, greeting us as if she'd never imagined she would see us again. Andie. I hadn't quite factored her in. No problem, I will adjust.

Frank is concealing his surprise. 'Thea. Hey.' A creditable attempt, masking an undercurrent of something or other. A cocktail of discomfiture is my guess. I don't think he expected this. Probably feared the party had queered his pitch irrevocably. Instead of which, lo and behold, here I am, offering an olive branch.

There is no foreboding in his eyes, or not that I can see.

'I trust coffee's on offer as usual,' I say. 'It was so cold last night, wasn't it? I had a fire. Very cosy. First of the year.'

He ushers me inside, throwing an arm around my waist, which I do not shake off. Tells me they haven't tried out their fireplace yet. Oh, it will draw very well, I assure him – I made sure of that.

Let's get this baby going, he says to the coffee machine with a show of enthusiasm. He apologises for the mess. He and Kim did a lot of clearing up after the party, the Wombat especially, but the kitchen's still a bit of a pigsty. It's incredible, right, the amount of damage a bunch of able-bodied dudes can do in twenty-four hours? Came from good homes too. Well, most of them did. He grins. He is uneasy, I can tell. I have an urgent need to reassure him.

People's capacity for destruction beggars belief, I agree. So, I could assume it was a good party? They'd all worked on the movie, I imagined. Yeah, they had, actually. It was a blast, kind of a wrap party, music-wise.

We sip our coffee looking out on the gum trees. I think of Kim, and take special account of the texture and the taste. I am living in the moment. My sensation level is high.

Frank is sitting on the same sofa, his legs crossed. I keep my eyes averted from his skimpy dressing gown. I am uncertain whether he has anything on underneath. Marlon's hunky physique is still in my mind. Compared with his, Frank's body is really quite scrawny.

'It's such a pleasant morning,' I muse, watching the play of the thin autumnal sunbeams on the leaves. 'But it's going to change later. Storms predicted. I think we've had the last gasp of summer.' I can't resist a sly dig. 'No more sunbaking in your birthday suit, I fear.' A flicker. He is not sure how to respond.

And how is Ellie going, down in Melbourne? I enquire genially. I am full of goodwill and the milk of human kindness. Relieved, he gives me a run-down. A few more medical technicalities I don't want to hear. But I am interested in one piece of information. It is highly likely Ellice will have to spend the last part of her pregnancy under observation in hospital. Maybe as much as the last trimester, having what they call bed rest. This information is pleasing to me.

'More quality time with the Wombat,' Frank avers. This is not the moment to disillusion him. He proceeds to rub salt in one of my wounds by adding, 'You were right to say she needed more attention, Thea. I took that to heart and we're chilling, like you suggested. She's more at ease with me. Loosening up a lot.'

Now is my chance, perhaps the only chance I will get. I seize it, with both hands.

I assume a pensive expression. 'I'm glad to hear you say that, Frank. And I think there's something that must be done.'

He looks at me, eyebrows raised. Wary, anticipating a broadside. Put them on guard and then confound their expectations, I always found, when you want something from them.

'There shouldn't be secrets between us, is what I'm thinking,' I confide, leaning towards him a little. 'But most importantly, between you and Kim. Don't you agree?'

He nods, still cautious. 'I'm an open book, Thea. You know that.' A little smile, tailored, it seeks to convey, especially for me. His charm seems contrived now, his wiles blatant. Being Frank, though, I think he is also faintly titillated.

'So, I'm thinking I should take you somewhere, while we have the chance.'

'*Take* me somewhere, Thea?' He gives me a deadpan look.

'I think I should let you into the secret. Show you what I showed Kim.'

'You mean, on that walk she clammed up about? The big mystery? Huh.' He is intrigued. He mulls over this. 'What about the Wombat? The way she was, it sounded like something happened, like she'd had some kind of,' he looks at me, 'some kind of an – initiation. She mightn't be cool with me being in on it.' He is keen to parade his sensitivity and regain some points.

'You're quite right. We won't tell Kim,' I say truthfully. 'It's best that we don't. Your initiation will be just between the two of us.' And the two dogs, I think. But they will not tell anyone.

I see he still has a sliver of doubt.

'It's rather important for you to have seen this. Not just Kim, Frank. When we get there, you will understand why, believe me.'

He hesitates. I give him a winning smile. 'And it's a lovely walk,' I say.

A flash of pale thigh as he uncrosses his legs. I look away. Kim would have seen this inadequate dressing gown, I am thinking, on a regular basis. I put down my empty mug. 'Maybe we should go now, what do you think? I'm not sure the weather's going to hold for too long.'

He capitulates with a shrug and gets up. 'Well, okay then. I'll go and fling on some gear.'

I remind him to get Andie's lead. Forgetting Andie's lead would put a spanner in the works. Then I concentrate on the task at hand. On holding my nerve.

Frank returns in the familiar uniform of form-fitting jeans, with a long-sleeved check shirt over his T-shirt. Pats me on the shoulder. 'I'm all yours, Thea,' he says.

We exchange a few words as we push our way through the scrub. The walk has put him in a romantic frame of mind, as it happens. He reminisces about the day he and Ellice came upon the house. That was a find, he says. Changed their lives.

The spicy scents of the bush, the colours of the wildflowers and the scudding clouds are particularly pleasurable to me today. I wonder if they seem that way to Frank. We are treated to a fly-past of yellow-tailed black cockatoos. Later I draw his attention to a pair of spectacular king parrots. They are putting on quite a display for us this morning, I remark. And I point out some reticent autumn flowers that can be missed by the untrained eye. I want him to pay attention, to take the trouble to savour this experience while it lasts.

And when we arrive at the sandstone rock I am pleased to see he is suitably impressed. He is very taken by its shapely sinuousness. He wants to linger. It's a surprise, I agree – you'd never imagine it was here, would you? I tell him how Teddy and I came across it, many years ago. How Kim found it.

It is a remarkable formation, it's true, but this is not where we are heading. We should move on, Frank, I say. I'm concerned about the weather.

I am lying, the weather is on my side. It has clouded over and there is a light breath of mist. Mist is often the prelude to fog.

Teddy thinks we are going to the cave. I call him back. We skirt the perimeter of the rock and press on. Frank is walking close behind me, holding Andie's lead. She is definitely pulling less, I tell him. She is a very responsive puppy and Kim is a natural trainer. Maybe that's what she'll do, he says. Work with animals.

No, Kim will be a writer, I say. All the signs are there. Sometimes children find their vocation early – or it finds

280

them. He laughs and says he doesn't think of her as a child. I do not pursue the subject. This was the trouble all along, I reflect, this is where you went wrong. You and Matthew. Some children find their vocation early, only to lose themselves. This will not happen to Kim. I shall not let it.

So, is she formally adopted yet? I inquire casually. Not yet, it seems; anything in this area is a grindingly slow process. I consider the news with interest. I have been aware lately of the need to redraft my will. Apart from providing for Teddy, I have not felt this need before.

We forge downhill, following the icy path of the creek. It is a thin stream, as it usually is after the summer, and the route is easier to negotiate than it is in the muddy winter months. I am so familiar with it now that I forget, sometimes, how steep it is in parts. Frank, though, is regarding me in some amazement, revising his mental picture. No wonder you're so fit, Thea, he says. This is quite a workout. Are we there yet?

And we emerge where the ground levels out between towering cliffs. Ahead is the grand arch, the semicircle with the view of rippling gorges and valleys beyond. It's interesting, the way the two halves don't quite meet in the middle, I say to Frank. It always reminds me of the iconic paintings and photos of the Sydney Harbour Bridge when it was being built, with the incomplete spans leaning towards each other like two outstretched arms.

'But the two arms would have met once, of course,' observes Frank. 'Over time, the pinnacle's eroded away.'

As he makes that chance remark, that simple, obvious comment, something clicks into place. I utter an involuntary exclamation. Frank asks if I'm okay. He thinks I've hurt myself. I'm quite all right, I assure him. It's just that I suddenly understood something that's had me baffled for years.

'There's this little sketch I've been looking after,' I say. 'It's unique, but I never knew quite what it was. When you said that the arch had once been complete – an inspired observation, by the way – I realised in a flash that the drawing is a shorthand for it. Only it was sketched long, long ago when the rock arch was still intact. It shows the vault as it was, a frame for the view beyond. The successive folds of valleys and mountains.'

I draw breath. 'You see, Frank, I'd never known whether the artist actually came here. I suspected it, and I felt in my bones that she did. Now I am certain of it. She stood here. She knew this place.'

Frank looks at me oddly. He thinks I am rambling. And indeed I *am* rambling. It is, and rather inappropriately when I think about it, a briefly happy, burbling ramble. I am quite lightheaded over this.

I cannot wait to tell Kim my discovery. She will be miffed, temporarily; she wanted to be the one to solve the mystery. However, I shall not tell her today, because I never came here today. I won't tell her, perhaps, for some time. I should wait for the dust to settle, as it were, before I return to this sacred place with her.

But I digress. This is where, at all costs, I must not come unstuck.

Better tie Andie's lead to this tree, I tell Frank. We need to go over there under the curve of the arch, so I can show you the full impact. The creek becomes a waterfall. You will never see a more spectacular vista in your life, Frank. I can promise you that.

He is cheery, eager to oblige. I check on the knot. Teddy leads the way forward. I look back at Andie, tugging, desperate to follow us. I order Teddy to go back. To stay, and sit with her.

She came back alone, I shall say later, shaking my head. Young puppy, damp, exhausted, no lead. The lead must have got caught up on branches. Puppy wriggles out of

282

collar and takes off. Any number of scenarios. No way of knowing which way they went, I'm afraid. I didn't see them leave.

'You're right. This view is bloody incredible. I had no idea,' Frank enthuses as we approach the edge of the escarpment and the unfurling, primeval vastness. The silence holds us in its grip.

'Feel it,' I tell him. 'Let it envelop you.'

And already the mist is rolling in along the valley floor. It has obscured the ocean of rippling leaves. Frank is standing next to me, not wanting to appear wimpish. But as I step forward boldly he puts out a shocked arm to stop me. 'Hey, hang on, Thea.'

'It's all right,' I say. 'I'm used to this.'

He drops his arm. 'I don't have your head for heights,' he says. But he shuffles a little closer to the edge.

I am on the rim of the precipice. My fix floods over me in a rush. I am exultant. This is my warrior moment, Oscar, if only you were here to witness it.

It doesn't need a shove. It needs only a small, firm tap. But the last thing I want, in the future, is to be unsure of my role. I have learnt to become proactive in my old age, and I am glorying in my newfound nerve.

So I exert a little force. Not too much. Not enough to send myself tumbling after him. He tries to clutch me, something I had not foreseen. I waver, and recover my balance. He utters a sound, but it is muffled by the swirling fog.

I cannot see his diving figure. But I know what will happen to him. The green sea will part for him and swallow him up. The heaving waves of leaves will close over his head.

The surface of the valley floor will be pristine again. Untouched and shimmering, as it has been for millennia.

•

Teddy is on his feet. He has taken a few steps towards me and stopped. He looks into my eyes with an unfathomable expression, and licks my hand.

When we get home I leave the dogs in the garden and put Andie's lead in a plastic bag. I drive to the village and drop the bag in a rubbish bin.

People do wander into the bush, as Sandy is aware. When you've lived here for as long as we both have, you know that. Sometimes they disappear and they're never found again. They get lost, the cloud comes down and they panic. It's rare, it's not common, but it does happen. The bush just swallows them up.

Acknowledgements

Many people gave me unstinting help, both personal and professional – as well as the constant encouragement a writer depends on – during the writing of this book. I should especially like to single out Ann Blaber, Anne Chisholm, Sara Colquhoun, John Duigan, Penny Gay, Nammi Le, Robert Milliken, Drusilla Modjeska, Caroline Moorehead, Kathy van Praag and Lizzie Spender.

At the business end, my editors at Random House – Meredith Curnow, Brandon VanOver, Roberta Ivers and Catherine Hill – have been as exemplary as before in transforming business into pleasure.

Thank you all.

Also by Virginia Duigan

The Biographer

He was there to uncover the past . . .
She wanted it left a secret

When Greer Gordon met Mischa Svoboda, a driven Czech-born refugee painter, he was unknown. His debut show at the small art gallery where she worked created a sensation, and their explosive love affair caused Greer to abandon her husband and career and embark on a nomadic life with Mischa.

Twenty-five years later, Tony, a young art critic who is researching a biography of Mischa, arrives in the small Italian hilltop community where Greer and Mischa now live. Greer is consumed by anxiety, fearing the biographer may have unearthed the secret she had always intended to write out of her life story. A gripping cat-and-mouse game plays out, and with it the growing suspicion that Tony may be manipulating a dramatic outcome on which to build his career.

Virginia Duigan's intimate and enthralling portrait of the relationship between an artist and his lover will have readers examining how their own biographies might be written, for who amongst us has nothing to hide?

'A clear light on the ruthless habits of biography. Marvellous.'
Drusilla Modjeska

Days Like These

There are certain friends with whom you don't have to pretend

Lou, a freelance journalist, leaves New York after the breakup of a long relationship. Taking refuge in Mim's North London house, the nerve-centre for a group of old university friends, she becomes drawn into an escalating series of personal dramas.

Days Like These is about women behaving badly. It is about love and loyalty, deceit and disaster, and the onset of moral choices. In a world where you can touch most things, what – and who – is untouchable?

Told with wit, humour and sophistication, *Days Like These* tests the bonds between friends.

'A tremendous first novel possessing real charm, a kind of freshness and guilelessness that is very potent – and a toughness and reality that I genuinely applaud.'

William Boyd